Mission Hollywood

"With wit and gentle humor, Michelle Keener whisks readers from the glamour, flashing lights, and empty promises of Hollywood to the beautiful truth of God's grace. Her emotionally-engaging, relatable characters captured my heart from the first page. This tender story of love despite the odds and faith during life's difficulties will be a sure hit for fans of inspirational romance."

—KELLIE M. PARKER
2018 Daphne du Maurier winner

"*Mission Hollywood* is my favorite kind of contemporary fiction, the real sort. Keener avoids the pitfalls of Christian romance and creates relatable characters with flaws intact and gives them the room to grow in their faith through their struggles. You will definitely fall in love with Ben and root for him and Lily to get their happily-ever-after. With a fast-paced plot, the story keeps you hooked, turning the page to see what happens next."

—CHRISTA MACDONALD
Author of *The Broken Trail*, 2017 ACFW Carol Award finalist

"A romantic tale that truly deserves the label 'Inspirational.' Ever the skeptic, I worried that not all the characters would be willing to change or grow but *Mission Hollywood* proved me wrong, illustrating the transformative power of faith. A charming and thoughtful read to spend the weekend with."

—ALLISON PEARL
Author of *Glazed Suspicion*

Mission Hollywood

MICHELLE KEENER

a Red Carpet Romance
Book One

AMBASSADOR INTERNATIONAL
GREENVILLE, SOUTH CAROLINA & BELFAST, NORTHERN IRELAND

www.ambassador-international.com

Mission Hollywood
A Red Carpet Romance - Book One

© 2019 by Michelle Keener

ISBN: 978-1-62020-930-1
eISBN: 978-1-62020-946-2

Cover Design & Typesetting by Hannah Nichols
Ebook Conversion by Anna Riebe Raats
Edited by Daphne Self

AMBASSADOR INTERNATIONAL
Emerald House
411 University Ridge, Suite B14
Greenville, SC 29601, USA
www.ambassador-international.com

AMBASSADOR BOOKS
The Mount
2 Woodstock Link
Belfast, BT6 8DD, Northern Ireland, UK
www.ambassadormedia.co.uk

The colophon is a trademark of Ambassador, a Christian publishing company.

For Emily

With all my love

Chapter One

LILY SWUNG HER CARRY-ON BAG over her shoulder and waited for the slow moving line of passengers to shuffle down the aisle. There was no need to fight her way into the crush of people trying to make connections. She wasn't in a hurry. Yawning and rubbing the stale airplane air from her eyes, she glanced out the tiny, plastic window. The lights of Los Angeles glittered in the distance, an endless field of manufactured stars that lit up the night. She smiled at the distant neon glow as a single word whispered through her mind. *Home.*

It had been a long day, followed by an even longer flight from Boston. Her annual pre-Christmas visit with her former college roommate had been fun, as always, but she was ready to see her family again. They never complained about her yearly trip to Boston. Kate was family in every way except genetics, but Lily also knew that she was needed back here. And quite frankly, jumping into Kate's fast paced lawyer life had been exhausting.

As she walked through LAX, carefully dodging tourists with their amusement park hats and giant cameras, she wondered how big the pile of dishes waiting in the sink would be and how many pizza boxes would be stacked up beside the recycling bin. Her dad and brother were good at a lot of things, but housework and cooking were nowhere on that list. If her mom were still alive things would be different. The thought leapt to her mind before she could stop it. Taking a deep breath, she waited for the sadness to pass. It didn't matter how many years went by, losing her mom was a wound that would never heal.

She rode the escalator down to baggage claim, letting the frantic passengers pass her as she stood to the side, content with the slow descent. As she stepped off the last metal stair she spotted a handsome chauffeur holding a white sign with "Brat" written in flawless penmanship. Rolling her eyes, she headed straight for him.

"Nice, Noah. Way to make your baby sister feel loved."

"Of course, you're loved. It doesn't say Spoiled Rotten Brat, does it?" Noah wrapped her in his arms and lifted her off her feet. "Welcome home, Brat. How's Kate?"

She surrendered her bag to him and they walked towards the passenger pick up exit. She had made this trip enough times to know better than to check a bag. It was easier to travel light. The automatic doors slid open and she breathed in the exhaust and smog of a winter night in Los Angeles. Honking horns and the squeals of family reunions bounced off the concrete walls and slammed into each other in a symphony of chaos.

"She's good. She enjoys her job at the law firm, but it's been crazy busy for her. I think she's pushing herself too hard. She has no idea how to slow down."

Noah's face wrinkled into a frown. "You should tell her to come out here for a few days. A nice vacation would do her some good."

Lily glanced at her brother. "And seeing her again might do you some good too, right?"

Noah bumped her with his shoulder and avoided her gaze. "Shut up."

She giggled and let it go. Her brother had been nursing a crush on Kate since their junior year in college. He had been devastated when Kate packed up and moved to Boston to attend Harvard Law School and Kate had been happily oblivious to his broken heart. Now there was a continent sized pile of pride and regret between them. Noah refused to come with her to Boston and Kate refused to come back to Los Angeles. Lily sighed, trusting God had a plan for both of them. She hoped that plan might someday bring them together.

"So how's Dad?" Instead of pressing, she opted to change the subject. Noah's shoulders relaxed and he was able to make eye contact again.

"He's fine. He's working around the clock on the church's block party. He'll be happy to see you and your organizational skills again, that's for sure. Here . . . " He reached into his jacket and pulled out a folded brochure. "This is what he's been working on."

Lily glanced through the advertisement for the upcoming event, a free block party for the residents of their low-income Hollywood neighborhood. It was a rough area and most of the kids living there witnessed, or experienced, a crime before they ever made it to their first day of school. Her parents had built the Hollywood Mission together smack dab in the middle of the poverty, crime, and graffiti, believing that was exactly where God wanted them. After her mom died, Lily and her brother joined the staff to help their dad keep it going.

Noah clicked a button on his keys and the black, stretch limo in front of them beeped. He popped the trunk open and dropped her bag inside before opening the rear passenger side door.

"Your chariot awaits, Madame," he said in his best limo driver voice.

Insecurity tugged at her as she tried to ignore the curious stares from people on the sidewalk. It would have been helpful if she had a sign that simply said, 'I'm nobody.' Then maybe she could go back to being invisible and anonymous.

"You know, you could have brought the truck."

"This is more fun. " Noah grinned and offered her his hand. "And it gets me great parking."

She slid into the dark, plush interior, and Noah closed the door. The irony of it wasn't lost on her; she was probably the only girl in Hollywood who had never dreamed of being a movie star. Fame, celebrity, interviews, and photographs all sounded more frightening than exciting to her. But as she let her hand run down the soft leather seat and breathed in the lingering perfume from whichever celebrity Noah had last driven, she thought she wouldn't mind a little bit of pampering every now and then.

Tossing his chauffeur's cap onto the passenger seat, Noah jumped behind the wheel. He looked over his shoulder. "Ready to go home, Brat?"

Before she could reply, flashes sparked outside the limo, bright white lights danced off the tinted glass like tiny fireworks. A roar of voices and the slap of feet against pavement washed over the car. The rear door flew open and a man leapt into the limo beside her. An endless stream of camera flashes blinded her as dozens of paparazzi surrounded the limo. The car shook as they leaned against it and banged on the glass.

"What happened in Rome?" someone shouted.

"What do you have to say about Giselle's interview?"

"Do you think the scandal will hurt your new movie?"

"What are you going to do now?"

The questions tumbled together as the reporters shouted and shoved each other, fighting to get closer. Camera lenses and flashes invaded the limo and Lily shrank back against the leather seat. Nerves exploded in her stomach and her heart raced in the chaos.

"No comment!" The man who had jumped into the limo snarled the reply and yanked the door closed. The sudden quiet was like finding a sliver of shade in the desert. She blinked her eyes, trying to get rid of the glowing, white circles that swam in her vision.

"What are you waiting for?" The stranger yelled at Noah. "Let's go."

Lily looked at Noah who was staring wide-eyed at the man beside her. She followed his gaze and her mouth went dry. Sitting next to her in faded jeans and a rumpled black shirt was none other than Ben Prescott, movie star and Hollywood A-lister. His chestnut brown hair was a tousled mess, as if he had spent the past few hours running his hands through it over and over again. Dark circles shadowed his deep brown eyes and several days of rough stubble covered his clenched jaw.

She blinked again, certain her eyes were playing tricks on her. How could one of the biggest movie stars on the planet be sitting next to her? Opening her eyes, she found herself staring into the face she had glimpsed on posters at the movie theatre and passing buses chugging through the crowded downtown streets. Her heart skittered.

He was staring right back at her.

Outside, the paparazzi yelled and the limo rocked. Noah cleared his throat. "Mr. Prescott I think there's been a mistake. I'm not your driver." He nodded his head towards Lily. "I'm hers."

Ben Prescott tilted his head as he turned the intensity of his gaze on her. "And who are you?" he asked.

She stuttered and for a second, she forgot her own name. Nobody, she thought, I'm nobody. She opened her mouth and hoped words would come out. "I'm Lily. Lily Shaw."

Ben smiled and took her hand, shaking it once. "Hi, Lily Shaw, I'm Ben Prescott. It's nice to meet you." She felt the heat of the contact zip all the way up her arm. "Do you mind if we get out of here?"

A reporter slammed his camera against the window and she jumped. "No. I don't mind at all."

"Great." Ben turned to Noah. "I will give you a thousand dollars to drive me anywhere but here."

Noah hesitated, his glance darting back to his sister.

"Please," Ben looked at her, desperation coloring his words, as he gripped her hand, the warmth of his touch enveloping her fingers. "Please don't make me get out of the car."

Flashes popped and not even the solid walls of the limo could stop the sound of the endless questions being thrown at Ben. In the dim light of the limo, Lily could see the weariness in his eyes, the lines of fatigue that crossed his face. He held her hand solidly, like it was a lifeline he was afraid to lose. Turning to her brother, she prayed she wasn't making a huge mistake.

"Get us out of here, Noah."

Chapter Two

NOAH GUIDED THE LIMO THROUGH the crush of paparazzi and reporters. As the cameras faded into the distance, Lily relaxed against the seat, grateful for every mile Noah put between them and the paparazzi. How awful it must be to be chased and hounded like that. Just the thought of that many people watching her made her stomach queasy.

"Thanks for sharing your ride." Ben smiled and she wanted to melt. Then she scolded herself for being such a girl. He was just a guy. Just a guy who happened to be a movie star. Anxiety rippled through her again and she swallowed the dryness in her throat.

Clenching her hands, she forced a calm she didn't feel into her voice. "It's no problem. That was quite a scene back there."

Ben rubbed his temples. "Yeah. I wasn't expecting it. I thought I was sneaking back into the country, but no such luck." He pointed towards the mini-bar on the side of the limo. "Do you mind if I get a drink?"

"Oh, no. It's fine." She ignored Noah's narrow-eyed stare in the rearview mirror.

Ben shuffled over to the row of tiny bottles. "Do you want anything?"

"Just water, please." He handed her a bottle of water from the mini-fridge. "Thank you."

Ben grabbed a bottle of something and sat back down. He unscrewed the lid and took a deep drink. "What a day."

Lily took a sip of water and searched for something to say. "Where did you fly in from?"

"Rome. You?"

"Boston. I was visiting a friend."

Ben nodded and took another drink. "Boston is nice. I was there a few years ago shooting *World at War*."

The insanity of the situation hit her, and she started to laugh. She'd seen that movie on cable not long ago. And now the dashing Army captain who'd crossed enemy lines to rescue his men was sitting in a limo next to her trying to escape an onslaught of reporters.

"Oh sure," she said with an air of sophistication. "I film there all the time."

Ben studied her, his brow creased as if he were trying to figure out if he should recognize her. Grinning, she held up her smart phone. "Just yesterday I was filming my friend Kate while she was drinking coffee. The day before that I was filming this cold, white stuff that falls from the sky. It's cutting edge movie making."

He laughed and the relief in the sound loosened the ball of nerves in her stomach. "Ah, so you're a funny one. Actress?"

She rolled her eyes. "Definitely not."

Ben finished the drink and tossed the bottle into the trash. "Producer? Director? Unpaid intern?"

"None of the above. I don't think I'd do well in the movie industry."

"Yeah." Ben examined the labels on the bottles in the mini-bar. "Me neither."

"I think you'll be all right." Lily picked at the wrapper on her water bottle. "So what were you doing in Rome?"

"I was there for a movie premiere. A quick trip in and out." Ben grabbed another tiny bottle from the bar. "Red carpet, do a few foreign press interviews, and then home." He sat down and pinched the bridge of his nose. "It didn't exactly go as planned."

"What happened?"

"I may have been dumped by my girlfriend in the middle of the premiere." He closed his eyes and leaned back against the leather seat. "I also may have been escorted from the building by the Rome police."

"May have?"

"Either that or I was arrested." He shrugged, seemingly unconcerned by his possible arrest on foreign soil. "The details are a little foggy. You know how those premieres go."

Lily opened her mouth, searched for something to clever to say, then gave up. "I have no idea what to say to that."

"Why?"

"Well, I've never been to a movie premiere and I don't normally have conversations with the actors who attend them."

"Oh that." Ben waved his hand dismissively. "I do it all the time, it's not hard. Ask them a few questions about themselves and they'll do all the talking. Eventually you can walk away and they won't even notice you're gone."

Noah snorted in the front seat.

"See," Ben said and pointed at the back of Noah's head. "He gets it." He twisted the cap off the small, glass bottle and threw it in the direction of the trashcan. It hit the rim and rolled across the carpeted floor. "Of course when I left Rome, I didn't realize my girlfriend, who is now apparently my ex-girlfriend, was planning to give an interview about the demise of our relationship while I was in the air. And I certainly didn't expect to be ambushed by the paparazzi as soon as I hit the jetway."

"I'm sorry." Lily thought back to the scene at the airport. The yelling and shoving, the barrage of questions. Even now it made her stomach flip. "That's awful."

He shrugged again. "That's Hollywood."

Noah turned the limo onto the 405. "Mr. Prescott, you're in the Hollywood Hills, right?"

"Yeah. Thanks." Ben turned towards to her. "Well, Miss Shaw, you know my sad story. What's yours?"

Lily blinked and shook her head. "I don't have one."

"Oh come on, this is LA, everyone has a sad story."

"Not me. I live in Hollywood and I work at my dad's church."

Ben stiffened. "Church?"

Whether he meant to do it or not she noticed he slid back a few inches, as if the word was contagious.

"Yes, the Hollywood Mission. We've been there for about ten years." She handed him the brochure for the block party. "This is our church."

He flipped through it, but she could tell he wasn't reading any of it. She saw the hard line of his mouth as his eyes darted across the photos of the bounce house, face painters, and the hot dogs sizzling on the grill. "Looks like fun. My church never did anything like this."

"Which church do you go to?"

He snapped the brochure closed. "None. I don't go to church."

Lily recognized the bitterness in his voice. This was a man who didn't want anything to do with church. But years of ministry were as ingrained in her as good manners. "Well, you're welcome to come to ours anytime. We'd love to have you."

"I'll keep it in mind." He offered the brochure back to her, but she put her hands up.

"Keep it. You never know when you might need it."

He slid the brochure into the back pocket of his jeans. "Thanks, but church really isn't my thing."

Headlights passed in a blur as the Los Angeles landscape flew by. "What do you mean?"

Ben shifted in the seat so he was facing her. "I don't see the point. There's nothing in a church I can't get from a friend or a therapist. And at least the therapist would be honest about wanting my money."

Sarcasm laced his words, but she didn't retreat. "That's a pretty jaded view of church."

"As jaded as one of those green Chinese dragons." Smiling at his own joke, he gave her a mock salute.

"I'm sorry you feel that way."

Ben shook his head, ignoring her sympathy. "Don't be. It's not like I'm missing anything. If I want boring music and guilt, I can go to my mother's house." He drained the small bottle in one swallow and threw it towards the trashcan. He missed and it ended up near the discarded cap on the floor, rolling along the plush, carpeted floor with every turn of the limo. "Look, church is just a lot of people pretending to be good for one day of the week and then going home and doing the same garbage they always do. I've got enough hypocrites in the movie industry to deal with. I don't need another crowd on Sunday mornings."

Lily sipped her water and said a silent prayer for wisdom. "It must be really hard, trying to do everything on your own."

Resting his arm on the seat behind them, he leaned towards her. "Sweetheart, that's why I have an agent, an assistant, a publicist, a personal trainer, and a whole pack of lawyers from the studio who as we speak are smoothing out whatever stupid thing I did in Rome. I'm never on my own." As he scrubbed a hand over his eyes, she wondered if being surrounded by that many people who depended on you for their livelihood was a good thing.

"So you see," Ben said with a tipsy smile. "I have enough people telling me what to do without tossing God into the mix." The words were delivered with confidence and practiced ease but the emptiness behind them was louder than anything else.

Lily caught Noah's eye in the rearview mirror. The limo had started a slow climb into the hills above Hollywood. The bright lights and crowded streets giving way to expensive homes guarded by iron gates and high walls.

"God doesn't want to tell you what to do." She softened her tone and looked the movie star straight in the eye. "He just wants to bring you home."

Ben fidgeted in his seat, refusing to meet her gaze. "Well, I don't need His help. I've got a pretty nice house already."

She opened her mouth to continue, but he reached across her lap and pressed the button to raise the partition glass between them and Noah. For a brief moment the heat of his body washed over her. But instead of leaning into the heat of his presence, Lily pulled back, alarm bells ringing in her head.

"So, Lily Shaw, tell me," his words came out coated with alcohol and cynicism. "Do you think I'm worth saving?"

Dread coiled in her gut as she stared back at him. "Everyone is worth saving."

He gave her a magazine cover smile, fake and insincere, and slid his arm along the seat behind her head. "Would you like to come to my place and tell me more about why I'm a lost little boy who needs to go back to church?"

Lily scooted into the corner, as far from him as she could get.

"You know," his words were slurred and sloppy. "It's been a pretty rotten day. Maybe we can make each other feel better." He slid closer and Lily jumped off the seat.

She banged on the partition glass. "Noah, stop the car."

The limo pulled sharply to the right and screeched to a stop. The driver's door slammed and there was a rushed crunch of rocks before the rear door flew open.

Noah's hand shot through the open door. Without a word he grabbed the collar of Ben's shirt and yanked him out of the car.

Lily followed just in time to see him haul a very confused Ben Prescott off the ground and shove him against the limo.

"What—" Ben started, but Noah cut him off.

"Don't say anything. Lily, are you okay?"

Ben interrupted. "She's—"

"Stop." Anger flared in Noah's eyes and his knuckles turned white as he tightened his grip on Ben's shirt. "What my sister says next will determine how hard I'm going to hit you."

"Sister?" Ben choked on the word.

Noah took a step closer, his voice low and menacing. "Sister."

Ben kept his mouth shut as both men turned their gazes to her.

"Let him go. He's drunk." She looked at Ben. It wasn't fear or even anger she felt. It was sadness. Sadness that someone who had been given so much was unwilling to acknowledge the One who had given it all to him in the first place. She couldn't imagine a life without God and she wouldn't wish it on anyone, not even a drunk movie star.

Noah was still staring at her, his eyes flying from the top of her head to her feet searching for injuries, worry etched on his face. "I promise," she said, "I'm fine. Let him go."

He kept Ben pinned against the car, clearly looking for a reason to punch the dumbfounded and bleary-eyed movie star. Then he spun him away from the limo and let him fall to the ground. "Ride's over, Champ."

Ben sat on the asphalt and looked up at them. "You can't just leave me here."

"Actually I can. My limo, my rules. And my number one rule is no one hits on my sister without her permission."

Noah walked her to the front of the limo, his arm resting protectively against her back, and opened the door. She hesitated, giving Ben a long look, wishing there was something she could say, something that would reach him, before she shook her head and disappeared into the passenger seat.

Noah closed the door and walked around the front of the car. "Have a good night, Mr. Prescott." He waved once before climbing into the driver's seat and slamming the door. Then the limo headed back down the hill towards Hollywood. The last thing Lily saw of Ben Prescott was him sitting in the middle of an empty road, his reflection slowly fading in the rearview mirror.

*****

Ben stood and a wave of drunken dizziness clutched his head. Once the world stopped spinning and the hills were right side up again, he stuffed his hands into his pockets and looked up and down the road. The December air was cold and seeped through his t-shirt. Scattered lights from distant houses cast eerie shadows and the sky above was black. The frantic pace of Los Angeles suddenly seemed much further away. The road he was on was empty and lonely.

Kicking at a rock on the ground, he sighed. When had life gone so wrong? He knew he was screwing everything up. He just didn't know how to stop. Giselle had staged that fight at the premiere, he was sure of it. She was smart and she wanted her shot at stardom. Over the few months they had been together, he had given her plenty of ammunition for a fight. Now he was going to pay the price for it.

Mentally, he checked off the collection of crises he was facing. His girlfriend had dumped him and spilled the story to the press. He'd been kicked out of his own movie premiere, ambushed by paparazzi at the airport, and then ditched on the side of the road by an uptight pastor's daughter and her overprotective brother. It wasn't the worst night of his life, but it certainly wasn't what he had been expecting when he packed up to go to Rome.

Who knew staying in the spotlight would be so much work? He felt his grip on his own celebrity slipping. He didn't mind being Hollywood's bad boy, but he wouldn't mind being himself for a little while. The problem was no one cared about Benjamin Prescott from Nowhere, Indiana, they cared only about Ben Prescott movie star.

Everyone is worth saving.

Whispered words drifted on the breeze. The conviction in her voice, the certainty of her belief, unnerved him. It tugged on his heart like a dream he couldn't escape. The words burrowed down deep and refused to be uprooted. A memory stirred at the edges of his mind. The warmth of his grandmother's house, the comfort of her arms, the gentleness of her voice when she sang, "Yes, Jesus loves me."

Ben closed his eyes, forcing the memory back into whatever box he had locked it away in.

Everyone is worth saving.

He shook his hands, chasing the words away. He knew better. Christians were judgmental hypocrites and salvation was just a word they used to con gullible people into showing up at church and turning over their money. Nobody cared what you did as long as you said the right words and wrote the checks.

His dad had said all the right words to the people at church. Then he went home and drank himself into a stupor and hit anyone who didn't do as they were told. It was the Christians in their church who looked the other way and told his mom to keep going back to the man who beat her. Those same Christians told Ben he was going to Hell while his abusive father was assured a place in Heaven just because he let them dunk him in a pool one Sunday morning.

He didn't want anything to do with a God like that. And if he was going to Hell, then he'd go there as a free man.

Ben ignored the chill of the winter night and let resentment keep him warm. This was better. He didn't need charity from anyone, especially not a pastor's daughter who thought he needed saving.

He dug his phone out of his back pocket and stared at it. He could call a cab, but even in his inebriated state he knew this was a story he didn't want in the press. *Drunk Celebrity Needs a Ride Home* wouldn't play well in the tabloids and the studio was going to have enough on their plate trying to spin the problems he had in Rome before the new movie opened.

The dull glow of the phone waited in his hand. He could call Zoe, but even as he thought it, he dismissed the idea. He wasn't in the mood for his agent's micro-management of his life. Not tonight.

That just left Derek. Ben laughed, the sound echoing in the blackness. Isn't this exactly the type of thing a personal assistant is good for? He started to pull up Derek's number, but then stopped.

Crystal blue eyes danced across his mind. Eyes that had been filled with laughter and then turned to pity. He remembered the look she gave him before she slipped into the limo and disappeared back into the crowded streets of Hollywood. Some poor pastor's daughter felt sorry for him. Him. He was one of the biggest movie stars on the planet and she thought he was lost and alone.

He refused to listen to the whisper that said she was right. He was Ben Prescott. He had everything he ever wanted. He didn't need saving and he didn't need to be rescued.

He stuffed his phone back into his pocket, blew out a breath, and looked up the winding road. The movie star was going to be walking home.

Chapter Three

POUNDING.

Even before Ben opened his eyes, the pounding sent bright, white lightning bolts of pain through his skull. Someone with no understanding of how hangovers worked was pounding on his bedroom door. And that pounding was going to kill him.

He mumbled a curse into his pillow and cracked his eyelids open. Thanks to his heavy curtains, the room was blissfully dark. He had no idea what time it was and he didn't care. All he wanted to do was go back to sleep, but the horrible pounding started again.

"Ben Prescott, you better not be dead in there!"

He flopped onto his back and put his hands over his ears. There was no escaping it.

Zoe had found him.

"Ben, you open this door right now or so help me I will hire someone to break it down." Then the awful pounding started again. How could someone so little make so much noise?

He swung his legs over the side of the bed and slowly leveraged himself into a sitting position. He was still wearing the clothes he had flown home in, with the exception of one sock that had somehow gone missing. Standing, he winced at the fresh stab of pain in his head. As he stumbled to the door, he swore he would never drink again.

He flipped the lock and opened the door, closing his eyes against the too-bright sunlight that came streaming in. His bedroom was at the end of a hallway that faced the living room. The morning view from the panoramic windows that overlooked the hills was amazing, unless you were a vampire . . . or hungover.

"For crying out loud, Ben, I thought you'd overdosed in there."

Zoe Waltham was standing right in front of him, her perfectly manicured hand still raised in a fist to continue her assault on his bedroom door.

He rolled his eyes at her and instantly regretted the movement. "You know I don't do drugs."

"Well, after everything that happened yesterday I wouldn't blame you if you started."

Disjointed memories danced across his mind as he shuffled his way to the kitchen. The premiere in Rome, landing in LAX and getting hit with a barrage of texts and emails all demanding a comment on the story of the week, Giselle's tearful face as she told a morning talk show host about how his neglect and indifference pushed her into the arms of her co-star. It was all coming back to him and he wished it would go away.

"How did you get in here?" he asked as he squinted his eyes against the glare. He should really have Derek put up some curtains.

"Derek let me in."

Ben spotted his assistant slipping around the corner to the kitchen. "Traitor."

Derek's head popped back around the corner, his perfectly styled blond hair shining in the sun. "She's scary. And she's the one who hired me."

Ben made it to the kitchen and almost wept with gratitude when he saw the full pot of coffee already waiting for him. "You are an angel, Zoe."

She waved the compliment away. "I take care of my stars."

Derek opened his mouth then shut it quickly. He crossed his arms and narrowed his eyes at the preening agent. Ben ignored them both, not caring who actually made the coffee. He grabbed the largest mug he could find and started pouring.

Zoe drummed her red nails against the quartz countertop as he sipped the steaming cup of coffee flavored happiness. "Feeling better?" The saccharine in her voice was his first warning sign. "Ready to face the real world again?"

Dread coiled in his stomach. He swallowed a scalding gulp of coffee, his burning tongue briefly distracting him from the pounding in his head. "Why?"

"Well," his agent cooed. "I want you to be fully awake when you try to explain this." She reached into her purse and slapped down the front page of *The Inside Scoop*, one of the nation's biggest tabloids. The magazine trafficked in gossip, half-truths, and outright lies about celebrities. More than one career had been destroyed in its pages.

He peered at the photo. That was very clearly him right after he had jumped into the limo. He looked travel weary and frustrated. And sitting behind him was the outline of a woman. Her face was hidden in shadows, but it was obvious he wasn't alone in that car. The headline in giant print screamed: "Ben's Secret Affair."

Derek looked over his shoulder at the tabloid. "Who's the girl?"

"Oh no."

Ben's head started pounding again, and he felt sick.

"Oh yes. And look . . . " Zoe reached into her designer bag and slapped down four more front page stories. "There's more." All the photos were a version of the same scenario. Ben in a limo with a mystery woman. "How did this happen, Ben? As if we weren't in enough trouble with the catastrophe at the premiere and Giselle's interview. Now this." She jabbed the photo with her finger. "This complicates everything. Who is she?"

"I don't know. I just met her last night."

Derek's eyes widened. "That was fast."

"Oh Ben." Zoe Waltham, agent to the stars, straightened her shoulders and pulled out her cell phone, ready to defuse whatever public relations nightmare was about to unfold. "So what are we talking about here? Are we paying off a one night stand or burying a body?"

Ben wanted to believe she was joking, but he'd never had the nerve to ask how far she was willing to go to protect her clients.

"No, it's not like that." He rubbed his hands over his tired eyes and wished he could have a do-over for the past few days . . . maybe the past few years.

"Did you sleep with her?" The detached, business tone in Zoe's voice made him nauseated. Sometimes it was easy to forget that she wasn't his friend. But she wasn't, she was his agent. And he was her prized possession.

"No, I didn't. When I landed at LAX I got your text warning me about the story. So I stayed on the plane to watch it. By the time I left the terminal the paparazzi were everywhere. I don't know how they knew my flight, but they were waiting for me. I saw a limo parked outside, and thought it was mine and jumped in, but this girl was in it and her brother was driving."

"And," Zoe prompted.

"And nothing."

Zoe narrowed her eyes at him like a cat stalking its prey, and even Derek started to fidget under her chilly gaze.

Ben cleared his throat. "Well, nothing major. I begged him to get me out of there. The paparazzi were swarming and this girl . . . " Her name leapt to his mind, like a breeze blowing through his memory. He might not remember everything, but her name was seared into his brain, a brand he couldn't escape. "Lily. She was scared. She convinced her brother to take me home."

"And," she prompted again.

"And . . . " Ben hesitated. "I'm not entirely sure, but I may have hit on her. She was going on and on about her church and how great it is—"

"You hit on a nun?"

Ben had never seen the unflappable agent so surprised. If his head hadn't been pounding and his career wasn't on the line, he would have found it hilarious.

"She's not a nun. Her dad is the pastor of some tiny church in Hollywood. She works there. Anyway, I had too much to drink and suggested she come back to my place and she kicked me out of the car. Left me right there on the side of the road. After her brother decided not to break my face, I walked home."

Zoe set her phone down and placed her hands on the counter. Derek mumbled something about checking email and disappeared back to his office. Ben winced. He recognized the look. It was her take charge look. He was about to get a serious lecture, and he hadn't had nearly enough coffee yet.

"So let me get this straight. You got into the wrong car, proceeded to drink yourself stupid, and then you hit on a preacher's daughter while her brother was watching."

He grimaced. That sounded a lot worse than he remembered. "In all fairness I was being chased by a pack of paparazzi. I didn't have time to check itineraries with every limo driver at LAX."

"Ben, they have photos." Zoe spat the words and paced away. "What if this girl comes forward as your mystery woman? Do you have any idea of the amount of trouble she could cause to rain down on you if she doesn't keep her mouth shut?" The sharp click of her heels on the wood floor snapped like a perfectly executed military parade.

"She won't do that. I told you, she's a pastor's daughter. She works with disadvantaged kids. Look." He fumbled in the back pocket of his jeans and found the brochure Lily had given him.

Zoe snatched it and resumed her pacing. Back and forth she went, clicking a path from the kitchen to the living room and back again. Halfway through her third pass she stopped. Turning back to him, she tapped the brochure against her palm, a slow smile spreading across her face. "This looks like a very expensive event for such a small church. I'll bet they could use a big payday to make it all happen."

He shook his head. He knew where she was going. He could see the calculating wheels whirling in her brain. The nausea that rose in his stomach had nothing to do with lack of sleep or alcohol. "You've got to be kidding me. She's sweet and kind. She's like a real life Christmas movie."

Zoe walked around the kitchen island and stood beside him. She set the brochure down and laid her hand on his arm. "If the tabloids find this girl, if she gives them a story, this whole mess with Rome and Giselle will blow up in your face. There is a fine line between an attractive bad-boy and unmarketable, box office poison. And you're right on the edge." Softening her voice like she was talking to a child who was close to being sent to the principal's office, she pushed the photographic evidence of his mistakes towards him. "I can sell you as Hollywood's rebel. I can't sell you as the guy who gets caught having a one-night stand at LAX with a preacher's daughter. Do you see the problem here?"

Trapped. The word closed in around him. He was trapped by his career, by the persona Zoe had created. Trapped with no way out except to lose it all. "I told you, I didn't sleep with her."

"And you also didn't get arrested in Rome, but it doesn't matter. The only thing that matters is what it looks like. And right now it looks like your life is out of control. These photos . . ." She stabbed the tabloids with her fingernail. " . . . could end your career. There are only so many scandals you can afford, and you used up all of your freebies in Rome. You're not a stuntman anymore, Ben. You're a leading man. You've got an image to maintain."

The coffee turned sour in his mouth and he set the cup down. He hated this part of the business. He loved being an actor. He loved being on set, the lights and the chaos, and the crazy pace of it all. But the rest of it . . . the carefully crafted charade that he had to keep up every day, the constant need to maintain his celebrity image was draining. What did it matter if he ended up in the wrong limo? What did any of it matter? He missed the simplicity of showing up to the set, getting lit on fire or jumping off a building, and going home with his paycheck and his anonymity.

He looked at Zoe, the agent who had plucked him out of obscurity and made him a star, and he realized he didn't know if he could keep up the pretense of perfection much longer. The line between Ben Prescott the movie star and Ben Prescott the man was blurring, and he wasn't sure he could tell the difference anymore.

Unbidden, Lily's face swam through his memory. The echo of her laugh lingered at the edge of his mind, just out of reach. She had an honesty that was rare in Hollywood. He wondered what it would be like to live with that kind of freedom, no lies, no charades, no media ready smiles. "What if we just tell them the truth? The reporters, the studio, the gossip sites. What if we just tell them I had a bad day in Rome, got dumped, and got in the wrong car?"

Zoe gave him a condescending smile, as if he had suggested they make the Easter Bunny his next co-star. "This is Hollywood. The only truth here is the box office returns."

Ben pulled away and crossed to the expansive windows that overlooked the hills. How many years had he dreamt of being here? He had come a long way from the sixteen-year-old kid who left home with a broken-down car and fifty dollars in his wallet. How many nights had he slept in his car imagining what it would be like to have a home of his own, to have enough money that he would never be hungry, and never be dependent on anyone's mercy again? Now he was here. He had it all. And in the blink of an eye, or the flash of a camera, it could all come crashing down.

He turned his back on the sun and faced his agent. "Fine. What do you want me to do?"

She grabbed the brochure and handed it to him. "Go find this girl. Make nice. Apologize for being a drunken idiot. Then try to find out if she's talked to anyone about last night."

"I told you, she's not like that." He looked at the brochure and remembered the feel of Lily's delicate hand on his. The girl who didn't know how to talk to movie stars, the one who thought that he was worth saving.

Zoe rolled her eyes. "I'm sure she's just as sweet and innocent as a fluffy kitten, but you'd be amazed at what people will do when money is on the line. Look at this as a chance to do some good. Offer to pay for this block party thing. Write the church a big, fat check if she agrees not to talk to the press."

Bile rose in his throat. He didn't know if it was from the hangover or the cold calculation in his agent's eyes. "You want me to buy her off?"

Zoe shrugged and tossed her blonde hair over her shoulder. "You have money, they need money. Everybody wins."

He sank down the sofa and closed his eyes, wishing he could go back to sleep and wake up when it was all over. "It doesn't feel like winning."

Zoe sat beside him and took his hand. "It doesn't matter what it feels like. It only matters what it looks like."

Chapter Four

THE HOLLYWOOD MISSION OCCUPIED THE building that used to be Anderson's Plumbing Supply on the corner of Madison and Eleventh. Standing outside the door in the early afternoon light, Ben looked up at the church, swallowing the disgust that crawled its way up his throat. They may have added a cross to the front of the building and planted some pretty flowers on the outside, but it was still just an old plumbing supply building filled with people who would smile to your face then stab you in the back.

His grandmother would hate that he was so jaded. She'd probably love the building. She'd fuss over the flowers and the pretty touches on the outside. But she'd never seen the ugliness inside the church. She died before she saw what happened to her daughter and grandson. She thought all Christians were like her. She didn't know the truth.

Ben rolled his neck and blew out a deep breath. Better to get it over with. He walked up to the heavy wooden doors and hesitated. Should he knock on the door or walk right in? Deciding a church was basically a business, he opted to walk in.

The foyer was cool and quiet. Wooden tables topped with poinsettias and holly branches lined the hallway. A large Christmas tree decorated with handmade paper ornaments and a silver star twinkling on top stood in the corner. The smell of the holiday season lingered in the air—cinnamon, pine needles, and hot chocolate. It was the smell of an old-fashioned Christmas, the kind with snow on the ground and wood popping in the fireplace. Without warning, childhood memories danced through his mind. They squeezed his heart and stole his breath and for a moment he was back in Indiana, a little boy hoping for cookies and presents. And a moment was all it took for the remembered stench of alcohol and cigarettes to chase away the foolish fantasy of every Christmas joy he prayed for and never had.

He stepped further into the church, fleeing the shadows that had surrounded him. Large oak doors loomed in front of him and just beyond them he heard the faint sound of singing. He didn't recognize the song, but still he stood there, transfixed, not by the words, but by the purity of the voice that sang them. The song seeped through the weathered wood and saturated his soul, like a balm being poured over a burn. He drank in the song like a desert absorbs the rain. And when the words finally drifted away even the silence left behind was sacred.

Before he could question his decision, he opened the door to the sanctuary and walked in. The lights were dim, but he could make out the rows of chairs set up facing the stage. He was surprised to see drums, guitars, and a keyboard. It looked more like a concert stage than a church. A simple wooden cross was hung on the back wall, flanked by two large screens and standing in the middle of the stage, frozen behind a slim microphone stand and staring at him with a mix of shock and embarrassment, was the very woman he had been searching for.

Lily.

Her light brown hair was pulled up in a loose ponytail. She was wearing faded jeans and a bulky, ivory sweater. The blue eyes that had seared themselves into his brain stared at him and she clutched a stack of papers tightly in her hands. He couldn't tell if she was preparing to yell at him or run away. The stunned silence stretched on as he fumbled for something to say.

"That was beautiful." His words carried across the rows of chairs and filled the room.

Even from this distance, he could see the rush of pink that colored her cheeks. "I was just practicing for Sunday. It's a new song and—" The words tumbled out in a nervous flood. She stopped and shuffled the papers in her hands. "Thank you."

Ben began the long walk towards her, aware of her eyes following him as he walked down the aisle. "Do you sing in church?"

She nodded, glancing to the side like a rabbit preparing to run and weighing her escape routes. "I sing with the worship team."

"From outside that door it sounded like you are the worship team." Ben reached the stage and looked up at her. "You have a beautiful voice."

Blushing again, she intently studied the ridges of her tennis shoes. "That's nice of you to say. I didn't think anyone was here. I certainly didn't expect to see Ben Prescott come walking into the sanctuary."

Hearing his name broke whatever spell had woven its way through his mind. He was here for a reason. Ben Prescott had a job to do. He couldn't afford to be distracted by an enchanting voice and pretty eyes.

He walked up the stairs. He was an actor; he knew how to use a stage. "Actually, Lily, I came to apologize. I acted terribly last night. You were nice enough to bail me out of a rotten situation and I repaid you by acting like a . . . a . . . " He searched for the word.

"Jerk?" she supplied.

He smacked his hand over his heart. "I was hoping for something less harsh, but we can go with jerk." Stepping forward, he took her hand, surprised by how small it felt in his. "I really am sorry. I hope you can forgive me."

"Of course." She pulled her hand back and shuffled the sheet music again. "I can't believe you came all the way down here."

"I had to. I didn't want your one impression of me to be that I was a . . ."

"Jerk?" she said.

"There's that word again." He smiled like a boy caught sneaking an extra cookie. "Yes, a jerk." Unable to stop himself, he reached for the acoustic guitar resting in a stand nearby. "May I?"

"You play?" The surprise on her face made him laugh.

"It's been a while. So it might not count as playing anymore. It might be more like attempting to play."

Lily nodded, and he picked up the guitar and strummed a few notes, relishing the familiar feel of the strings. His fingers found the chords like a traveller coming home. Music was one of the few things he hung on to from his youth, the last vestige of the boy who would grow up and become Ben Prescott. He hadn't found a role that would let him play on screen, but maybe someday.

He looked at Lily across the guitar, the simple notes he played fading into the background. "I was wrong and I'd like to make it up to you."

"It's not necessary, Mr. Prescott—"

"Ben."

She blinked and stuttered as if she were trying the word out in her mind before saying it out loud. "Ben. You don't have to do anything else. It means a lot to me that you came down here."

"Well, I still want to do something . . . even out my karma and all that." He set the guitar back in its stand.

With a smile, she shook her head. "I don't believe in karma."

"And I don't believe in anything. But this will make me feel better." Ben reached into his back pocket and pulled out his checkbook. "I had a chance to look through the brochure you gave me. It looks like you guys are doing really important work in this community. So, I'd like to pay for it."

Her mouth dropped open and he was sure the surprise on her face had made the entire trip worthwhile. "You want to pay for it? The whole thing? With a check?"

"Don't worry, it won't bounce." Grinning, he raised his hand in a boyish promise. "Overpaid movie star's honor."

Confusion wrinkled her forehead, uncertainty creeping in where surprise had been. "I don't understand."

"Look, you were nice to me and I was, as you have repeatedly pointed out, a jerk. I want to make up for it. Besides, I still owe you for the ride."

"But you got only half of a ride."

"Well, your brother didn't run me over so a nice, long walk home was getting off pretty easy."

"Sorry about that."

"Don't be. I deserved it." His pen slid across the expensive paper. He glanced up at her as he wrote. "I'll bet it makes one heck of a story, too."

"I suppose so. My friend Kate will laugh until she cries when I tell her about it."

Tension seized in his gut, but he didn't let it show. "I'm happy to know I will be fodder for all of your future family dinner parties."

"Not all of them." Lily smiled mischievously. "Just for the next two or three years."

Ben laughed. It was the same laugh he used when producers thought they were being funny: forced, practiced, and fake. "I'm sure there are plenty of people who would love to hear it. So," he paused and tore the check out, "has anyone asked you about it?"

"Like who? My dad?"

Ben raised his hands in mock self-defense. "Dads are already scary enough without them finding out about your worst moments. No, I mean has anyone else asked about it?" He folded the check and tried to sound casual. "Reporters, media, anyone like that?"

Tilting her head, she pursed her lips. "Are you asking me if I've talked to the press about you?"

"Well, it's just . . . it was a crazy night . . . all those reporters . . . and I'd hate for you get caught up in all that garbage." He leaned against the podium, crossing his ankles with a nonchalance he didn't feel. "I mean you saw how it works, it's awful. You don't want to get hounded by reporters or photographers, right?"

Her eyes narrowed, her carefree smile had vanished. "No."

Ben ignored the guilt twisting in his stomach and forced an encouraging smile on his face. "Of course not. It's the worst part of my job. They take something so innocent and turn it into something awful." Rounding the podium, he held out the check to her. "So it'd probably be for the best if you didn't tell anyone about it. That way you don't have to worry about being plastered all over the papers and gossip sites."

Lily started rolling the papers in her hand, smaller and smaller, until they disappeared into a strangled cone. "So you're worried about me, is that it?" She took a step towards him, faint embers of understanding sparking to life in her eyes. "You came all the way down here to make sure I wasn't being hounded by reporters . . . for my own sake, right?" Stopping a few feet from him, she crossed her arms. "How very noble of you."

"Lily, I—"

"Let me tell you what I think, Mr. Movie Star. I think you're worried I'm going to spill your little story to the press. You came down here to save your own sorry reputation. You came down here—"

She glanced at the check in his hand, then her gaze flew back to his, and he knew the moment it all fell into place. The pieces fit together and the shy sweetness behind her eyes ignited into an angry, wildfire of flashing blue. "You came down here to pay me off."

"Lily, it's not like that—"

"Oh really? Then what's it like? You happened to have a change of heart on your long walk home last night. You were so moved by the brochure I gave you," she took a step towards him, "the one you didn't even read, that you want to hand me a big, fat check and at the same time, you just happen to mention I shouldn't talk to the press about you? Who do you think I am?" She jabbed him in the chest. "Who do you think you are?"

"Look, I really am sorry. I was having a bad night. I messed up. I'm trying to make it right."

"No, you're trying to avoid making it worse." Lily stomped away and tightened her ponytail before facing him again. "Mr. Prescott, we don't need your money. Our church will be fine without you." Ben opened his mouth but she threw up a hand to stop him. "And I certainly don't need to waste my time talking to the press about you. If your reputation suffers, it won't be because of me."

Cold, hard regret gripped him. He was a fool.

"I'm sorry, Lily." They were the truest words he had ever spoken, but it was too late. Sometimes "sorry" isn't enough.

Hurt and anger warred in her eyes. "You should go."

Ben looked at the check in his hand. He held it like the obscene thing it was. With a nod, he turned away. His footsteps didn't make a sound as he walked back up the aisle and out the door. There was no reason to look back.

Chapter Five

LILY WATCHED THE DOOR TO the sanctuary swing closed. Anger coursed through her veins and she squeezed her hands to keep them from shaking. She wanted to race up the aisle and give that arrogant movie star a few more choice words. The nerve of him suggesting that she was after a quick buck. As if she would ever stoop to selling out another human being for money.

Frustration propelled her off the stage and into the backstage room. She dropped the sheet music onto a small coffee table in the center of the room. The pages were hopelessly mangled; she'd have to print out new ones before Sunday morning. And that would be Ben Prescott's fault, too.

"Maybe I'll run to the gossips and tell them that, too. Selfish, stupid, rude movie star causes worship leader to destroy sheet music." She made a face in the empty room. "How much would you pay me for that one, you big jerk?"

She plopped down onto the ancient sofa that took up one wall of the small room and tried to calm down. This room was normally her safe haven, a respite from the hectic pace of ministry and teaching. It was quiet and filled with the echoes of hundreds of hours of laughter and prayer. The worship team met here, they prayed here before service, humbled themselves before God and readied themselves to go on stage and worship Him.

She took a deep breath. She didn't take her responsibility as a worship leader lightly. It was a privilege to lead the congregation in song. It wasn't a right she had earned; it was a gift she had been given. A gift she was profoundly grateful for. She wanted to protect that platform, to keep the sanctuary a place that honored God, thanked Him and worshipped Him.

And that self-obsessed actor had strutted in and turned it into some sort of bargaining table.

Lily grabbed the discarded sheet music and wadded the papers into a ball. She flung it across the room just as the door opened.

"Whoa!" Noah ducked behind the door. "What did I do now?"

Lily flopped back against the sofa cushions. "Sorry. It's not you."

"Glad to hear it." Noah picked up the ball of crumpled papers and dropped it into the trashcan that she had missed by several feet. "At least I don't have to worry about your aim." He leaned against the wall and crossed his arms. "Want to talk about it?"

She pursed her lips into a pout. "Not really."

"Okay." Noah pushed off the wall and headed for the door.

"Ben Prescott was here."

Whistling, he turned back around. "You could have led with that. What did he want?"

Fresh irritation drove away the little bit of calm she had found, and she gave the frustration free rein. "He wanted to buy our silence." She waited for her brother to be offended, to join her in her righteous indignation, to be equally mad at Ben Prescott and his self-centered narcissism.

But he considered the information and then shrugged. "That makes sense."

His matter of fact tone shocked her. She hadn't expected him to be so calm about Ben's proposition. Given how upset he'd been last night, she thought he would take the news much worse, that he'd be her partner in justified anger. "How does this make sense? He thought I was going to run to the press and tell them all about his stupid behavior . . . for money. How could he think that? How rude can he be?"

Noah crossed the room and sat beside her. "You don't know these people, Brat. I do. They're used to being manipulated and played and having to keep up a façade. They can never be who they really are. What you saw last night was probably the most honest he had ever been and that scared him. His whole career is built on what people think of him, on letting the world see only certain parts of him." He rested his arms on his knees. "And you heard him, he's surrounded by people who make money off of him. Of course, he'd be freaked out that you might see a chance for getting a quick payday off his name."

His words made sense but she wasn't ready to be mollified by any amount of logic or understanding. "I'd never do that. And neither would you."

"No. But he doesn't know that. He doesn't know us at all."

"You'd think the fact that we work at a church would have given him a clue."

"You heard him last night. It doesn't sound like church is a big selling point for him."

She tried to imagine what it would be like to hate the church so much. What had happened to make him turn his back on God? She didn't want to admit it, but the thought had plagued her all night. What hurts were hidden in Ben Prescott's past?

She tried to hold on to her anger, but the gentle nudge of the Holy Spirit was there, urging her to release it. The simple truth was that she was disappointed. For one wild moment when she saw him walk into the sanctuary, she hoped that he had come to visit the church, that her words from last night had struck a chord with him, that maybe, just maybe, she had planted a seed of God's love in his heart and she was going to see a miracle of God's salvation. But none of that happened. God hadn't used her at all.

But she had no right to be disappointed that things didn't work out according to her plan. God was in charge and He knew what He was doing. Her anger faded, replaced little by little with peace. "Fine," she conceded. "Maybe it was understandable, but it was still rude."

"I'm not saying it wasn't." Noah rubbed his chin. "So how much did he offer?"

"Noah! What would Dad say if he heard you?" Laughing, she swatted his shoulder.

Wrapping his arm around her, he gave her a hug. "You did good, Brat."

Lily exhaled and let it go. After all, it wasn't her fight. Ben Prescott was in God's hands. If she couldn't reach him, maybe someone else would.

Chapter Six

BEN STOOD IN THE EMPTY foyer of the church, feeling the solidness of the closed door behind him. The story wasn't going to get out. Zoe would be thrilled. He leaned back against the door to the sanctuary. With the story contained, he could move on and focus on the premiere. He should be happy. The pressure was off, the danger averted; he should feel relieved.

But he didn't.

He felt awful. The look in Lily's eyes had been enough to show him how wrong he was. Zoe might know how to control Hollywood, but she didn't know anything about the people who lived and worked outside of the bright lights and shady deals of the movie industry. Maybe he didn't either.

Stuffing the check in his pocket, he headed out a glass door that led to the side of the church. It opened onto what must have been an old loading dock. The concrete platform and sloping, delivery ramp were still there, but the space had been transformed into a garden in the midst of the city. Potted plants and raised beds surrounded a collection of mismatched picnic tables and rocking chairs. A well-used grill stood off to the side against the church's outer wall. Beyond the loading ramp, a playground sat like a colorful island in an asphalt ocean. Swings, teeter-totters, and a large jungle gym with slides and a bridge connecting two plastic turrets sparkled in vibrant contrast to the drab greys and browns that lay just on the other side of a chain link fence that surrounded the church property.

It looked nothing like the white clapboard church of his childhood. That church had hard, wooden pews, no air conditioning and certainly no playground. Vivid memories of being shuttled down to the basement for his Sunday school class drifted up from his past. The dark, steep staircase had always frightened him, and his mother had kept her finger firmly pressed between his shoulder blades to keep him moving. But the Hollywood Mission was different. There were no dark staircases here, no sense of dread that followed him around. The church was welcoming, as if it had been waiting for him.

Taking a seat at one of the tables, he pulled out his cell phone and dialed Zoe's number. She picked up on the first ring. "Well?"

"It's done. She isn't going to say anything." He decided not to mention the fact that Lily turned down the money. Zoe might understand the movie industry better than most people, but he doubted she'd understand Lily's integrity.

"Good job, Ben. I know you don't like my methods, but they work. Now you can forget this whole thing." Even as she said the words, he wondered how easy it was going to be to forget Lily.

He pinched the bridge of his nose. "Look, Zoe, I'm still at her church. Can we talk later?"

"Of course," she purred. "Let's meet for dinner tonight at The Bistro and we can talk about how to respond to Giselle's interview. We need to stay on top of it and make sure we take control of the story. Giselle may have dumped you, but we'll make sure everyone knows it was because she couldn't handle your fame."

Zoe's voice grated on his nerves. Lies, lies, and more lies. "That's not what happened."

"It doesn't matter. Once you sign the contract for your next film, we'll have a year to recover before the movie comes out. We just need to get the studio to commit, then we can take a breather. And now that we don't have to worry about this mystery girl showing up in the press, we can spin those limo photos any way we want. Maybe we call her your assistant."

"There's nothing to spin. Leave Giselle alone and leave this girl out of it. It's over." The words came out harsher than he intended, but he didn't care.

There was a pause and then Zoe spoke, her words coated in a fake sweetness that he recognized as her placating voice. "Okay, Ben. I know this has been a tough few days for you. Why don't you go home and get some rest. I sent over some scripts for you to look at. Let's focus on capitalizing on the buzz around *Blood and Honor*. This could be your biggest year ever. I've got a feeling great things are coming your way." He rolled his eyes. Was he really that easy to manipulate? "You're an amazing actor and we're going straight to the top."

Apparently, Zoe had no problem including herself in his career trajectory. He needed her and she needed him. They were stuck together as long as he wanted to keep working and stay famous. "Thanks, Zoe. We'll talk later."

"The Bistro at seven. Remember, you're my super star, Ben. Kisses." She made a kissing sound into the phone and hung up.

Jamming his phone back into his pocket, he closed his eyes. Everything about the past few days felt wrong. The world had shifted around him and he didn't know where the pieces fit anymore. He had everything he ever wanted, but he felt hollow inside. His life had imploded and he didn't know how to fix it, but he knew Zoe's plans weren't helping.

Dating Giselle had been Zoe's idea and it was a mistake from the beginning. They didn't have anything in common except their longing for fame and the fact that they looked good together in photos. He was pretty sure Giselle had staged the break up at the premiere for exposure and it had worked.

The sad truth was that he didn't miss her. He was battling an emptiness he didn't understand and the only thing he had learned was that the answer wasn't at the bottom of a bottle. He had tried that and this is where he ended up, scandal plagued and sitting at a church he didn't believe in. If he'd had the energy, he would have laughed at the situation.

"Well look at that . . . I don't remember ordering a pompous movie star." The limo driver and over-protective brother appeared from around the corner. "What brings you to our quiet corner of Hollywood? I doubt you're here for another ride."

"It's Noah, right?" Ben walked towards him and extended his hand. Noah shook it with a little more force than necessary.

"Very good, Mr. Prescott. Is there something I can help you with?"

"No. I just came down to apologize to your sister for last night. I was a . . . "

"Jerk?"

Ben sighed. "That does seem to be the consensus."

"Yes, you were." Noah regarded him with cool appraisal in his eyes. "But," he said, his tone suddenly friendly and light, "we all have bad days."

Ben squinted at the limo driver. He was prepared for another fight. He was even prepared for the guy to follow through on his threat to break his nose. He was not prepared for a friendly conversation. "Yeah, that's true . . . thanks."

Noah started walking towards the parking lot and Ben fell into step beside him. A large carport was set up in a far corner of the lot and Noah's limo was resting in the shade. Pulling a rag out of his pocket, he wiped at a faint smudge on one of the tinted windows. "I started driving part time when my parents planted this church. Money was tight and it was a good way to pick up some extra cash. I worked for another guy's company until I could save up the money to buy my own car."

Ben watched him wipe away tiny specks of dirt. He remembered being able to buy his first new car. He had paid cash for it with the paycheck from his first speaking role in a movie. He'd driven off the lot feeling like a king. "It sounds like interesting work. Meeting new people, seeing the city."

Noah shrugged. "It has its moments." He walked to the back of the limo and Ben followed. "You know, driving a limo is really just like driving an expensive cab. We have to be licensed and all the cars are registered." Ben looked at the bumper and saw the white numbers stuck there. "So it's pretty easy to track down a particular car. If someone was interested in it and willing to do a bit of research."

The anxiety Ben had set aside was back, clawing its way up his throat. He kept his face passive even as his palms started to sweat. "That's good to know." He started searching for a way out. "Well, I don't want to take up anymore of your time."

"Oh it's no bother, Mr. Prescott." Noah reached into the backseat of the car and retrieved his cell phone. Even from this distance, Ben could see the voicemail notifications. "It seems I've become very popular this morning."

He tapped the screen and a woman's voice filled the air. "Hi there, this is Alyssa Harrison from *The Inside Scoop*. I would love to talk to you about having Ben Prescott and his friend in your limo last night. That must have been exciting. Give me a call and let's talk." Noah started the next message before she finished leaving her phone number.

It was another's woman's voice. "Good morning, this is Janie Gibbs from *Celebrity Exclusive*. I saw that you picked up Ben Prescott and a young lady in your limo at LAX last night. I'd love to get your side of the story. Our paper offers a substantial payment for exclusive stories, so give me a call and let's make some magic."

He tapped the screen again.

"That's enough," Ben said.

Noah glanced down at the phone. "Twenty-six voicemails and more texts than I can count. I had to stash the phone in the car before my head exploded from the constant ringing."

The trap was closing in around him. Noah had a story that all the gossip blogs and tabloids would pounce on and the limo driver knew it.

"Look," Ben said. "I'm sorry you got caught in the middle of this. It certainly wasn't my intention. I'm trying to keep this out of the press, too."

"Hence your noble and selfless offer to pay for our block party?"

He winced. Bad news traveled fast around that church. Rubbing the back of his neck, he wished for coffee. The morning was not going well. "Look, I wasn't trying to offend anyone. I was just trying to apologize."

Noah smirked at the feeble excuse and Ben tossed his hands in the air. "Fine and also keep my name out of the papers. Is that so terrible? Things are bad enough already."

The limo driver studied him, a cat toying with a mouse. "I think we can come to an arrangement."

"Great." Ben dug in his pocket for the check Lily had rejected. But Noah stopped him. "Oh, I don't want your money."

"Then what?"

He leaned against the limo and crossed his arms. Noah tapped his finger against his lips, pretending to think it over. "You know, I was just thinking how amazing it would be if we had a big name celebrity, maybe even a movie star, helping us out with the block party."

Taking a step back, Ben laughed. "You can't be serious."

"I understand if you're not interested." Noah looked down at his phone. "What was the first girl's name? She sounded really nice. Was it Amy? Audrey?" He started to scroll through the messages.

"Isn't blackmail against your religion or something?"

Noah grinned. "This isn't blackmail. I'm just giving you a chance to do a good deed."

The impossibility of the situation wrapped around him like a hungry snake. He didn't want to work at a church. When he left home he told himself he'd never go back to a church, he'd never be a part of the hypocrisy that kept his mother chained to an abusive husband. His grandmother may have found her joy in the Bible, but it wasn't for him. "It's not that simple. I have to be very careful about what I get involved in. I can't have people thinking I'm a . . . a . . . " He waved his hands helplessly.

"A Christian?"

"Look, it's nothing personal. But that's the way it is in this business. I've got a certain image, a reputation."

"It isn't much of a reputation right now, though, is it?"

Ben clenched his jaw, but he couldn't deny the truth of those words. "Look, Hollywood isn't big on conversion stories, okay?"

Noah pushed off the car and started walking towards the church. "Well, if that's how you feel about it." He started scrolling through his phone again.

Ben chased after him. "Wait."

But Noah kept walking. "No. No. We'd hate to bother you. I'm sure you're going to be very busy in the next few days." He made it to the top of the loading ramp and paused. "Good luck, Mr. Prescott."

As Noah walked to the glass door that led back into the church foyer, Ben cursed under his breath and ran up to the ramp. He slammed the door shut and kept his hand against the glass. "Fine. Fine I'll help with your block party thing. Just delete the voicemails and texts."

Noah smiled and held up his phone. "Already done."

"What?"

"Mr. Prescott, I'm not interested in making a quick buck and I'm not interested in ruining your precious movie career. I am, however, deeply interested in helping the people of this community. You said you wanted to make up for last night. This is your chance."

Someone started knocking on the glass. Ben peered inside and saw Lily standing on the other side, a deep frown on her face. He dropped his hand and stepped back.

She shoved the door open and stared at the two men. "What's going on out here?"

"Hey, Brat, guess what?" Noah threw an arm around Ben's shoulders and flashed a brilliant smile. "Ben is going to help with the block party. Isn't that great?"

The color drained from Lily's face. She looked as sick as Ben felt.

Zoe was going to kill him.

Chapter Seven

LILY GLARED AT HER BROTHER across the dinner table. "This is a terrible idea."

"No, it's not," he replied and stuffed a forkful of salad into his still grinning mouth.

"Dad." Giving up on reasoning with Noah, she turned to her father instead. "Do you really think this is good for the church? Having some playboy celebrity slap his name on our event? He isn't even a believer."

But, in truth, it was more than that. The bitterness in his voice, the poorly concealed contempt he had for Christianity. Ben Prescott wasn't just an unbeliever; he was as far from God as he could get and he had no interest in coming back.

Pastor Evan Shaw propped his elbows on the wood dining table and steepled his fingers. His sandy hair was sprinkled with grey and fine lines creased the corners of his eyes. "I haven't made up my mind about it yet. I'd like to meet the young man and get to know him a bit more."

"What more do you need to know? He hates church and I'm pretty sure he hates God." She was stunned by her dad's reaction. Ben would be a disaster for the church. And if she had to see him all the time, she would probably end up throwing something at him. "He came down here to buy our silence, to make sure we didn't tell the paparazzi about his awful behavior last night. He isn't interested in doing a good deed, he just wants to keep his image intact." Pushing her plate away, she crossed her arms, ready for a fight.

Her dad's eyebrows rose as he looked at the mutinous expression on her face. "You remind me so much of your mother. You have her kindness and her fierce passion."

Some of the defiance she felt dissipated at his words. Her mother had taught her what it means to serve, to reach out to those in need. She swallowed past the lump that rose in her throat. "Thank you, Dad."

He laid his hand across hers. "But you also have her stubborn streak."

Lily tried to deny it, but Noah was laughing too hard. Frustration clawed its way through her veins again. Why was she the only one who could see the catastrophe this would be? "How is it stubborn to want to protect the church? He doesn't care about the ministry or the neighborhood. The only thing Ben Prescott cares about is his reputation."

Sitting back in his chair, her dad's gaze was measured and steady. "So you don't want him here because you don't think he's sincere?"

"Exactly." Was she finally getting through to them? It didn't matter how much fame or celebrity Ben could bring to the block party. They would be fine without him.

Dad nodded thoughtfully. "What about the parents who drop their kids off for children's church on Sundays and then leave? Those parents aren't sincerely seeking God either. They're not even staying for the service. They just want free babysitting for an hour. Should we turn them away, too?"

Noah whistled and gave her a triumphant look. She sent him an icy stare in return.

"That's not the same. Were here to minister to the neighborhood. Teaching the children, opening our doors to the parents, sharing the Gospel with them, that's what we're called to do. Maybe they're not staying for the service now, but that might change."

"And you think we aren't called to minister to Ben Prescott? He doesn't live here so he doesn't count?" There was no judgment in his voice, no condemnation, but her dad had never shied away from the truth.

Lily squirmed in her chair. "Of course, he counts, but he isn't . . . he doesn't . . . "

"Doesn't what?"

"He doesn't belong here." The sentence died on her lips. Guilt and conviction stole the heat from her words. She knew how it sounded and she knew how wrong it was. After all, she was the one who told Ben that everyone was worth saving. If she truly believed that, then she had no right to close the doors of the church to him, no matter how arrogant or angry he was.

Her dad laid his hand on her shoulder and squeezed gently. "Don't let the money and fame fool you, Sweetheart. He might need this church more than you know."

Sighing, she knew she had lost. But she didn't like it. It still looked like a disaster in the making, but the only thing she could do was trust God. Well, trust God and keep a close eye on Ben Prescott.

"There you go, Sis," Noah said with a grin. "Turns out, I was downright brilliant."

"Not so fast." Noah froze as their dad directed his pastor's voice to him. "I'm happy to give Ben the opportunity to help, but I don't feel comfortable using his celebrity to advertise the event."

Noah choked on his water. "What? Do you have any idea how much free publicity having Ben Prescott on board can bring us?"

Her dad held up his hand and Noah fell silent. "I understand what you're saying, but it isn't right to bring him in for the sole purpose of exploiting his name. If he truly wants to help, we can always use an extra pair of hands when it comes to prepping and running the event."

Noah blinked in disbelief. "You want to use a no-kidding movie star to grill hot dogs and set up bouncy houses?"

"If that's where the needs are."

Lily laughed and gave her big brother the sassy little sister look she knew he hated. "Well, there you go, Noah. You're responsible for recruiting the most famous hot dog griller in the world."

"Oh shut up, Brat."

"Noah Shaw!" her dad scolded.

"Sorry," Noah mumbled in half-hearted apology.

Their dad reached over and ruffled his son's hair. "But first things first. I want to meet this young man. Let's have him over."

Lily and Noah stared at each other across the table.

"Well, I'm not calling him," she said.

"But I'm sure he'd rather hear from you than me."

"Too bad. He's your new best friend. And this whole stupid thing was your idea. You can call him."

Noah sighed. "Fine. I—" He stopped and laughed.

"What?"

"I don't have his number."

Dropping her forehead into her hand, Lily sighed. Of course, her brother had forgotten that one little detail. "Well, I doubt we'll ever see him again."

"He'll be back," Noah said. "You'll see."

"Not likely." She rose to clear her plate from the table.

"Okay, that's enough." Her dad ended the discussion. "If he comes back, make sure you invite him over for dinner. Let's get to know him better and see what God is doing."

Lily rinsed the dishes in the sink, happy her dad couldn't see her roll her eyes. What were the chances Ben Prescott would ever show his face at their church again?

Chapter Eight

"YOU ARE NEVER GOING THERE again," Zoe hissed. She grabbed her wine glass and took an unladylike gulp.

Ben saw the flash in her plastic-surgery-preserved eyes and knew he had been right to break the news to her in a public place. They were seated at a corner table in the trendy Bistro restaurant. The smooth, brown leather bench seats complimented the neutral colors of the dining room. Dark wainscoting lined the walls and the butter yellow glow from hanging pendant lights was a welcome reprieve from the harsh neon bulbs glowing on the streets outside.

As always, the restaurant was full. Actors, directors, and power players sat beside the hopeful up-and-comers looking for a break and the once-famous faces trying to find a way back into the spotlight. Conversations were animated, but quiet. He had the feeling that every table was putting on a show. It was the type of place people went to be seen, to be noticed, to remind the world that they were still alive. It was one of Zoe's favorites.

Ben took his eyes off the dozens of dramas going on around them and focused on Zoe's irritated face. "You told me to make sure they wouldn't talk to the press. I did."

"I told you to write that girl a check and be done with it. Not get wrapped up in some holy roller street revival." She drained the rest of her wine and started searching for the waiter.

He sat back and smoothed his shirt. It wasn't going quite as badly as he imagined. A few years ago, when he was still an unknown actor looking for his big break, a producer had offered him a role and he had been so excited he had accepted without talking to Zoe first. When she found out, she threw a framed photo of her and the President across the room. Ben was pretty sure she hadn't been aiming for him, but he hadn't had the nerve to ask. Since then, he had never accepted another job without talking to her first. Until now.

"Look," he said, unconcerned by both the blackmail and his agent's reaction. "It's going to be fine. I'll shake some hands, take some photos, and go home. It will be good publicity."

"It's a church." She spat the last word like it was a disease.

As the waiter refilled her wine glass, Zoe made eye contact with a producer who had been hounding her for weeks and gave him a subtle nod of her head. The producer smiled and lifted his glass in a silent toast. The unspoken communication between power players was sealing deals and setting new projects in motion. In the back of his mind, Ben wondered if Zoe had just signed him away for another project. Who was he being sold to and for how much?

He tried to shake the melancholy thought away. He was an actor and she was his agent. They both had a serious investment in his career. When she first spotted him working as a stunt double for one of her clients, she offered to sign him on the spot. And Ben, a struggling stuntman who knew nothing about the industry, agreed. Truthfully, he doubted he could have said no. Zoe was like a force of nature blowing through the set and touching down right in front of him, sweeping him up in her whirlwind of plans and calculations. When he signed the contract, tying his career and his life to her, she promised that if he did everything she said, she would make him a star and she had. He had no reason to doubt her now.

Fixing a smile on her face, she turned her attention back to him. "We have worked for years to get you here. You're Hollywood's rebel. You can't go changing your tune now. If you wanted to be the sweet, Christian boy you should have thought of that years ago."

Ben swirled his water glass, watching the ice cubes bump and clink. "I'm not joining the church. I'm showing up to help under-privileged kids. What's not to like about that?" He took a sip, searching for more reasons to get Zoe on board so she'd stop making it such a big deal. "Besides, it's Christmas, no one is going to care."

"I care," she snapped. "This isn't part of the plan. It's a PR nightmare. You have to get out of it." She said the words like a pronouncement, an executive order he was expected to follow.

"No."

Her eyes narrowed to slits and she glared at him. "Excuse me?"

"No. I said I'd do it, and I will. I'm keeping my word."

The waiter returned with their entrees. Zoe pursed her lips in tense silence as she waited for him to leave. Ben thanked him and almost begged him not to go.

Zoe leaned across the table, her voice dropping to a sharp whisper. "This could ruin your career."

"You're being overly dramatic," Ben whispered back and winked.

But she wasn't mollified. "Coming on the heels of the whole debacle in Rome and Giselle's theatrics in the press, this is going to look like some desperate conversion story. Is that what who you want to be?"

Picking up his fork, he pushed the risotto around his plate. Who did he want to be? If Lily and Zoe were two extremes, he was somewhere in the middle, caught in a no-man's land of emptiness, wandering like a stranger through the landscape of his own life.

When he didn't answer, Zoe sighed and picked up her wine glass again. "Fine, but don't come crying to me when you end up blacklisted by every major studio in town. If you want to find Jesus or whatever, do it behind closed doors. No one cares about your faith as long as they don't have to see it."

Ben flashed her his most charming smile. "Who else would I come crying to? You know you're my rock."

She took a sip of her wine, placated by the compliment. "I still don't like it."

"I know. And I promise I will do everything you tell me to do from now on."

Zoe snorted. "I'll believe that when I see it."

He laughed, relieved the worst was over. It might not be the best solution, but he'd make it work. And, as much as he hated to admit it, he wouldn't mind seeing the blue-eyed pastor's daughter again.

The door to the Bistro opened and his smile vanished. A hush descended on the restaurant as every eye turned to the door and then swung back to him.

Like an empress entering her throne room, Giselle sauntered into the restaurant on the arm of Liam Donovan, her co-star turned boyfriend.

"Well, this should be fun," Zoe said and raised her pencil-thin brows.

Liam and Giselle were shown to a table in the center of the room. Ben felt the eyes of everyone in the room watching him, gauging his reaction. Giselle reached across the table and rested her hand on Liam's wrist. He said something that made her laugh and wag a finger at him. The ordinariness of it all, the carefree picture of them together, after all the turmoil she had caused struck him with the force of a slap.

His memories of that last night in Rome were sketchy, but he clearly remembered Giselle showing up at the premiere and picking a fight. True he'd had a star-struck tourist on his arm at the time, but it hadn't meant anything. When the fight turned into a break up, Ben had been escorted from his own premiere by the Roman police while Giselle shed tears through her waterproof mascara, and the press devoured it all. Her interview and the photos of Ben being led away by the police had set him up for the paparazzi ambush at the airport.

So while he was a scandal waiting to explode, she was the darling of the gossip sites. The poor girl who got her heart broken by Hollywood's bad boy. Except, she didn't look too broken hearted as she stared dreamily across the table at that pretty boy Liam.

Emotion beat logic and he tossed his napkin on the table. "Excuse me," he said as he stood.

"Ben, don't," Zoe said, but her protest was too late. He strode across the dining room. Giselle didn't see him coming until he had already reached their table. When she looked up, no doubt expecting to see the waiter, her eyes widened in shock. It was almost enough to make him forgive her. Almost.

"Hello, Giselle. Liam." He didn't even look at his replacement. "Fancy meeting you here."

She swallowed hard. "How are you, Ben?"

"Cold and indifferent, according to the last interview I read."

Giselle shifted in her chair and played with the edges of her napkin. "Look, I'm sorry about the whole thing in Rome. I know it was bad timing."

Ben laughed, aware that everyone was watching, and not caring one bit. "Bad timing?"

"Would you keep your voice down?" She demanded, but he saw her eyes slide to the audience that was hanging on their every word. Giselle may not have been the most talented actress, but she knew the value of a good headline.

"Did you need the publicity that badly?"

Giselle recoiled from the blunt honesty of his words and he knew he had stumbled upon the truth. It had all been a publicity stunt. He shouldn't have been surprised. He'd seen it play out countless times before, but it still stung. He'd never loved Giselle, but he wouldn't have sacrificed her on the altar of gossip, no matter how badly he needed the press.

Liam leapt to his feet. "That's enough."

"Sit down, Donovan." Ben's eyes were cold and hard as he stared at Liam. Blood pumped through him, hot and angry, ready for a fight. Echoes of his father's cruel words and the stunning pain of his fists broke through the frozen ice of his memories. He wasn't helpless, not anymore, and he wouldn't be helpless ever again. Moving of their own volition, his fists clenched at his sides.

"Stop it!" Giselle grabbed his arm. "This is not the place." She plastered a smile on her face, posing for the cameras she couldn't see but that she knew were snapping away.

Like a light exploding to life in a darkened room, the whole situation was suddenly, amazingly clear to him. It was ridiculous, all of it. The drama, the cunning photo ops, it made him sick. His life had become as fake as the movies he made. Staring down at his ex-girlfriend, he tried to find a flicker of emotion, a remnant of anything they shared, but found nothing. "I hope the payday was worth it."

A gasp echoed from a few tables over and Zoe appeared at his side. "It's time to go, Ben."

Slowly, his fist unclenched. The other patrons were watching him with hunger in their eyes, waiting for the scene to unfold. He could hear the stories being written, the captions and comments being composed. They were all watching, entitled to be observers to his pain because of who he was. He had given them that right, he'd signed up for it and he had no way to escape it.

Though he ached for a fight, he simply nodded. He turned his back on Giselle and the time they had spent together. None of it had been real, none of it mattered.

"Yes, Ben," Liam said, a patronizing tone oozing from the words he cooed to his back. "Run along home. I'm sure you won't have any trouble finding another woman to disappoint."

Ben resisted the urge to respond, resisted the taunt of his father's words dancing in the corridors of his mind.

"Coward." Liam spat the words, then reached out and shoved Ben in the back.

Ben stumbled forward, colliding with the table in front of him. The two women seated there yelped in surprise, their water glasses tipping over, and soaking the tablecloth. He gave them a dashing smile as he straightened. "Good evening, ladies. I highly recommend the risotto." Then he looked at his agent. "Sorry, Zoe."

"For what?" she asked.

"This."

The Battle for Giselle

By Alyssa Harrison

Trendy LA eatery, The Bistro, was unprepared for the brawl that broke out last night between Ben Prescott and Liam Donovan. Prescott was having dinner with his agent when his ex-girlfriend Giselle Ferris arrived with her new beau. Giselle made headlines earlier this week when she very publicly broke up with the star at the European premiere of his latest movie, *Blood and Honor*, and her subsequent interview in which she blamed Prescott's distance and neglect as well as unproven accusations of infidelity for the demise of the Ben-Elle relationship. Prescott has thus far refused to comment on the story, but he is clearly taking it much harder than anyone thought.

Witnesses say Prescott was obviously upset when Giselle arrived on the arm of hunky Liam Donovan, looking thoroughly smitten with the handsome newcomer. According to one diner, Prescott confronted the couple and an argument ensued. After some heated words were exchanged, Prescott reportedly threw the first punch, hitting Donovan in the face. Donovan retaliated, and the brawling boys broke at least one table during their fight. The two men were escorted from the restaurant by the wait staff and management. Police were called to the scene, but no arrests were made and neither man required medical attention. There's no word on whether charges will be filed in the future.

A representative for Team Gi-Li, issued this statement, "This has been an extremely difficult and emotional time for everyone involved and we ask that everyone respect their privacy." Mr. Prescott has not responded to requests for comment.

Chapter Nine

"HOW ABOUT A WESTERN SET on Mars?"

Ben stared at the ceiling of the living room. He was stretched out on the sofa while Derek sat in a chair beside him going through another stack of scripts Zoe had sent over. She must be furious because she hadn't spoken to him since she talked the police out of arresting him and then sent him home to lay low until his black eye was gone.

She had obviously been in touch with Derek since he showed up every morning with a new collection of scripts for him to read. Zoe might be mad at him but she was still in charge of his career and she wasn't about to let him forget it.

"Maybe," he replied without any enthusiasm.

Derek sighed. "Okay, we'll add that to the maybe pile."

It had been three days since the ill-fated dinner at The Bistro and he had been stuck in the house ever since. Photos of the fight were still playing on every morning talk show and entertainment news channel. They were plastered across the tabloids and decorating the cover pages of gossip sites. He didn't need to look out the window to know the paparazzi were staked out in front of his gates. If it wasn't for his housekeeper doing the grocery shopping, he would starve to death before the photo hungry sharks left their makeshift camp.

"What about that one?" Derek pointed to the script that was lying forgotten across Ben's chest. "What did you think of it?"

He picked it up and stared at the unfamiliar cover. He hadn't actually read the script. It was just there. Just words on a page that didn't make any sense. It might have looked like he was working, like he actually cared about his career and was engaged in choosing his next big project. But in reality, he was sitting in silence, staring at words he wasn't reading, counting down the hours until he could go back to bed and forget about the day.

There was nothing he could depend on, nothing solid in his life, no rock to cling to, no foundation to stand on. Everything was shifting, blown about by the fickle winds of fans and focus groups. His grip on life was tenuous. He was at the mercy of public perception and media hype. He was an actor reading lines someone else had written, waiting to see how it would all turn out, waiting to see if he would survive the final act or end up one more useless character killed off and forgotten by the time the credits rolled.

"I don't think it's right." He tossed it on to the pile of all the other scripts he hadn't read. Then he leaned back against the sofa cushions and closed his eyes again.

Derek fished it out of the pile. "Did you even read it?"

"No."

"Then how do you know you don't like it? There might be an Academy Award in here."

He didn't bother to open his eyes. "What's the title?"

He waited in silence, listening to Derek flip the script over. *"Captain Courage and the Chipmunk Squad."*

He slid his eyes to Derek.

"Well," his assistant cleared his throat. "We can probably pass on that one." The script landed on the floor with a thump. "Look, I know you're going through some stuff here, but you've got to focus. You need to pick something. If you don't stay in the game, everyone will forget you."

Ben sat up and dropped his feet off the sofa. He faced his young and ambitious assistant. "Do you want to be an actor?"

Derek looked taken aback by the question, fiddling with the script he was holding before answering. "Yes. Eventually."

"Then why are you here? Why work full-time as my assistant? Shouldn't you be out auditioning?"

"Everyone has to pay their dues." Derek stacked the scripts on the floor into a neat pile. "If I can prove myself to Zoe here, she'll sign me as a client. I mean, we can't all get discovered by one of the biggest agents in town and become an overnight star."

An overnight star. Ben let the words hover between them. He thought back to the nights he spent in his car, being paid under the table in cash for his first construction jobs in Hollywood, the broken bones and bruises he got doing stunts. But none of that mattered now that he was famous. No one cared where he came from, only where he was.

He wondered briefly how he'd never heard the bitterness in Derek's voice before. Derek wanted what he had. He wanted to be the one casually rejecting scripts and letting someone else tidy up the messes he made. Ben thought back to the guy who first introduced him to a stunt coordinator. One introduction, one handshake, and his life had been changed forever. Derek was looking for that same moment, that same stroke of luck. And if luck wouldn't seek him out, he would go find it.

Studying his assistant again, he saw the hunger and the desire hiding there, and he recognized it. "Let me know when you're ready," he said. "With or without Zoe, I can line up some auditions for you."

Derek's eyes widened. His mouth opened and closed before he could speak. "That would be amazing."

Ben shrugged. "I can get you in the door, but the rest will be up to you."

A wide smile broke across Derek's face. "Thank you so much." He scooped up the scripts in the rejection pile. "I'll just tell Zoe these ones are a no and that you're still looking." He raced from the room and Ben wondered briefly who it was he wanted to call to share the good news. A sudden pang of loneliness swept over him. What would it be like to have someone to share that kind of news with? To have someone you couldn't wait to call, someone who would be there for both the good and bad news.

He rose and stood in front of the windows, trying to run from the melancholy thoughts that weighed on him. It was the view from these windows that made him buy the house. The sweeping panorama of Los Angeles was spread out before him. It was a movie star's house and that was what Ben had wanted, a house that would remind him everyday of how far he had come.

But how far was it really? Giselle was gone. His career was hanging by a thread and his eye hurt. He was trapped in this movie star house listening to his housekeeper sing in the kitchen while he pondered the meaning of life.

He had to get out of the house before he went crazy. Crossing to his office, he flipped on the security camera monitors and grumbled in frustration. The photographers were still there, waiting like vultures for their next meal. So much for the plan to jump in his car and drive up the coast. Rubbing his uninjured eye, he tried to think of a place to go, a place where no one would think to look for him.

The suddenness of the idea startled him. He knew exactly where that was. He just didn't know if a certain blue-eyed pastor's daughter would open the door. The thought of seeing the fire flash in her eyes and the stubborn set of her jaw made him like the idea even more.

He smiled as he grabbed his cell phone and wallet and went to the kitchen. His mother hen of a housekeeper was scrubbing the spotless sink as she danced along to a Spanish pop station playing in the background.

"Maria, I need a favor."

Chapter Ten

LILY SAT CROSS-LEGGED ON THE colorful carpet, surrounded by a circle of four and five-year olds listening intently to her tell the story of Noah's ark.

"Then the lions came walking up." She roared and the children laughed.

"Then the horses galloped in." Neighing loudly, she shook her long hair.

"Then the cows and the chickens." She mooed and clucked and the children echoed her farm animal noises.

"The rain started to fall and God shut the door of the ark. It rained and rained and rained, but God kept Noah and his family and all the animals safe and dry inside the ark."

Little Gabi raised her hand. "Miss Lily, how come the animals didn't eat each other?"

Tilting her head, Lily pursed her lips as she considered the little girl's question. "That is an excellent question, Gabi. I have no idea."

"But you're the teacher. You're supposed to know."

Lily smiled. "Well, I do know lots of things. I know you love chocolate milk." She wagged a finger at Gabi and the little girl giggled. "And I know Zeke wants to be a fireman when he grows up." The future fireman nodded with a serious expression. "And I know that Nate's birthday is in two days." Nate squealed and clapped his hands. "But, here's the truth," Lily leaned in and dropped her voice to a whisper, ready to share a secret with her class. The enraptured kids scooted closer and she glanced over her shoulder, checking for eavesdroppers. The eyes of her class widened the longer they waited to hear their teacher's big secret. She pressed in closer and whispered, "Only God knows everything."

The children gave a collective, "Oh," and sat back.

Lily smiled as she looked at them. She loved this class. She got to see them in the morning before school and again in the afternoon for after-care. Her mother had started the classes not long after the church first opened. It had taken only one conversation with a mother who admitted that her kids had to stay at home by themselves after school while she worked and Lily's mom knew she could help. Most of the elementary schools in the area offered something similar for the older grades, but the younger kids didn't have many options.

When her mom died, Lily took over the class and she had never regretted it. These children with their endless questions and wild stories brought her so much joy. She couldn't imagine closing the doors and leaving them to sit at home alone.

"Miss Lily?"

She turned to the young girl with dark braids and big, brown eyes. "Yes, Stella?"

"Who's that man?" Stella pointed to the door and Lily turned and gasped.

Ben Prescott was standing outside and grinning at her through the small window in the door. Her heart skipped and for a moment she had no idea what to do. Should she let him in? Should she tell him to go away? Where was Noah? He was the one who thought having the movie star around would be a good idea.

He was back. The words reverberated in her brain. After everything she had said to him, Ben Prescott was back. And he was waiting for her to open the door.

She cleared her throat and tightened her ponytail. "Okay," she said to the class sitting at her feet. "Let's have fifteen minutes of playtime while I talk to our visitor." The children cheered and raced for the toy bins and bookshelves as Lily walked to the door.

Ignoring the nervous tremble in her hand, she opened the door about halfway. Whether that was to keep the kids in or keep Ben out, she wasn't sure. She searched for words, but the only one she could manage was, "Hi."

"Hi. Sorry for the interruption. I didn't know you were a teacher, too." He glanced over her shoulder at the class. The kids were happily absorbed in the unexpected free time and weren't paying any attention to their teacher as she stood trying to figure out what to say to a famous actor.

Lily blinked, then blinked again, trying to make sense of Ben Prescott standing outside her classroom. But nothing about this situation made sense. "What are you doing here?" She asked, keeping the door braced against her side like a shield.

Ben stuffed his hands in the front pockets of his jeans and shrugged, looking more like one of her students than an international celebrity. "I was in the neighborhood."

She highly doubted that was true. And yet, there he was, standing in the doorway in faded jeans and a black t-shirt looking like he had been out for a stroll and just decided to stop by. The idea was ridiculous, and she knew it, but she couldn't help the flutter in her stomach as she stared back at him. Then she saw his eye.

"What happened?" Before she could stop it, her hand flew to his cheek.

The ugly black and blue bruise under his eye had spread to the side of his face. His breath stilled when she touched him and her hand warmed as it rested on the yellowing bruise. The stubble beneath her fingers was sharp and hard and it matched the piercing look in his eyes. Reality hit her and she dropped her hand, embarrassment sinking into her bones as she stared at the floor.

Raking a hand through his already tousled hair, he grinned. "You should see the other guy."

"Seriously?" She paused, glancing over her shoulder before whispering, "You were in a fight?"

"It was more of a heated discussion that didn't end well." He seemed so unconcerned about it that she wasn't sure what to do. If he'd been one of her students she would have sent him to time out. What was she supposed to do with a grown man who got in a fight? She was pretty sure she didn't have time out jurisdiction where Ben Prescott was concerned.

"Are you okay? Do you want some ice for that shiner?"

Ben shook his head. "I've had worse." He didn't pause long enough for her to ask about that sentence. "Other than being trapped in my house for the past few days, I'm fine."

She felt her forehead wrinkle as she tried to keep up with his end of the conversation. "Why were you trapped in your house?"

He leaned against the doorframe. "The paparazzi have my house surrounded. Apparently punching my ex-girlfriend's new boy toy in the face makes for a good story. I'm supposed to be in hiding."

"So how did you get away?"

"My housekeeper smuggled me out in the back of her Prius."

Lily opened her mouth to say something, then changed her mind. The image of Ben Prescott, all six-feet and muscle of him, stuffed into the hatchback of a Prius flashed in her brain and she struggled not to laugh.

She took a quick look at the classroom behind her and checked the time. The kids were playing quietly for now, but that could change at any moment. She couldn't stand here talking to an escapee movie star much longer.

"Mr. Prescott—"

"Ben." He pushed off the doorframe and smiled at her.

She clasped her hands and forced herself to focus. "Ben. I'm glad you're here, really, but—"

"Lily," he interrupted her, his voice suddenly bereft of bravado and charm. "I don't have anywhere else to go."

The plea in his words moved her more than the bruise on his face. It was loneliness and sadness that had driven him here. She pulled on the ends of her scarf until she nearly strangled herself as she considered what to do with the movie star who showed up at her classroom door looking lost and alone.

Caution warred with compassion as she stalled. How could she turn him away? "I guess you could hang out here. If you don't mind a room full of preschoolers."

A smile broke across his face as relief flooded his eyes. "Sounds like my last press conference."

She laughed, as nerves and doubt winged through her brain. But it was too late now to change her mind. She stepped away from the door and let him in. Moving to the wall, she flicked the fluorescent lights off and on. The kids stopped what they were doing and looked at her. "Class, come back to the rug please." The kids plopped down into a ragged circle on the colorful rug and looked up at her expectantly. "This is my friend, Mr. Ben. He is going to visit with us today."

A dozen little faces swiveled from Lily to Ben. "Is he your boyfriend?" Gabi called.

The kids burst into giggles and she felt the telltale warmth of a blush engulf her cheeks. This was a bad idea. She should have locked the door and ignored those pitiful brown eyes in the window.

Ben stepped forward. "No, I'm not Miss Lily's boyfriend, but wouldn't I be lucky if I were?"

She didn't think it was possible to blush even more, but judging by the heat flooding her face, she had found a way. Ben winked at her and then found a spot on the rug and sat down between Nate and Stella, leaving Lily standing by the light switch with no idea what to say next.

Chapter Eleven

BEN COULDN'T REMEMBER WHEN HE had felt so relaxed. Watching Lily teach had been incredible. Her face was alight with joy as she told the story of Noah's Ark. Then she led the kids in singing "Yes, Jesus Loves Me." The beauty of her voice seeped into his soul, mingling with the memories of his grandmother singing the same song. He had a wild and sudden thought that his Granny would have loved Lily. They would have made quite a pair, his gentle, but spirited grandmother and Lily, a woman who had shown him the same qualities. What would his life have been like if Granny had lived, if she had been the one to teach him about God instead of the closed fists of his dad and the helpless defeat of his mom. Would he have believed then? If he'd met Lily's God as a child, would he have ended up on a different path?

Not that it mattered now. He'd made his choice and things had worked out great. He may have hit a rough patch lately, but he certainly didn't need to go looking for God to find his way out of it. One more hit movie, one more award, and everything would be fine. He didn't need God for that; he just needed a few days to rebuild his image.

He shook off the thought and focused instead on stacking colorful wooden blocks with three of the boys. He was helping his new friends build a castle. Or a spaceship, he wasn't really sure what it was, there seemed to be a bit of a debate about the structure. All he knew was that no one cared about his name or his last movie or his ex-girlfriend here. Here the only thing that mattered was that he knew how to stack the blocks so they didn't fall over.

"What happened to your face?" Nate was a bubbly four year old and he had taken an immediate liking to Ben. Nate had been one of the loudest singers during circle time and he hadn't cared one bit if he forgot the words or sang off key.

Ben turned the blue rectangle block in his hand over a few times as he considered his answer. "I got into a fight," he finally said.

"Tommy Johnson once tried to take my cookie at lunch time and I hit him. I got in big trouble and had to sit in time out." Nate added a red block to the tower and then looked at Ben. "Did you get put in time out?"

All three boys stared at him, waiting to hear if grownups got in trouble, too. Ben nodded solemnly. "I did. I was in time out for three days."

Their eyes widened. "Three whole days?" Nate asked.

"Yep." He added the block to the castle/spaceship, aware that he had just shattered the world time out record. He might have just achieved legendary status to these preschoolers.

"Wow." One of the other boys whispered the word with awe. "Your mom musta been real mad."

Ben laughed. His mom probably would be mad at him if she knew. But he hadn't seen her or his father in almost a decade. The last he saw of them they were both passed out in the living room. They didn't even notice when he left. He hadn't waited around to graduate high school. He couldn't take one more day in that house. Once he'd saved enough money for a car, he'd packed his clothes and his guitar into the backseat and headed west. He hadn't intended to go to Los Angeles, he hadn't thought any further than getting to the next big city and losing himself in it, but that's where he ended up.

He'd called home a few times the first year after he left, but the calls always ended in fights, so he'd stopped calling. It wasn't until after his first movie came out that his parents showed any interest in finding him and by that time Ben had no interest in being found.

"Did you say sorry?" Nate asked as he added a green triangle to the top of the tower. "Miss Lily says that if you hurt someone you have to say you're sorry."

Ben looked at the wooden block in his hands and struggled to find the right words to say. He wasn't sorry and he doubted he'd ever feel the urge to apologize to Liam Donovan. In fact, he was certain he'd rather punch him again than apologize to him.

The heavy hand on the clock ticked and Ben felt a touch on his shoulder. He looked up and found the blue eyes that had inspired him to crawl into the trunk of a Prius like a stowaway. Of all the dumb things he had done in his life, Ben knew he would never regret that one.

Lily was standing over their block building crew, her hand still resting on his shoulder. He kept himself still, unwilling to risk her moving. She smiled to the building crew and then spoke softly, her words meant for him alone. "Parents are going to start arriving in a few minutes."

She didn't say anything more, but Ben knew what she meant. The kids might not know who he was, but their parents would. "Thanks." He passed the blocks in his hands to Nate. "Looks like it's time for me to go."

All three boys made a disappointed sound and Nate crawled over to him. "Will you come back someday, Mr. Ben?"

Ben looked at Lily, but her face was unreadable. "I'd like to," he said. "If Miss Lily will let me."

"Yay!" Nate threw his arms around his neck and squeezed tight.

Ben hugged him back. The innocence of the gesture tugged at his heart. Here he was unknown, no fame, no celebrity, and he had nothing to offer but himself. And for these kids that was enough. Zoe wanted his career, Derek needed his paycheck, and the media wanted his life. But Lily, she hadn't asked for anything.

Standing up, a slice of disappointment cut through him. "See ya buddy." He patted Nate on the shoulder and gave fist bumps to the other two builders as he stood up.

"Bye, Mr. Ben." Nate said it first, then the words picked up like chorus and echoed through the room as all the kids yelled their goodbyes.

Lily walked him to the door. "If you don't want to go home yet, you can go around the back of the church." She pointed towards the door at the end of the hallway. "It's out of sight and you can hang out until after the kids are picked up."

He was surprised by her offer, but he wasn't about to pass it up. "I'll do that. Thanks."

The moment stretched on between them. Words stuck on his tongue. He didn't know what he wanted to say. He only knew he wanted to make the moment last.

Her eyes darted down the hallway and she twisted the door handle in her hand. "So, I guess, I'll see you there in about twenty minutes."

Recognizing his cue to leave, he stepped away from the door. "Okay. See you then."

Lily turned back to the classroom, pulling the door shut behind her. Ben stood on the outside, listening to the laughter hidden in that room. He checked his watch and then headed down the hall to the door Lily had pointed to.

The sun was heading to the horizon as Ben walked down the short flight of steps that led to the asphalt parking lot. He walked towards the playground and then decided against it. If he were a kid getting out of school he'd head for the swings as soon as possible. So he turned to the left and went around the corner instead.

Up ahead, a handyman was working on a window frame. Perched on a rickety metal ladder, balancing a hammer under one arm, he was trying to pull the top of the window frame off with the other. It was a dangerous looking operation.

"Need a hand?" Ben asked. Old habits from working construction kicked in and he walked closer to steady the ladder.

"That'd be great." The handyman passed him the hammer and used two hands to remove the top of the window frame. "This window's leaking. Lily's been after me to fix it before it rains again and floods the music room."

Ben looked to the Southern California sky. There wasn't any rain in those puffy white clouds, but Lily definitely seemed like the better to be safe than sorry type.

"Here, can you take this?" He handed Ben the top of the frame. Ben grabbed it and set it on the ground. "Pass me the caulk," the handyman said.

Ben dug around in the ancient tool bag planted at the base of the ladder. The thing had seen better days. Two of the side pockets were missing and the handle was being held together with duct tape. He found the caulk, snipped the top off with a knife and loaded it into the caulk gun before passing it up the ladder. "Here you go."

The handyman gave him an appraising look. "You work in construction?"

Ben steadied the ladder again, his hands loose but secure on the cool, metal sides. "A long time ago. When I first got to LA it was the only work I could get."

"It's honest work." The handyman laid a line of caulk along the top of the window, sealing the edge where the frame fit into the side of the building.

"Yes, sir," Ben agreed. "I liked that it was straight forward. Find the problem and fix it. No games or agendas, just hard work and then a good night's sleep."

From atop the ladder, the man grunted in agreement and continued to trace a long line of sticky, white caulk around the window frame. When the handyman completed the circuit, Ben handed him a rag. He used it to clean up around the window and then passed it back.

"That should do it. Once that dries, I'll put the fame back up and cross that off the to-do list." He climbed down the ladder and wiped his hands on his ripped and paint-stained jeans, then reached out to Ben. "I'm Evan. Thanks for your help."

Ben shook his hand. "Ben. It's nice to meet you."

Evan cleaned up his tools and put them back in the bag while Ben collapsed the ladder. "Where to?"

Evan pointed to a garage and they started walking. "So what brings you here?"

"I stopped by to see Lily. But parents are coming to pick up their kids so she suggested I wait back here."

Evan gave him a sideways glance, his eyes subtly appraising. "Lily told you to wait for her?"

Ben cleared his throat and shifted the ladder in his arms. "I've been kind of a pain. She probably wants to make sure I don't get into any more trouble."

Using the end of the hammer Evan pointed to his cheek. "Looks like trouble already found you."

"Yeah. That's been happening a lot lately."

They reached the garage and Evan rolled the door up. It was a mess of mismatched tools, car parts, pieces of wood, and a collection of odds and ends that would make a tinker proud. Ben couldn't see any organization to it, but Evan didn't seem at all bothered by the chaos. He stored the tool bag on a shelf near the front, dropping it into an empty place between a table saw and what looked like an old record player. "The ladder goes there." He pointed to a pair of hooks on the wall. Ben lifted the ladder and hung it up.

"Water?" Evan asked and Ben nodded. Evan opened a small refrigerator and pulled out two bottles of water. He tossed one to Ben, then leaned back against a workbench. "So, did you throw the first punch?"

Taking a long drink of the cool water, he nodded. There was no sense in lying about it. "I did."

"Was it worth it?"

Ben considered the question. He thought of the backlash, the days stuck in his house, the stress. Was it worth it? There are some things that couldn't be undone, some things that couldn't be explained away. The only choice was to accept the consequences and move on. "Probably not."

"Hmmm. That's too bad. Shiner like that should be for a good cause." Grabbing a slightly less dirty rag from the table, Evan wiped the rest of the dirt off his hands. "Worst fight I ever got in was back in high school. I was at a school dance and some guy started putting the moves on my girlfriend. I don't remember his name now, but I do remember him putting his hands on her. I punched him as hard as I could." A smile tugged its way across his face at the memory. "I'd never punched anyone before. Had no idea it was going to hurt that much." He shook his hand as if the pain was still there and laughed. "He went down then jumped back up and tackled me. We both ended up with some bumps and bruises and a week's suspension. That was before my mom found out and grounded me for the rest of my life. In fact, I might still be grounded." Laugh lines crinkled the corners of his eyes as he wrapped up the story.

"So," Ben asked. "Was it worth it?"

"Sure was." Evan smiled, pride and contentment radiating from his expression. "I married that girl."

Ben tipped his water bottle towards the handyman in salute. "Not me. I got the black eye, but I still lost the girl."

"Well, maybe God has something better in mind for you."

Ben scoffed, not wanting to offend the man, but not about to buy into his theories about God either. "I don't think God has much of a plan for me at all."

"You might be surprised. God doesn't give up on any of us."

Ben brushed at the dust on the workbench, oddly embarrassed by the conversation. "I wouldn't blame Him if He did. I tend to mess things up."

"I've messed up a time or two myself. Fortunately God takes the messed up and broken things of this world and fixes them. That window we worked on? It wasn't hopeless or useless. It just needed someone to repair the broken parts so it could shine again."

Ben wanted to believe him. He wanted to hear those words and believe that they applied to him. But he didn't. He couldn't. He'd fallen too far, run too long. Some people were way past saving, no matter what Lily might think. "And sometimes you have to throw the whole thing away."

Evan looked like he wanted to say something more, but he stopped and looked towards the church. "There she is now."

Ben turned and saw Lily coming towards them. Gold and red from the setting sun glinted off her hair and the breeze coming from the hills pulled the loose strands into a dance.

She strode across the parking lot and slipped into the garage. "So, Dad, it looks like you've met our movie star."

Ben's eyes widened and he turned back to Evan. "Dad?"

"Guilty as charged." Evan smiled sheepishly.

Ben glanced from Evan to Lily. Once he started looking for it, the resemblance was there. "I thought you were the handyman."

"I am. Handyman, plumber, cook, gardener, and whatever else needs to be done."

"And the pastor," Ben added. He studied Evan again. He wasn't what a pastor was supposed to be. He didn't wear fancy clothes and he didn't talk down to him or make him feel inferior. He was on a ladder, getting his hands dirty, doing the same work Ben used to do.

"That, too." Evan led the way out of the garage and rolled the door down. He snapped the lock in place. "Sorry I didn't mention it sooner. Sometimes it's nice not to have to be Pastor Evan all the time."

Ben shook his head. "The pastor who does construction work and gets in fights over a girl. That's a new one for me."

Lily whirled on her dad. "You got in a fight? Over Mom?"

Evan patted Lily's shoulder. "Don't worry, it was a long time ago. And I won. She married me didn't she?" Evan shook Ben's hand again. "Thank you for your help with the window. I appreciate it."

"Anytime, Sir."

"Be careful or I'll take you up on that. Especially now that I know you're good with tools." Lily's shocked expression darted from her dad to him.

"You don't have to act so surprised. I wasn't always a lazy celebrity."

Evan clapped him on the back. "Are you hungry? You should come over for dinner."

"Tonight?" Lily gasped. The panicked look on her face reminded Ben of the first time he did a screen test. Staring into the camera like it was a black and glass monster ready to devour him and hoping, just a little, that the floor would open up and swallow him whole before he made a fool of himself.

Her father laughed. "Why not? It's pasta night. There's going to be plenty to go around. What do you say, Ben? Are you up for some spaghetti and garlic bread?"

He knew Lily wanted him to refuse. And he should refuse. He should make up some excuse about work and figure out a way to sneak back into his house. There was no reason for him to say yes. Except that he actually was hungry and he couldn't resist the pull of those wide, blue eyes.

"Absolutely. I'd love it."

Lily blinked once, then twice. Then she spun on her heel and started walking away. He heard her mumble under her breath. "Ben Prescott is coming to my house for spaghetti. I can't believe this is happening."

He smothered a laugh. This was turning out to be a great day.

Chapter Twelve

LESS THAN A MINUTE AFTER her dad invited Ben over for dinner, Lily fired off a series of desperate text messages to her brother.

Ben Prescott is coming over for dinner. TONIGHT. Please make sure the house isn't a mess.

Seriously, Noah. Move your laundry pile and do the dishes.

We'll be home after Dad locks up. Please, please don't let the house be an embarrassment.

I am actually begging you.

When she didn't get a response to any of her texts, she pulled out her ace in the hole. The threat to be used only in the direst of circumstances.

Noah, if you don't clean the house I will call Kate and tell her you have a massive crush on her.

Ten seconds later her phone beeped.

The house will be clean. You're a brat.

A little after five p.m., her dad switched off the lights and locked the doors to the church. The December air was crisp, and the sky was deepening into darkness as the sun disappeared below the horizon of jagged buildings.

"Do you ever get nervous living here?" Lily wasn't surprised by Ben's question. He'd been checking out the neighborhood ever since they left the church. It was only four blocks from the church, but it was a world away from the gated mansions of the Hollywood Hills. The houses were old, but most of them were cared for. Graffiti marred the walls of the other buildings and many of the storefronts were empty and abandoned.

This area, hidden behind Hollywood's glittering lights and glamorous façade, had been struggling for decades. The wealth that filtered down from the movie industry and the tourists who flocked to the Walk of Fame, didn't make it here. Here the families had to fight to stay afloat. Parents working and barely scraping by, bills that never ended. They battled the temptations of gangs and drugs and the allure of a quick buck on Hollywood Boulevard.

Lily had been shocked when her parents bought the small house near the church. They had raised her and Noah in the security and safety of the suburbs up north, surrounded by cul-de-sacs and manicured lawns. But her parents had thrived in the little yellow house. The joy of serving God had filled every corner of their home. Most of Lily's college friends had taken one look at the neighborhood and never came back. All of them, in fact, except Kate. Kate hadn't minded the sirens or the run-down buildings or the graffiti. She stuck around.

Lily snuck a sideways look at Ben. Would he be the one who runs, or the one who stays?

"We've had a few scary moments." Her dad answered the question honestly. He was never one to hide from the truth. "But my wife and I felt strongly that we wanted to live in the community we served. The people who come to our church aren't just church members. They are our neighbors, our family. And it helps to be so close to the church. You never know when someone is going to see that cross and ask for help."

Ben nodded, his gaze sweeping the street, taking in the cracked sidewalk, the tenacious weeds that pushed their way through the fractured concrete. "It actually reminds me a bit of my hometown." Lily held her breath, caught off-guard by the comment. It reminded him of home. Sirens wailed in the distance, but they also heard the sounds of laughter, the shrieks of kids playing in the dry grass of their backyards, the rattle of skateboard wheels as they zipped along the uneven asphalt. Lily hoped that was what he was thinking of, happy moments that broke through in the midst of struggle. But from the dark look in his eyes, she was certain he was remembering something else, something far from laughter.

"Why did you build the church here?" Ben asked her dad. "Of every place in the world you could have gone, why here?"

Looking up at the sky, her dad peered beyond the haze and the clouds. She'd seen that look before. He was having a private conversation with God. Asking Him for the right words, waiting for God to show him the way.

"My wife, Amy, and I had no intention of planting a church. We lived up in the Valley. She was a teacher, I was a lawyer and that was it. We attended a great church, had a wonderful pastor, and we were involved in everything. The kids grew up in the church. They went to school there, they served there. Lily started singing in the worship team when she was still a teenager."

Lily felt Ben's stare, but she ignored him, her gaze fixed on the chain link fence to her right.

"Then one day, Amy and I went on a mission trip. We came face to face with people who were hurting, people who were starving. I didn't speak their language, but I could recognize pain. After we came home, I couldn't sleep. I couldn't erase those images from my mind and I didn't want to. I looked at our house, everything I had taken for granted, and I knew I wanted something different. I had no idea how I was going to explain it to Amy, but in the end I didn't have to. She came to me one night after the kids had gone to bed and said she felt the Lord was calling us to ministry."

Tears shone in his eyes and this time when he looked up, Lily knew he was seeing her mom's face. They had been such a wonderful team, supporting each other, encouraging each other. Even when they argued, the love they felt for each other was there. She learned what marriage was meant to be, what love should look like by sitting in the kitchen and watching her parents. She wouldn't settle for anything less than what they had shared.

"Well, we prayed and prayed about it. The idea of leaving our careers, leaving our home was terrifying. We asked our pastor to pray. We asked Lily and Noah to pray. And with every passing day we felt it more and more strongly. God was calling us to plant a church. So we started looking at third world countries, we started praying about where He wanted us to go and over and over the same city kept coming to us. Hollywood." He laughed, as if he was still as dumbfounded by the idea as he had been ten years ago. "Hollywood of all places."

Lily picked up the story as they walked through the hazy, yellow circle of a streetlight. "I was still in high school at the time and I thought my parents were crazy. With all of the need across the world, why would God send them to Hollywood?"

Her dad nodded. "We fought it. But then I realized, sometimes the biggest mission field is the one in our own backyard. We drove down here and looked around. I saw the same pain, the same need, the same heartache right here that I had seen on that mission trip. Amy felt it too and we knew. This was where God was calling us. So we sold the house and moved here. After Amy got sick, Lily and Noah moved in to help take care of her and help with the church."

Silence settled over them. A few more steps and they left the circle of light on the sidewalk and stepped into the lengthening shadows of night. Ben's voice dropped when he spoke, filling with a quiet reverence, the sympathetic tone Lily heard from everyone when her mom passed away and she knew what he was going to ask.

"When did she die?"

"Two years ago." Her dad didn't seem to mind the tears that slipped from his eyes. "If I'd known we were going to have so little time together, I would have brought her here sooner. She was a light in a dark place. And someday . . . someday I'll get to see her shine again."

Lily reached out and took her dad's hand. She remembered the day she heard the diagnosis. The word *cancer* changed everything. They had all prayed, they prayed with every ounce of faith in their hearts and her mom fought hard. But in the end, God brought her home. Lily had never doubted God's love, but there were many days she doubted His plan and her own strength to get through the grief. Why, out of everyone in the world, had it been her mom? Even in the face of chemotherapy and pain, her mom had never lost her faith. She had never doubted, never drifted. So why her? She knew there wasn't an easy answer, but it didn't stop the questions.

Her dad squeezed her hand in silent communication. They had made it through. They had God and they had each other. And so they got up each day, they took one more step, they breathed one more breath, and they kept going. And as her dad said, someday she would see her mom again.

Lily wanted to believe she had that same strength, but she wasn't sure. Her mom said that it was the trials that refined her faith and brought her closer to God. Lily hoped she would never have to go through that kind of struggle. She wasn't naïve enough to believe that her faith could protect her from every bad thing in the world. She just hoped she wouldn't falter when the trials came.

Chapter Thirteen

DINNER THAT NIGHT WOULD FOREVER be one of Ben's favorite memories. They sat around the kitchen table, sharing stories and laughing until their sides hurt. Ben, who had eaten in five star restaurants across Europe, wouldn't have traded Lily's spaghetti and homemade garlic bread for anything in the world. No one asked about his movies, no one pitched him a script, no one asked him for money. It was like a scene from a family friendly movie, and he hoped the movie would never end.

Evan sat back and patted his stomach. "Lily, that was delicious. Thank you."

"It was the best dinner I've had in a long, long time," Ben said, enjoying the way her cheeks turned pink at the compliment.

Noah stood and slapped him on the back. "I'm glad you liked it. Because now you have to pay the price for such good food. You get to help with the dishes."

"That sounds fair," Ben said and reached for Lily's plate.

"You don't have to do that." She grabbed the plate, refusing to let him take it. After a short tug-of-war, he yanked on it, and it slipped from her hand.

"Sure he does." Noah grinned and passed Ben another plate. He stacked the dishes on the counter while Noah filled the sink with water and a little too much soap. Lily and Evan sat back and watched.

"So, Ben." Evan sipped from a coffee mug that had a faded family photo on the sides. Ben had been entranced by the young Lily staring up at him from the coffee mug all through dinner. The family on the mug looked so happy. Even after all they had lost, they still did. He had a hard time imagining that kind of childhood, what that kind of contentment would feel like. "How long have you been in LA?"

Noah handed him a glass and Ben busied himself drying it with a Christmas-themed dishtowel as he debated his answer. There was the official, agent approved story and then there was the truth. According to his official biography, Ben moved to LA when he was twenty. He worked as a stuntman until he was discovered by a famous director and cast in his first movie. That first movie led to another, then another and within three years, Ben was a leading man. As far as the press knew, Ben had skyrocketed to success. As long as no one looked any deeper, that's the way the story would stay.

But he thought about how much Evan and Lily had been willing to share with him, they hadn't hesitated to share both their joy and their sadness with him. So he decided on the truth.

"I came out here about eight years ago. I had been moving steadily west for two years and finally ended up in Santa Monica."

"Where's home?" Evan asked.

Ben hesitated. Home. He wasn't sure he had one. There was the house he grew up in, but that had never been a real home. There was his house in the Hollywood Hills, but with his shooting schedule he was hardly ever there, and when he was there it was quiet and lonely. The truth was, he didn't think he had a home, just a mismatched collection of houses he no longer lived in.

He accepted another dripping plate from Noah and dried it off. "I grew up in Indiana." That seemed like the safest answer he could give.

"Are your parents still there?"

Ben shrugged and stacked the dried plate with the others. "Probably. I left at sixteen and I haven't been back since."

He heard Lily's sharp intake of breath. He didn't need to turn around to know it was her, to imagine the shock on her face. To someone who had grown up with parents who loved her, who wound up smiling in photos on coffee mugs, of course his life would sound sad and tragic. Tension tightened his neck and he focused on the dishtowel in his hands. He didn't want her to feel sorry for him. His life might have been a mess, but he was getting by.

"You were only sixteen?" she whispered.

He saw Noah glance his way, and he felt the heaviness in the air. He hadn't meant to open up his past, it had slipped out, drawn up from the dark corners of his memories by the warmth of this home and the kindness of this family. He folded the towel and turned around. Lily and Evan were watching him from the table and he felt Noah's solid presence beside him. There was no going back now. "I didn't have a great childhood. For a few years I stayed with my grandmother. But when she died, I was sent back to my parents. Unfortunately, neither of them were very interested in being parents. They both drank. There was a lot of fighting and a lot of hitting. Once I got a driver's license and saved up enough to buy a car, I couldn't take off fast enough."

"That's a hard way to grow up," Evan said. Ben looked at him, expecting pity, maybe even disgust, to be written on the pastor's face. But he didn't see either of those things and relief washed through him.

He rubbed his hand on the back of his neck. He hadn't talked about his family in years. He hadn't wanted to think about them in years. All of his good memories ended when his grandmother died. Everything after that day was covered in a haze of anger, pain, and resentment. "That's just the way it was. My dad worked and then came home and drank himself into a stupor. My mom drank to keep up with him. We'd show up to church on Sunday and listen to a preacher tell us all the things we weren't supposed to do and pretend like we were a happy family. Nobody cared that my mom and I showed up every week with bruises."

Ben paused, expecting the pastor to jump in and defend the church. He was ready for a long lecture on why he needed to start going to church immediately. But Evan didn't comment on it at all. The Shaw family was hard to offend and even harder to understand. "Well, the prospect of packing up and hitting the road sounded pretty good compared to all that. For two years I just drove until I ran out of money. I'd stop in whatever town I was in when the car ran out of gas and then work odd jobs until I could afford to hit the road again. Once I got to LA, I worked construction for a while and then one of the guys I worked with hooked me up with some small time stunt work for extra cash. I didn't mind jumping off buildings or taking a punch so I was able to keep working. After a few years of stunt work an agent spotted me on set. I don't know what she saw in me, but Zoe signed me on the spot and a few months later got my first speaking role. I guess the rest is history."

Evan nodded thoughtfully. "Well, I'm glad you made it here."

Ben glanced at Lily. Her innocent gaze met his and held. "So am I," she said.

Ben had never felt his heart stop beating before. But in the sweetness of her smile, time itself stood still.

"You should come over again," Evan said.

Ben handed the clean plates to Noah so he could put them away.

"I'd like that very much."

"Great. What are you doing on Monday?"

"Dad," Lily put her hand on her dad's arm. "Monday is Christmas."

Evan smacked his forehead. "You're right. I'm losing track of the days. So, Ben, what are you doing for Christmas?"

Ben stared at him for a moment. Was he really inviting him to spend Christmas with his family?

Lily interrupted his thoughts. "Dad, I'm sure Ben has plans for Christmas." She looked at him. "Right? Jetting off to some tropical hot spot. Or skiing in Aspen. Maybe filming in the Tunisian Desert."

He had planned to go to Barbados with Giselle and spend Christmas on the beach. Now it looked like Giselle would be sitting on the beach sipping margaritas with Liam instead. He hoped they both got sunburned.

"Actually, I'm in between films at the moment, I don't know how to ski, and I'm not a fan of tropical islands." Lily pursed her lips, waiting as Ben stumbled over his words. Ben gave her an innocent smile as he continued, "I'd love to spend Christmas with you. Thank you."

Evan clapped his hands together. "Great. Church starts at ten a.m. We'll see you there and then we'll head back here for Christmas festivities."

"Church?" Ben stuttered, tripping over the excuses that flew to his lips, but the words wouldn't come out.

"Yep." Evan kept going, unaware of, or choosing to ignore, Ben's stammering. "Ten a.m. sharp. It's crowded on the big holidays so don't be late."

Now it was Lily's turn to flash Ben that oh-so innocent smile. But if she thought one little church service would keep him away, she had another thing coming.

Noah laughed and slapped him on the back. "Don't worry, you'll survive. Dad keeps the sermons short on holidays."

"Hey!" Evan protested, but Ben could hear the humor in his voice. There was no anger, no offense.

"So, do you need a ride home?" Noah asked.

"Oh." Ben rubbed his hands against his temples, allowing the real world to invade this hidden oasis of anonymity. "I forgot about that. I guess the photographers are still there."

"You could spend the night here," Noah offered and Lily sputtered into her water glass.

Ben took a step towards her. "Are you okay?" But she waved off his concern, coughing into her napkin. "I appreciate the offer, but I don't want to impose."

"It's no imposition. Plus whenever we have company Lily makes pancakes for breakfast. You don't want to miss that." Noah elbowed him. "I've got clothes you can borrow."

Ben looked at Evan. "It would be a big help. I could avoid sneaking into my own home for another day."

"Of course you're welcome to stay, Ben. We're happy to have you."

He glanced in Lily's direction. Her coughing fit had subsided and she sighed. "Looks like I'm making pancakes tomorrow morning."

Chapter Fourteen

LILY WAS SPRAWLED ACROSS HER bed, her feet up on the wall behind the headboard, with her cell phone pressed to her ear. Even though Kate was snowed in across the country, it felt like they were back in their dorm room at UCLA. And given the day she'd had, she was in desperate need of some best friend time.

"I can't believe Ben Prescott is in your house. *The* Ben Prescott. Just hanging out with you, eating garlic bread, and washing dishes. That's crazy!" Kate's incredulity made Lily giggle. She couldn't blame her. It's not everyday you find out your best friend is feeding a movie star and letting him crash in her guest room. Of course, if the tables had been turned, Lily wouldn't have been nearly as surprised. Kate was the one who managed to find adventure and mischief. Lily had always been the quiet and reserved one, she was the one who made sure everyone got home all right and made it class on time. Kate was the one who made things fun.

"It wasn't what I expected to happen today, that's for sure." It was as far from the expected as she could get. Lily expected her life to be simple, normal, and ordinary. She wasn't destined for fame or fortune and she was fine with that. As long as she could sing and serve the Lord, she didn't need anything else. She certainly didn't need a handsome, non-believing movie star mucking up her perfectly quiet life.

"So he's seriously in the guest room?" Kate pressed for details. "The same guest room I used to sleep in?"

"The very same."

Kate squealed into the phone and Lily laughed. Then she clapped her hand over her mouth to stifle the sound. The guest room wasn't that far away.

"What's he like?" Leave it to Kate to get right down to the nitty-gritty. As they spoke, Lily could picture her best friend curled up under a blanket, the snowy, Boston winter covering the world outside her window in a frozen sheet of white. What she wouldn't give to have her here beside her. Kate would know exactly how to handle her famous houseguest.

"He's . . ." She stared at the ceiling as she contemplated her answer. She didn't know where to start. How could she sum him up when she hadn't been able to figure him out? Ben Prescott wasn't at all what she thought he was. He made his feelings about the church pretty clear. He obviously had a bad experience with church growing up and he didn't want anything to do with it now, but he was willing to come to a Christmas service.

After dinner, she had listened to him and Noah talk about the upcoming football game, and she couldn't help but think that Ben didn't want to leave. The man with a mansion in the Hollywood Hills and more money than she could imagine wanted to stay in their simple house eating spaghetti and talking football. It didn't make any sense.

"He's nice. And he's really funny. He was so sweet with the kids in aftercare today. Just sitting on the floor playing with blocks. Oh, and you should have heard him talk about his family. It was so sad. And—"

"Oh my gosh," Kate interrupted. "You have a crush on Ben Prescott."

"No, I don't." Lily made the protest, but even as she said the words, she knew she wasn't being entirely truthful. She didn't have a crush, not yet. It was more like she was excessively noticing him. She enjoyed his company, and now that she knew he wasn't a complete jerk, she liked being around him. But that's all it was. It didn't matter how funny or smart he was, he was still an unbelieving movie star and that made him a big no-no on two counts. Maybe she did have a slight attraction, but it was just a tiny one and it wasn't going to go anywhere, so what was the big deal?

"Lils." Kate used the nickname she gave her on the first day they met, two nervous young girls in the middle of a sea of college students. They had found each other during orientation and then clung to each other as the reality of college life descended on them. "I can hear it in your voice. You talk about him the same way you talked about Joshua Lang in your Spanish class."

Lily winced at the reminder. She had gushed over Joshua Lang for months, and she was certain he had never even known her name . . . not in Spanish or in any other language.

"Your voice is all dreamy," Kate continued. "Not that I blame you. Did you see him in *Border Crossing*? Ben Prescott is seriously hot."

Lily sighed into the phone. "It's not a big deal. It's not like anything is going to happen between us. He's a superstar and I'm . . . well . . . just me." She tried to say it lightly, to pretend that her ordinariness didn't bother her. She knew God loved her and that was enough. So what if she wasn't glamorous and gorgeous. It's not like the kids in her class minded that she wore jeans and sneakers. She and Ben came from very different worlds, that's all it was.

Kate scoffed, the unladylike sound traveling across the country to defend her friend. "And he'd be lucky to have you."

Lily smiled, once again in awe of Kate's vibrant personality and her unapologetic bravado. "You have to say that. You're my best friend."

"Well, maybe you should remind him of the fact that you have a crazy best friend with a law degree. If he tries anything, I'll fly out there and teach him a lesson."

"Is that what it will take to get you back out here?" Silence settled on Kate's end of the conversation. "You're overdue for a visit you know."

Kate was quiet for a long time and Lily didn't press her. She waited for her to be ready. She knew it wasn't easy, but she also knew her friend needed to come to terms with her past eventually or it would eat her up inside.

"I know," Kate finally replied. "I'm just slammed at work. I have a pile of lawsuits sitting on my desk that I have to go through." Work was an excuse. They both knew it, but Lily played along. The hurt that kept Kate on the other side of the country, miles away from LA and all its memories, was still too near the surface. Kate had been devastated when her little sister had died. Lily had stood by her side for the funeral, holding her hand as clumps of dirt scattered over the coffin. And she'd been there when the family heard the news that the drunk driver wouldn't serve any jail time at all. Kate and her family had been furious. Her dad retreated into work and Kate dedicated herself to a law career as far from the place her sister died as she could get.

"I understand." And she did understand. She understood that kind of loss as only someone who had experienced it could. There were times she passed a shop or a restaurant that she had gone to with her mom and without warning the pain would come rushing back. She didn't blame Kate for needing to stay away. All she could do was pray that she would find her way home eventually. "You're doing a great job. I wish you could be here for Christmas though."

Relief filled Kate's voice. The sad moment had passed, swept back under the rug. "With Ben Prescott under your tree, I wish I was going to be there, too!"

The girls laughed, then she heard Kate yawn. The time difference was hard on their phone calls. "Okay, Super Lawyer, you should go to bed. I'm sure you're getting up early tomorrow."

"As always." Kate put on her serious voice. "Be careful with him, Lils. I don't want you to get your heart broken."

"I'm not going to get my heart broken. It would take a miracle for Ben Prescott to ever notice me." She ignored the sting her words caused. She wasn't interested in Ben's life. She didn't want to be a part of it. It shouldn't matter if he never noticed her. But deep down, she knew that it did matter.

"Well, you're the one who still believes in miracles. So be careful."

Chapter Fifteen

BEN PUSHED HIS PLATE AWAY. If he stayed with the Shaws any longer he'd be the fattest movie star on the red carpet. Staring at the pile of pancakes by the griddle, he considered the thought for a moment. It might be worth it. Although he was pretty sure his trainer would disagree. He could only imagine the cardio he was going to have waiting for him next week.

While they were devouring Lily's pancakes, Evan explained that they had a ministry event going on at the church that day. Several churches in the area teamed up every weekend to serve lunch to the homeless and once a month the Hollywood Mission hosted it. Today was that day.

"You're welcome to come, Ben," Evan said. "Or if you want to hang out here, that's okay, too. We'll be back in plenty of time for dinner."

Lily looked back from the stove. Ben might be done eating, but Noah was still putting away the pancakes and it looked like he had room for a few more.

She met his eyes briefly before she turned back to the griddle and expertly flipped another pancake. He watched her as she worked, the elegance of her movements capturing his attention, and the idea of spending another day with her was suddenly very appealing. "I'd love to come, thank you."

Though she tried to hide it, he caught the puzzled expression that drifted across her face. He was confusing her. And if he was honest, he was confusing himself. After years of avoiding church and God, he was sitting in a pastor's kitchen, helping with an outreach event, and he had plans to willingly attend a Christmas service. If he believed in God, he might think there was someone above orchestrating things. But, if God hadn't bothered to show up when he needed Him most, Ben doubted He was going to care enough to show up now.

Lily stacked the fresh pancakes on a plate and scooted it across the table to Noah. He grinned and grabbed the syrup. She caught Ben's gaze and smiled, a stray dusting of flour streaked across her nose and he had a sudden itch to brush it away. He didn't, but the itch still tingled in his fingers as she walked away.

It was going to be an interesting day.

*****

Once the volunteers arrived at the church, Pastor Evan introduced Ben to the team. He didn't mention Ben's last name, but a few eagle-eyed ladies spent a great deal of time staring in his direction.

After a quick meeting, the volunteers scattered like a championship team taking the field. Ben helped set up a series of long tables against one wall of the large room at the front of the church. It used to be one of the showrooms for the plumbing business, but, Evan explained, they now used it for youth group meetings, wedding receptions, and any other time they needed a place for a large group.

"Do you know you look just like Ben Prescott?"

Turing to the two women who appeared at his side, Ben smiled. "I get that a lot."

"Seriously," one remarked as they unfurled a tablecloth. "You could be his twin."

Apparently spotting the potential for trouble, Lily hurried over to join them. Although he wasn't sure if she was coming to protect him, or the sweet-faced women doing the interrogation.

"Actually," he said, before Lily could pull whatever distraction she had in mind. "I do most of the stunt work on his films."

How he managed to keep a straight face while looking at Lily's flabbergasted expression, he would never know.

"Oh wow!" Both women oohed and aahed over him and he felt a little guilty. It wasn't a complete deception, he did still do most of his own stunt work. "What's he like?"

Rubbing his chin, he pretended to give it some thought. "He's kind of . . ." Meeting Lily's gaze, he smiled. "A jerk."

Taking their disappointment to the next table, the women left him alone with Lily. Smoothing out the wrinkles on the white cloth, she whispered. "Maybe he's not a complete jerk."

Stepping closer, the vanilla of her perfume wafting around him, his hand nearly touching hers, he lowered his voice to match hers. "I'm sure he'll be glad to hear that."

He caught the briefest glimpse of light dancing in her eyes before she disappeared back into the crowd of volunteers.

After the serving tables were set up, they worked on dozens of small round tables for seating. Plastic folding chairs were pushed into place and even more crisp, white tablecloths fluttered open, covering the scarred wooden tabletops. Like a perfectly choreographed film shot, once the tables were ready, the food began to appear. Ben was astounded. More volunteers arrived in an unending procession carrying chafing dishes, bowls, and crockpots full of food. There was obviously a well-practiced system in place. People moved with efficiency, knowing exactly where they were going and where everything should be arranged. Ben found the best place to help and not be in the way was stacking the paper plates and plastic utensils they were going to use.

When the food was prepped and everything was in place, Evan gathered the group in the center of the room. "Thank you all for being here today. We are so grateful for your time and your willingness to spend your day here, serving the Lord. The people that we are going to serve today are deserving of all the love we have to give. Before we open the door, let's pray and invite God to be the center of this meal."

The team formed a circle and joined hands. Lily stood beside him and slipped her hand into his. He bowed his head with the others, but instead of closing his eyes, he stared at her delicate fingers enfolded in his hand.

"Dear Lord, lead us and guide us today. Help us to be Your hands and feet to people who need to know that You have not forgotten them. Remind everyone we meet today that You love them. Protect us as we serve Your people and give us the right words to speak. In Jesus' name, Amen."

Ben muttered an amen, already missing the warmth of Lily's hand in his.

"Here, you're going to need this." Noah handed him a plastic hair net.

Ben made a face as he stared at it. "You can't be serious."

Noah shrugged, not even bothering to conceal the smirk on his face. "Rules are rules, my friend," he said and sauntered off.

Ben wound up on the mashed potatoes station with a single mom named Jayda. She smiled broadly and called everyone "honey." Slipping on the disposable serving gloves, he tried to stop wondering how silly he looked with the hairnet tucked over his hair and around his ears.

Pastor Evan and Noah opened the doors to the church and a steady stream of men and women poured in. Ben was so busy scooping up mashed potatoes, he completely forgot about the hairnet. As he worked, he looked into faces he recognized. Not because he had met them before, but because he knew what it was to be hungry. He'd had that same look on his face the first time he ran out of money on his trip from Indiana. Between gas, food, and hotels, the money he had so carefully saved up ran out after only a week. Out of gas in a small town in Illinois with no food and no place to stay, he didn't know where to go.

The first night that he spent in his car, he didn't sleep. Living with his parents he had known fear. He had known desperation, but this was different. There was no one he could turn to, no one he could ask for help. He was on his own, and as much as he thought he wanted that, he couldn't stop the panic that wormed its way into the cramped interior of his beat up sedan. He was in a parking lot behind the local grocery store and when the store closed and the lights winked out, the darkness that settled around him was filled with terrifying stories and regret.

The next morning he crawled out of the car, exhausted and hungry. He went into the store as soon as it opened and asked for a job. He spent the next month stocking shelves and collecting carts from the parking lot. After that first night, Ben resigned himself to staying in his car. It was the fastest way to save up money so he could move on. The compulsion to keep moving hounded him. He didn't have anywhere to go, he just knew he couldn't stop. He had to keep driving, keep running, even though he didn't know what he was running from. But no matter how far he went, the emptiness followed him. There was no escaping it.

He forced the thoughts away and focused on scooping up mashed potatoes. He wasn't hungry, he wasn't lost, not anymore, but he knew how close he had been to being on the other side of the table.

As the line slowed down, he felt a hand on his shoulder. Lily was standing beside him and her presence banished the darkness.

"Want to get a plate and join us?" she asked.

Ben fixed himself lunch and joined Lily and Evan. They were sitting at a table with an older man wearing torn jeans and a faded sweatshirt. A knit cap covered most of his greying hair. Arthritis gnarled hands shook the fork as he ate.

"Thomas," Evan said. "This is our friend, Ben."

The old man looked up and nodded.

"Hi, Thomas. Nice to meet you."

They ate in silence and Ben was struck by the normalcy of it. The Shaws treated every person in the room the same way they treated him. There was no condescension, no pity, just simple acts of compassion and a willingness to listen.

Evan pushed away from the table and looked down. He frowned at whatever it was he saw. Ben followed his gaze. Thomas wasn't wearing any shoes. Two toes peeked out from the holes in his thin white socks. The bottoms were stained and caked with dirt.

"It's a bit cold to go around with no shoes," Evan said. "Do you have some in your bag?"

Thomas shook his head as he continued to eat. "I lost my shoes a way's back. I don't walk very much anymore so it's not too bad."

Evan stood beside him and compared their feet. Thomas flinched at the contact.

"You know what, we might be the same size."

Ben stared at the pastor. Evan bent over, untied his sturdy work boots and slipped them off. "Give these a try."

He held them out, but Thomas shook his head and pulled his hands away as if the boots would burn him. "I can't take those."

"You're not taking them," Evan said as he knelt down in front Thomas. "I'm giving them to you. Can I help you try them on?"

Thomas set down his fork and stared down at the pastor. Tears glistened, unshed in his eyes.

Evan gently took Thomas' foot and slipped it inside one of the boots. Then he did the same for other foot. "How do they fit?"

"They're good. Nice and warm."

"Excellent." Evan tied the laces and then stood up and laid his hand on Thomas' shoulder. "Is there some way we can pray for you?"

The old man kept staring at the boots as he wiped his eyes. "Maybe for my kids. I haven't seen them in years and I don't know where they are. Can you pray that they don't . . . that they don't turn out like me?"

Lily rose and stood beside her dad, resting her hand on his. Ben watched, uncertain. Should he stay or excuse himself? Then she inclined her head and drew Ben into the small circle they formed behind Thomas. Resting his hand on the man's shoulder, he felt the frayed cotton beneath his fingers and Thomas' thin back rising and falling with each breath.

"Heavenly Father," Evan prayed. "We thank You for our brother, Thomas. We thank You for the chance to meet him today. God we ask You to watch over his children. You have never lost sight of them. Even now You see them and You love them. Bless them we pray, protect them, and help them. And God we ask that You make a way for them all to be together again. Watch over Thomas. Keep him safe and warm and remind him how much You love him. In Jesus' name. Amen."

Ben kept his eyes open, watching them as they prayed. Evan's clear voice prayed without hesitation or reservation. He spoke boldly, talking to God like they were friends. Peace settled over Lily's face as she closed her eyes and tears rolled down Thomas' weathered and wrinkled cheeks. Ben felt the intimacy of the moment, the closeness they shared. He just didn't know how to be a part of it.

Chapter Sixteen

AS THEY CLEANED UP, LILY kept an eye on Ben. He'd been unusually quiet during lunch. She wondered if they had been right to invite him to help. Maybe it had been too much for him. Maybe this was a little too far from his mansion and red carpets. He'd worked hard and he hadn't complained. He was even still wearing the stupid plastic hairnet.

Lily forced herself to stop staring at Ben and focused on picking up trash. God was in control. She believed it. She trusted in that simple fact. The only thing she could do was give Him room to work.

She was dumping discarded plates into the black trash bag when the door to the church flew open. A young, athletic man walked in. His heavily gelled hair and skinny jeans screamed that he wasn't here for the free lunch.

She set down the trash bag and crossed the room. "Can I help you?"

"I'm Ben Prescott's personal assistant. Is he here?"

Before she could answer, his eyes darted over her shoulder. "Never mind." He strode past her and headed straight for Ben.

Ben was scooping leftovers out of the serving dishes when he spotted the man heading for him. "Derek?" he asked, a mixture of shock and horror filling his words. "How did you find me?"

Lily caught her brother's gaze across the room. He held his hands up helplessly, clearly as in the dark as she was.

Derek held up his cell phone and shook it. "Zoe is freaking out. Where have you been?"

"You tracked my phone?"

Derek looked at Ben like he'd lost his mind. "Of course I tracked your phone. You didn't call, didn't email. You just disappeared." He stepped back and looked Ben over from head to toe, his stare settling on the hairnet. "What are you wearing?"

Raising the phone, Derek snapped a series of photos.

Ben dragged the hairnet off his head and shoved it in his pocket. "What are you doing here?"

"Clearly, I'm saving you from indentured servitude."

Anger bubbled up in Lily and she took a step towards them, but a hand on her arm stopped her. She turned and faced a filthy man in disheveled clothes. He reeked of sweat and alcohol. Long, stringy, blond hair was matted to the sides of his face. The nails that gripped her arm were caked with dirt and his hands were scratched and scarred. Frantic desperation sparked in his eyes as he held her fast.

"I need money." His voice was raw and filled with the threat of violence.

Fear constricted her throat, but she took a deep breath. Scattered prayers bounced around her mind. This wasn't the first time she'd had to deal with a potentially dangerous person in the church. She reminded herself to remain calm as she looked at him.

He couldn't have been more than twenty. He was far too thin and his whole body thrummed with panic. Withdrawals. Lily could only imagine the pain he was going through as his body screamed for whatever drug he craved. She wanted to look for her dad, but she was afraid to turn away, afraid to take her eyes off him. Easing a gentle smile on her face, she adopted her mother's soothing voice.

"We don't have any money here. But we can give you lunch. Are you hungry?"

"No!" He yanked on her arm and she stumbled forward, the trash bag falling from her hand and spilling on the ground. "I don't want food. I know you have money. Give it to me. Please."

Heart racing, Lily tried to pull away but his grip tightened even more. His nails pierced the material of her sweater and dug into her skin. She bit back a cry as she dug her heels in, trying to stand her ground.

"Let her go." A solid presence appeared at her side. Ben.

He grabbed her assailant's wrist and Lily felt the pressure on her arm increase, the nails digging in deeper, a last desperate act, then she was free. Instinctually, she rubbed her arm, cradling it against her chest as Noah and her dad materialized on her other side.

"I'll burn this place down!" the drug addict screamed. "I'll burn it down!" Spittle dripped from his mouth as he fought Ben's hold like an animal caught in a snare. Rage contorted his face as he screamed obscenities at them, his skin stretching taut, revealing the wasted veins beneath.

Ben let go of his wrist and he bolted for the street, the front door slamming against the wall with a crash as his screams faded into the distance.

"Lily." Ben took her hand and turned her towards him. "Are you okay?"

The calm she had clung to vanished and tremors racked her body. She would not fall apart. She couldn't. Not when so many of their volunteers were still there, still looking to her. Later. Later she could collapse.

She forced her head to nod, once then twice. "I'm fine." She looked at his strong hand, the one that had rescued her, the one that held her own so gently. "Thank you," she whispered, wanting to say more, but not knowing where to start.

"That was incredible!" An excited voice tore through her mind, shattering the thin bubble of calm she was clinging to. Derek was holding his phone up, pointing the camera at her and Ben. Had he recorded the entire thing?

"Stop," Ben commanded, forcing the phone down.

"What? This is great footage. Hollywood Bad Boy Saves the Day. This is huge. Zoe will want to see it right away."

Lily swayed on her feet and Ben caught her against his side. "Put it away Derek. Delete it. This isn't a photo op."

"But—"

"Go home, Derek." Lily felt the tension in Ben's body as he stared down his assistant.

The young man tucked his phone away, a thunderous expression written on his face. He left without another word, stomping out the door, and she was glad to see him go. She let herself lean into the warmth of Ben's embrace even as her mind screamed for her to step away, to put on a brave face and walk away. But her heart longed to sink into the strength of his arm around her shoulder, to let herself be taken care of, to believe for just a second that he cared.

And so she did. She closed her eyes and let herself pretend it mattered to him, that she mattered to him.

Chapter Seventeen

BEN HAD DINNER WITH THE Shaws again that night. After the day spent at the church, he looked at the food on his plate differently. The sun was setting and his mind wandered to Thomas and the other people he met. Most of them were sleeping outside, finding shelter in the flimsy tents or scavenged pieces of cardboard and plastic they made into homes. Behind the billboards and the tourist spots, the lights of downtown faded. He'd spent years driving through the streets of Hollywood, ignoring the hidden world of poverty and despair that existed in the shadows.

He thought of all the charity galas he had attended, all of the checks he had written. None of that had seemed real to him then. He'd simply signed on the line, snapped a photo, and then promptly forgot the name of the charity he had just donated to. He'd never seen where the money went. But here, on this neglected and forgotten street, Ben knew he would never forget the people he had met. He would remember Thomas for the rest of this life. Staring into his water glass, he wondered if any check he had ever written had done as much good as that simple pair of boots.

"You okay, Ben?" Noah asked. He hadn't said much since they got back from the church. He had accepted their dinner invitation without hesitation. After what Lily had been through, he had no intention of leaving her before he knew she was home safe and sound. But even though he was sitting at their table, his mind was somewhere else entirely.

"What? Oh, I'm fine. It's just . . . " He paused. He didn't know what he wanted to say. How could he explain it? He went to clubs and awards shows and movie premieres only a few blocks away from the streets where people were starving, lonely, and dying. Not one of the people he helped feed today knew who he was. They didn't care about his movies. They cared only that he was there. Everything he had worked for, everything he had achieved seemed hollow compared to the simple act of giving food to a hungry person. His life of wealth and prosperity felt useless and empty.

"You did a good job today," Lily said. She hadn't eaten much, keeping her hands wrapped around a warm mug of coffee. "It isn't an easy ministry to do. Seeing so much hurt and knowing our resources are limited, but it does make a difference."

He looked down at Evan's feet. He was still walking around in just his socks, as if the loss of his boots hadn't even crossed his mind. Though Ben guessed that from his perspective the boots hadn't been lost at all. They'd been given. How much did he have in his home that could be given away? How many people could he have clothed or fed by now if he hadn't been so focused on himself?

"How do you do this every month? How do you not get swallowed up by the sadness of it all?" He'd been there only for one day and he felt like he'd never be the same again.

Lily smiled. "Because I have God with me. I don't have to do it by myself. I don't have to face it alone, God is there."

"God?" Ben demanded. "Where was God when that drug addict showed up? You could have been seriously hurt? Where was God in that? I didn't see Him show up and save the day." Bitterness tinged his words, but he didn't care. It was all further proof that if there was a God, He didn't care enough to get involved.

"He didn't have to show up. He sent you." Lily sipped from her steaming mug, her eyes daring him to object.

He took the bait. "That wasn't God. That was coincidence."

She smiled and shrugged, the motion buried under the thick sweater she wore. "Einstein said 'Coincidence is God's way of remaining anonymous.'"

Shaking his head, he glanced at Evan who remained quiet, watching the discussion. The man had lost his wife. He'd prayed for God to heal her and even though God was able to do it, He hadn't. He'd refused. He'd stood by and done nothing and yet Evan was still there. Still faithful, still willing to believe in the God who had let his wife die.

"But that's not God. That's not a miracle." His words came out sharper than he intended, but none of this made any sense to him. His instinct was to run away. To run back to his isolated house in the Hollywood Hills, to lose himself in a script and forget what he had seen. "All of this was your family, your church, doing all the work. And me being there to help Lily, that was luck."

"Ben, none of that happens without God." Passion shone in her eyes as she leaned across the table. "Sometimes God steps in and does something amazing, something people see and everyone calls it a miracle. And sometimes He works in smaller ways, sometimes He works through people who are willing to hear His voice and follow His leading. Feeding someone who's hungry, holding someone when they cry, that is just as much of a miracle as parting an ocean or stopping the sun."

Noah laughed. "Given the state of the world we live in, those small acts of kindness might be even more of a miracle."

Ben sat back in his chair and considered her words. He couldn't deny there was something special about Lily and her family. But he didn't think God should get the credit for it. They were good people doing good work. And for all the time he had spent with them he hadn't seen God actually show up and get His hands dirty. He was about to tell Lily as much when his cell phone rang.

He excused himself from the table and answered. "Hello?"

"Hi, Ben." A seductive breath drifted through the phone. "It's me."

"Giselle?" Ben thought about hanging up on her. Instead, he stepped out of the kitchen, but not before he saw Lily glance in his direction. He met her eyes and she quickly looked away.

"How are you, Ben?"

Her sugary sweet voice immediately irritated him. Why was she calling? Anger and resentment rose up as quickly as lava in a restless volcano. "What do you want, Giselle?"

"I miss you." He pinched the bridge of his nose and squeezed his eyes shut, regretting ever answering the phone. Her timing could not have been worse. "I want to see you. Can I come over?"

"Now's not a good time. I'm not at home. And I don't think it's a good idea for us to see each other." He lowered his voice, but he was sure Lily could hear every word. Noah was keeping up a steady stream of conversation from the sink where he was on dish duty again, but it was a small house. He stepped further into the hallway, keeping his back to the kitchen.

"Ben, I made a terrible mistake. The break-up, the interview. It was all wrong. I'm so sorry. Can you forgive me?"

"What?" Fractured, wild thoughts crashed in his head like waves in a storm. Giselle was purring into the phone, her silken voice bringing up old memories and times they shared. She wanted him back.

But even as she cooed and cajoled in the phone, Ben's eyes were drawn to Lily. Lily sitting at the table laughing at something Noah said. Lily who read Bible stories to children and brought food to the hungry. Lily with a voice like an angel and wildfire in her eyes. Nothing Giselle said could compare to that.

"It's over, Giselle. Go back to Liam. We're done."

Silence. Tense, heavy silence pulsed on the other end of the phone. Ben thought she hung up on him and he was about to disconnect when he heard her voice again.

"Let's talk about this in Barbados. We can spend the week there just like we planned and figure it all out."

Ben almost laughed. At that moment, nothing could convince him to go to Barbados, nothing could convince him to leave the warmth of the Shaws' home. "I'm sorry, Giselle." He walked back to the kitchen. Lily looked up at him and Ben knew exactly what he wanted to say. "I have plans for Christmas."

Chapter Eighteen

BEN WANDERED THROUGH THE TRENDY shops on Rodeo Drive. He hadn't planned on having a real Christmas. He'd planned on drinking something with an umbrella sticking out of it while he sat on a lounge chair next to a pool and tried to ignore the endless litany of gossip Giselle liked to share. There was no church, no carols, no holiday turkey in that plan. But everything had changed. All it had taken was Evan's invitation, and the puzzled look on Lily's face when he accepted, and suddenly he was like a kid counting down the days until Christmas morning.

A slow smile edged across his face as he strolled through the stores looking for just the right gifts for Lily, Noah, and Evan. He couldn't wait to spend the day with them, but he didn't want to show up empty handed. He picked up knick-knacks and belts and scented candles, but nothing seemed right. When he and Giselle had been together, shopping had been easy. Buy the most expensive of everything. But he didn't think Lily would appreciate that tactic. Giselle always wanted more. More shoes, more purses, more jewelry. Half of the clothes she owned she wore once and then they disappeared into a dark corner of her closet never to be seen again. Lily wasn't like that. Lily wasn't like any woman he had ever met.

He examined the sequined Chanel bag in his hand and put it back on the shelf. None of the expensive trinkets on display in Beverly

Hills belonged in the Shaw home. If he was honest, he wasn't sure *he* belonged in their home either. He was a messed-up kid from a messed-up family, and he had a history of mucking things up. The list of his regrets and mistakes followed him like a shadow. But the Shaws let him in anyway. For the first time in a long time, he had something to look forward to. He had people who didn't want to pitch him or sign him or use him. What kind of gift do you get for that?

He was staring at the black, velvet display of bracelets behind a glass jewelry case when he felt a heavy hand on his back.

"Hey, Ben, how's it going?"

One of the producers from *Blood and Honor* was standing beside him. His perfectly tailored suit and sharp red tie radiated power and influence. His company financed the movie and stood to make a hefty profit if it did well.

"James." He shook his beefy hand. "How are you doing?"

"Good. Good." The producer held his hand longer than necessary, pumping it up and down like an old-fashioned water pump. "I'm hearing some great early buzz about the film. Are you ready for the premiere?"

A knot he'd been carrying in his stomach since filming ended loosened. He liked the script and had enjoyed making the film, but there was no telling what the fans and critics would think. Good reviews were a great first step to box office success. And box office success meant another contract. Another contract meant another premiere and hopefully more box office success. It was a merry-go-round that just kept spinning. But one wrong move, one flop, and the ride could come to a crashing halt. So he plastered a smile on his face and let the man who bankrolled the film shake his hand as long as he wanted. "Can't wait."

"I'm glad you'll be there. Chris did a great job, but I can't put him front and center on this one. Not after he turned his last interview into a sermon." James gave him a pointed look.

Chris Johnston was the director and one of Ben's closest friends. He knew Chris went to church, but he didn't give it much thought. Chris didn't bring it up so he didn't either. As far as he was concerned, his choice of religion was in the same category as his choice of car. Neither made much of a difference on their friendship.

Ben waved the producer's snide remarks away. "I doubt it was a sermon. Didn't he just say something about Christmas?"

James sniffed and looked to the side. "Christmas is fine. Christmas is a money-maker for us. Everybody loves gifts and Santa Claus and happy elves making toys. But bringing up the name of Jesus is bad for business. No one wants to be told how to live their life." He looked at his cell phone, scrolling through several text messages, before continuing. "I know he's a great director, but if you're going to let your private beliefs become your public persona, well, then you need to be prepared for the fallout. I mean come on, if I wanted to hire a monk to make a movie for the prayer vigil crowd, I would have."

Ben forced a laugh, but he was ready for the conversation to be over. Zoe's warnings about his involvement with a church echoed in his head. "Chris is hardly a monk."

The producer dropped his phone back in his jacket pocket. "Really? When was the last time you saw him on a date?" He raised his eyebrows suspiciously. "I just wish he'd keep his religion to himself. I hired him to direct a movie, not become Hollywood's evangelist-in-chief."

Ben didn't reply. He thought of Lily and her family and how much they cared about the people who came to their church. They didn't hide their faith. Everything they did was because of that faith, and that didn't seem like such a bad thing.

"So." James peered in to the jewelry display case. "Are you looking for something for Giselle?"

"No." Ben's nerves tightened and he knew he was on dangerous ground. He had no desire to share his Christmas plans with the producer.

"Oh, right." James smacked a hand against his forehead in a gesture that was as fake as the veneers on his teeth. "I heard about the break up. That's too bad. You two looked great together."

Ben shrugged and stepped further away. He made a show of looking at the jewelry, but he was really looking for an exit. "Apparently she disagreed."

"Women, right?" The producer followed him, looking at the collection of sparkling gems in front of them. "So, for someone else then?"

The implication in the question hung heavy in the air, but he wasn't about to answer it. "Now, James, you know a gentleman never tells."

Laughing, the producer pounded him on the back. "It's good to see you bounce back so quickly. Just as long as this new girl doesn't ruin the premiere."

Ben didn't miss the subtle warning in his tone and he fought the urge to tell the producer to take a long walk off the Santa Monica pier. But Zoe wouldn't appreciate him burning bridges, even if this particular bridge was in desperate need of a match.

"Hey, you should come by the studio." James pulled his phone out again and started looking through his calendar. "I've got another project you'd be perfect in, a real action-packed flick. It's got blockbuster written all over it. What day works for you?"

Ben plastered a smile on his face. He knew how to fight this type of battle. "I'm pretty booked right now. Why don't you send the script over to Zoe? I'm sure she'll give it a look."

The producer's smile faded at the slight, but he forced a jovial tone to his voice. "I'll do that. See you at the premiere." He shook Ben's hand once again. "Remember, we've all got a lot riding on you."

Ben walked out of the store. He looked up and down the street. People brushed past him on the sidewalk as he stared at the endless parade of designer names and expensive stores. Anxiety vibrated around the edges of his mind. He got into his car and revved the engine as if the noise could silence the whispers of doubt that were starting to crowd in on him. He wasn't going to find what he was looking for here.

Chapter Nineteen

BEN ARRIVED AT THE HOLLYWOOD Mission at 9:30 a.m. on Christmas morning. He wasn't sure how to dress so he settled on khaki pants and a sweater. He sat in his car in the parking lot staring at the building, working up the courage to go in. Lily and her family had been kind to him. So for them he would sit through a Christian lecture. At least the chairs here were comfortable.

He kept his sunglasses on as he walked into the foyer. The Christmas tree in the corner was lit up and people were talking and drinking coffee cocoa from the little coffee table set up outside on the loading dock. The greeter at the door shook his hand and said, "Merry Christmas."

He worked his way through the crowd. Evan hadn't exaggerated when he said it would fill up. As he approached the sanctuary doors, he spotted Noah.

"Merry Christmas, Ben. I'm glad you're here." Noah enveloped him in a back-slapping hug.

"Thanks. Merry Christmas."

"Let's go grab some seats." Noah opened the door and led the way in.

"Aren't you supposed to be working or something?" Ben asked.

"Nope. I wanted to make sure you had someone to sit with this morning. Nobody should be alone on Christmas."

The sincerity of Noah's words hit him with an unexpected jolt, like he had stepped into a warm room when he didn't even know he was cold. His grandmother used to say the same thing. Her house was never empty on Christmas. There was Ben and his parents, of course, but she always managed to find a few other people to invite as well. She called them her orphans and she made sure they were loved. Service members who couldn't go home for the holidays, widows who would have been alone, a single mom struggling through her first Christmas on her own, his grandmother made room for all of them. As a child, he hadn't known how special, or how rare, that was.

And now he was the orphan being welcomed into someone else's family. Words stuck in his throat and he was glad Noah was focused on walking them through the sanctuary so he didn't notice. If it hadn't been for Lily and her family he probably would have spent Christmas in his empty house eating Chinese food, watching reruns, and wondering if he should have gone to Barbados with a woman who wanted him only for publicity.

Noah guided them to the front row and Ben hesitated. "The front row? Are you serious?"

"Best seats in the house. Besides, you're less likely to be recognized by the back of your head. And if we sit here Lily will come down and join us after worship." The idea of sitting next to Lily was enough to silence Ben's arguments. Noah took a seat on the edge of the middle aisle and Ben sat beside him.

Noah put his hand on his shoulder. "I'm really glad you're here."

At the muffled sounds of people shuffling in behind him, uncertainty settled in his gut. The worry that this was a bad idea grew with every passing minute. He hadn't attended a church service in over a decade, and as he sat in the front row feeling exposed and out of place, he knew there was a reason he had stayed away. His sweater felt too tight and his feet itched to race back up the aisle and drive home.

But when Lily appeared from the side door and the music started, his trepidation disappeared. He was captivated. It wasn't traditional music. Not like the old hymns from the church of his upbringing. The music was loud and exciting. And Lily's singing soared above it all. He was transfixed by the beauty of her voice and the radiance on her face as she sang. Music filled the sanctuary and stirred his heart. Words flashed on the screens behind the band and Ben was shocked when he started to sing along.

When worship ended, Lily and the other musicians came down the steps and sat in the front row. Noah had taken the end seat so Lily had no choice but to sit next to Ben. She gave him a shy smile as she leaned over. "Merry Christmas, Ben."

He didn't have a chance to respond because Pastor Evan was calling the congregation to prayer. Ben bowed his head with everyone else and let the pastor's words wash over him.

"Heavenly Father, we thank You for this day. We thank You for the gift of Your son Jesus Christ, who gave up the glory of Heaven to be born as a baby to save us and make a way for us to know You. We thank You and praise You for giving us the best gift of all, the gift of Your only son. Amen."

Ben was surprised that he didn't hate the service. In fact, he enjoyed it. Maybe it was because he knew Pastor Evan or maybe it was the woman sitting to his right, but all of the nerves and resentment he felt in the parking lot melted away as the service went on. Pastor Evan spoke about how much God loves people. He didn't talk about how God wanted to send everyone except for a few, perfect people to Hell. The God Evan described was a God who did everything He could, even allowing His own Son to be killed so people could find their way home to Him.

It was a God Ben had never known.

Pastor Evan's words were still rolling around in his mind when the service ended. Lily had gone back on stage to sing a final song and Noah nudged his shoulder. "Ready to go?"

Ben nodded and Noah led the way through the crowd towards the door. As they stepped out the side door into the loading dock garden, a small voice called out.

"Mr. Ben!"

He turned toward the high-pitched squeal. Little Nate was running up from the children's church classrooms, his unzipped, puffy coat flapping like bright blue wings around him. He threw himself around Ben's legs and squeezed tightly. "Merry Christmas, Mr. Ben!"

Ben picked him up and gave him a hug. "Merry Christmas, Nate."

"Look what I made." Nate waved a drawing in front of his face. It was a colored-in picture of the Nativity. All around the sides of the manger, Nate had drawn an assortment of animals.

"Is that an octopus?" Ben asked.

"Yep. And a dragon and a puppy. They're all wishing Jesus a Happy Birthday."

He set the excited boy back on his feet. "That is the coolest picture I have ever seen."

"Here, you can have it." Nate held the drawing out to him.

"I can't take your drawing. Won't your mom want to see it?"

Nate shook his head. "She's got lots of pictures on the fridge already. I want you to have this one. It's a Christmas present."

Ben took the picture. "Thank you, Nate. That's a really nice gift."

"Hey, there she is! Come meet my mom." Nate grabbed Ben's hand and started pulling him across the dock.

Stumbling behind the determined four-year-old, he looked back in time to see Noah's eyes widen in shock. He chased after them, but Nate wove in and out of the crowd like a race car driver, dragging Ben behind him.

"Mama! Meet my friend, Ben." Nate stopped in front of a cluster of women standing by the side of the dock. His mom turned with a smile on her face and then froze. Ben could see the war between recognition and common sense waging in her eyes.

It was too late to sneak away, so he smiled and offered his hand. "It's nice to meet you, Ma'am. I'm Ben. Nate is a wonderful boy."

She blinked and took Ben's hand. "Thank you."

"Ben built blocks with me in after-care. He's super nice. Can he come over and play?"

Laughing, Ben squeezed Nate's skinny shoulder buried beneath the heavy coat. "Not today, Buddy. It's Christmas. But maybe I'll see you back here again."

A wave of whispers started swirling around him. He'd been unnoticed, hidden in the crowd during the service, but word was spreading fast. He caught the stares and the quick glances being shot his way, the way the crowd started to gather around his conversation. Habit took over and he stuck his photo op smile on his face. "Thank you for the drawing, Nate. I love it." Then he turned to Nate's mom. "Merry Christmas, Ma'am."

"Merry Christmas." Ben tried to slip away, but her hand on his arm stopped him. "Oh, wait, can I get a picture of you with Nate?"

"Of course." Ben dropped to one knee and put his arm around Nate's shoulders. His mom took out her camera and it was as if that one simple act opened the floodgates. Cellphones appeared everywhere. Ben kept smiling, but Nate looked confused.

"Why's everyone else taking pictures?"

"Because you're so handsome." Ben stood and several people approached asking to take pictures with him. In the back of the crowd, standing a little further off, he spotted Lily. She was watching the scene unfold, a bemused smile playing across her lips. He winked at her, biting back a laugh as the smile on her face shifted into shock, and went back to posing and smiling.

Noah was working his way through the crush of people until he finally made it to Ben's side. "Merry Christmas, everyone!" He took Ben's arm and started to lead him towards the parking lot. He smiled and chatted with people as they walked, but he didn't stop until they were away from the crowd.

"Nice work, Noah. Very smooth," Ben said when they reached the safety of the parking lot. "If you ever want to give up driving the limo you could be a bodyguard."

Noah snickered. "No thanks. Where's your car?"

He pointed to the far side of the parking lot. "What about Lily and your dad?"

"They'll be fine. They'll be stuck answering a lot of questions about how Ben Prescott ended up at our church on Christmas morning, but they'll make it home eventually. Give me your keys."

"I don't think so." Ben dug the keys out of his pocket and closed his fist around them. "I'll handle the driving this time."

Noah shook his head. "You're not going to dump me on the side of the road out of revenge are you?"

"I wasn't planning on it. But now that you mention it . . . "

Chapter Twenty

CHRISTMAS HAD ALWAYS BEEN LILY'S favorite holiday. And at the Shaw house, it was a big deal. The tree was decorated, stockings were hung on the mantel, and Christmas carols played non-stop from the day after Thanksgiving until December twenty-sixth. The stocking for Lily's mom was hung up in its usual place and she had added a fifth stocking with Ben's name on it to the mantel. It even smelled like Christmas thanks to the pumpkin pie cooling on the kitchen counter and the hot chocolate in their Santa Claus mugs.

Ben and Noah were sitting on the sofa in front of a brightly burning fire, while her Dad was in an armchair that looked like it was older than his children. Lily sat on the floor eyeing the presents under the tree. She might be twenty-four years old, but Christmas always turned her into a child. She had wrapped most of the presents, but it was the three gifts Ben brought that caught her attention. The fact that he thought to get gifts for them made her nerves tingle, like a bird anticipating a change in the wind. Some cynical part of her wondered if he'd sent out his assistant to get them. Maybe he'd just given that blond Derek a list of names to shop for. Maybe the gifts would be just as much of a shock to him as they were to her. Of course, he was an actor so she probably wouldn't be able to tell the difference. The thought dampened her joy like water on a fire.

She furrowed her brows and glanced at Ben. He was laughing at something Noah said and she chided herself for her suspicions. She wasn't being fair. He was there and he had even come to church that morning. The man who said he didn't believe in anything had shown up at church on Christmas morning. A flutter danced in her stomach as she remembered sitting next to him. Then she thought of Ben holding Nate in his arms. He had no way of knowing that Nate had never met his father. He had no way of knowing how much that hug meant to the little boy. She couldn't stop the smile that spread across her face. Underneath all that Hollywood varnish, Ben Prescott had a soft heart.

"What are you smiling about, Brat?" Noah asked and kicked her foot.

"It's Christmas," she said and fussed with the ribbon on one of the presents, refusing to look at Ben, afraid her wayward thoughts were written on her face. "What's not to smile about?"

Her brother smirked at Ben. "That means she wants to open presents."

Grateful for the distraction, she picked up a rectangular box and handed it to Noah. "Here, open this one first. It's from me."

"See," Noah said as he set down his mug and took the gift. "She likes presents."

"Good to know," Ben replied and Lily pretended that she hadn't heard. Her dad sipped his hot chocolate and watched the exchange with a thoughtful expression, which she also ignored.

Lily stuck a Santa cap on her head and passed out one present at a time so everyone could watch the recipient open it. Noah laughed at the collection of Star Wars socks she gave him and thanked her profusely for the new book series he'd been wanting to read.

"With awards season coming up, these books will be a life saver."

"So that's what the limo drivers do during the awards shows," Ben said as Noah read the blurbs on the back of the books.

"That and we talk about how bad your cologne smells."

The mug in Ben's hands froze halfway to his lips and his eyes widened. "Really?"

"Don't worry. You're not on the cologne blacklist."

Ben didn't seem relieved, in fact he looked more worried than before. "Am I on some other blacklist I should know about?"

Noah shrugged with exaggerated implication and Lily smacked him on the foot. The look on Ben's face was priceless, but she didn't want his Christmas to be ruined. She scooped up a large box and shoved it in Noah's hands. He looked at the tag and passed it on to their dad. As he focused on unwrapping, Lily cast a surreptitious glance towards Ben. He seemed to be relaxing again and she was grateful her brother's quips hadn't stuck.

Her dad was thrilled with the coffee maker she and Noah had splurged on for him. "Coffee makes the world go round," he said.

Lily laughed when she unwrapped a scarf from Noah. Every year he gave her a scarf. It had become a Shaw family tradition. Fortunately, this year, he also found a cute purse to go with it.

As the collection of gifts dwindled and the pile of crumpled wrapping paper grew, she picked up a large gift bag. The tag read "To Evan, From Ben." She passed it to her father, curiosity bombarding her.

"Thank you, Ben." He pulled the tissue paper out of the bag and peeked in. "Oh my!" He lifted out a new tool bag. "Oh, this is a nice one."

He turned the black and red tool bag around in his hands, examining all the compartments and the sturdy handle that didn't need duct tape.

"Just think about all the things you can fix on the church now, Dad." Lily laughed.

"I'm sure you'll write me a list," he replied, still checking out all the pockets on the tool bag.

"Here, Ben," Lily said and handed him a wrapped box. It was from Noah. "Then grab that one over here," Ben said. Lily found the one he pointed to. It was almost the exact same size and it was for Noah from Ben. They opened their gifts at the same time revealing two equally ugly Christmas sweaters. Noah's was embroidered with dancing reindeer while Ben's had elves decorating a tree.

Ben unwrapped a framed print of a landscape scene from her dad. It was a beautiful painting of rolling meadows with a windmill in the distance. A mix of longing and loss passed across his face as he stared at the print, and she wondered what he saw when he looked at it. Did it make him miss the home he left, or was it a painful reminder of things he wanted to forget? But he sounded sincere when he thanked her dad and promised to hang the print in a place of honor.

With only two gifts left under the tree, Ben ducked under the pine needles and picked up a small square box that he handed to Lily. The card read simply, "Merry Christmas, Lily. From Ben." She tried to keep her hands from shaking as she unwrapped the pretty box. Her mouth dropped open when she saw the treble clef pendant and necklace lying against the black, velvet cushion. Tiny diamonds set in the white gold music symbol sparkled in the firelight.

Excitement and nerves raced through her as she touched the pendant. Ben was watching her, his brown eyes searching her face to gauge her reaction and she knew. He hadn't outsourced this gift. This was all him. That realization made it even more special. "It's beautiful. Thank you." She took the necklace from the box and unclasped it.

Ben stood and took it from her. "Let me." He walked behind her and the necklace drifted over her head. Breathing in the warmth of his arms, the strength of his hands, she resisted the urge to lean back against him as he secured the clasp behind her neck. She glanced up in time to catch the look that passed between her dad and brother. She'd have to tell them there was nothing going on between her and Ben. But not now. For this one day she'd let the impossible hope linger. When he sat on the floor beside her, she handed him her gift. He grinned and carefully unwrapped the heavy box. Inside was a black leather Bible with sticky notes poking out along the side. He flipped open to one of the marked pages. There was a verse highlighted in yellow. *I can do all things through Christ who gives me strength.*

Lily waited, worried she had offended him, hoping he wouldn't take her gift the wrong way. "I hope you don't mind," she said. "I highlighted some of my favorite verses. Just in case you needed a place to start."

Ben flipped through page after page, the crackle of the turning pages beating against her nerves. She touched the pendant around her neck, feeling the smooth metal warm under her fingers. Maybe she had gone too far. Maybe this was too pushy. She glanced at her dad for guidance but he was keeping his thoughts to himself.

Closing the Bible, Ben leaned over and gave her a hug. "This is wonderful. Thank you."

She felt so right in his arms. She rested her head against his shoulder and in that one perfect moment, the secret hope she had been hiding in her heart suddenly seemed possible.

"Merry Christmas, Ben."

Chapter Twenty-One

ZOE SAT ACROSS FROM BEN with her cellphone by her side and a black, leather portfolio spread across her lap. Her blonde hair was pulled up into a severe knot and designer glasses were perched on the edge of her nose. Ben knew she didn't need to wear glasses, but they certainly added to the no-nonsense look she was projecting for this planning meeting. Derek sat next to him with his tablet out, typing notes as Zoe went over the plans for the *Blood and Honor* premiere.

"So," she said crisply and Derek tapped away at the glass screen. "You will arrive at precisely 6:12 p.m. You will have twenty minutes for the television press and five minutes for photos. Wear the black Armani and keep the tie understated, got it, Derek?"

His assistant typed quickly and nodded.

"The movie will start at seven p.m., sharp. I'm going to put you between Chris and Nicole." With a quick flick of her wrist, Zoe checked off one of the boxes on her lengthy list.

He had no problem sitting next to Chris, in fact, he was looking forward to it. This was their third film together and he enjoyed working with him. Chris was a talented director and he kept the atmosphere on the set light and upbeat. Remembering his brief encounter with the *Blood and Honor* producer before Christmas, he wondered if Chris had taken any heat for coming out as a Christian in an industry that was built on lies and carefully crafted images.

"Nicole is bringing her husband." Zoe rolled her eyes dramatically. "And he'll be on her left. Don't get too close, he'll try to get you to partner in his latest investment firm and you'll be broke by the next day." The air quotes she used around the word investment told him enough.

"Really?" he asked.

Zoe peered over the thick frames of her glasses, her eyebrows raised in a knowing look. "They're flat broke. She'll be taking any project that comes her way for the next five years just to keep the tax man away. I imagine she'll be doing commercials for face cream or shampoo any day now."

Derek sniggered beside him, but Ben couldn't muster the energy to laugh at the mean-spirited joke. His co-star Nicole was nice. They didn't have much in common, but filming had gone well and he wouldn't mind working with her again. She was professional, she came to the set prepared, and she had been easy to work with. Now he was listening to her family's dirty secrets being discussed like the weather report. It was an awful feeling and he couldn't help but wonder what Nicole's agent was telling her about him. It was never enough to just show up and do the work. There was always something else going on, always an angle to play or a deal to make.

Derek spoke as he typed on the glass screen. "Don't give money to Mr. Nicole. Got it. What's next?"

Ben cleared his throat. He knew his next request was going to mess up Zoe's seating chart, but he didn't care. "I'll need another seat at the premiere. I'm bringing a guest."

Zoe's pen froze above her checklist. "Giselle?"

The hopeful tone in her voice irritated him, but he didn't let it show. Better to keep this conversation light and move on as quickly as possible. "Not in a million years."

Zoe took her glasses off and folded them slowly, the sides clicking into place. "Then who might this guest be?"

He held her gaze. She might be his agent, but he didn't need her permission for this. The idea had come to him on Christmas. Sitting in the Shaws' house beneath the tree with his arm around her, he knew he wanted her by his side. "Lily Shaw."

Derek froze and he could feel his assistant's eyes dart between the actor he worked for and the agent who hired him. And for a moment, he wondered where Derek's loyalties really lay.

"The pastor's daughter?" Zoe pursed her lips until they turned white. "You want to bring the pastor's daughter to the premiere of *Blood and Honor*?"

"Yes." He didn't bring up the fact that he hadn't actually asked her yet.

Closing the planner, Zoe leaned forward, an indulgent smile on her face. "Look, Ben. That photo op at the church on Christmas was genius—"

"It wasn't a photo op." He resented the implication that he had planned the photo with Nate going viral. One of the people who snapped a picture posted it to her Facebook account and within hours it was all over the news. Zoe might have thought the photo was a publicity stunt, she might have even kicked herself for not orchestrating it herself, but he didn't want to be thought of that way. He never wanted to be so desperate for attention that he'd use a four-year-old boy for publicity.

"Fine, it was a happy accident." Waving her hand, she dismissed his concerns. "However it happened, it made you look good. It's getting you positive press, but let's not go overboard. Bringing the pastor's daughter to the premiere of your biggest movie is not what you need right now. The press will eat her alive. And then they'll turn on you."

Uncertainty flared in his gut. Lily would hate the cameras and the questions, he was sure of that. But he had a plan. "After we arrive, I'll pass her to you and you can escort her in. I'll do the red carpet and the press by myself. No one in the press will even know she's there."

Zoe slid a piercing glance at Derek. The assistant excused himself and disappeared from the room. When he was gone, she clasped her hands and smiled like a mother preparing to lecture her wayward child. "Ben, you know I like you. You're one of the industry's top stars and you're not a high-maintenance pain in the neck to work with. You have your pick of scripts. But that works only as long as you stay on top. If you start dating some Bible thumping preacher's kid, how long do you think that will last?"

Anger flared, hot and bright, in his chest. Lily didn't belong to his world of celebrity and scandal, and he wasn't going to let his agent drag her through the mud. He might not have much to offer Lily, but he could protect her from this. "Choose your next words carefully, Zoe."

The Hollywood hardened agent sat back against the chair. Calculation glittered in her gaze, assessing the situation, examining options, running through the possibilities in her mind. It was the same look she had the day they first met. He was prepping for a stunt when Zoe waltzed across the sound stage looking for her client, a young actor clawing his way up from background parts to leading roles. They stood together behind the cameras and lights as he ran through a fight scene that culminated with him falling off metal scaffold and crashing to the ground. Fortunately for him the ground was covered in mats.

Even as he focused on the choreographed steps and the timing of punches with the other stunt man, he felt her eyes on him, assessing him, searching for something that only she could identify. At the time he didn't realize how much had been riding on that one moment or how much his life was going to change because of it.

The stunt went perfectly on the first take and as he pulled himself off the mats, Zoe was waiting, her manicured hand stretched out to him. She signed him as a client less than an hour after that first meeting.

That same expression was watching him now. "Is it serious?"

He pushed off the sofa and walked to the windows. The morning light was still golden, casting everything it touched in warmth while Zoe's question hung in the air. Crossing his arms, he stared out across the hills in the direction of downtown. Somewhere in the shadows of Hollywood, Lily was at the church. Maybe she was setting up her cheerful classroom or singing on the platform in front of an empty sanctuary. Was it serious? He didn't know the answer. He didn't know if she was thinking about him, if she had even given him a thought since he left her house Christmas evening. "It isn't anything yet."

"Then keep it that way. Your fans want a sex symbol, not a Sunday school teacher."

He turned and leaned against the glass. He'd always known Zoe had a hard edge, he just wasn't used to seeing it directed at him. From that first meeting on the set, he'd gone where she said, read the lines she had given him, taken the parts she suggested. She had made him a celebrity, there was no denying it. But looking at her across the room, he realized she had taken control of much more than his career. It was time that ended.

"You run my career, Zoe, not my life."

She met his stare without flinching. "And you still don't get it. The two are inseparable. I'm the one who keeps them together. I'm the one who gets you out of trouble and cleans up your messes. I'm the one who keeps you a star. You should remember that."

As if on cue, Derek reappeared and cleared his throat. He glanced from movie star to agent, but kept his distance from them both.

Ben crossed back to the sofa and sat down again. "Just make the change. I'm bringing Lily to the premiere."

With a sigh, she flipped the planner open. "Fine. But are you sure this girl is ready to be Ben Prescott's new girlfriend? Because as soon as she steps out of that limo, that's exactly what she's going to be."

He didn't answer. He had no idea if Lily was ready for that, but he intended to find out.

*****

There was dead silence over the phone. The kind of long, loud, poignant silence that usually comes before something bad. Lily's heart raced and she forgot how to talk. Words. She needed words. She was supposed to say something.

"Lily?" Ben's voice echoed in her ear. "Are you still there?"

Say something, Lily! The words crashed in her head. She was making a fool of herself. Clearly this was why she hadn't had a date in months. One phone call and she turned into a stammering simpleton incapable of forming complete sentences. *Answer the question!*

"Yes," she blurted out and immediately her stomach flipped. She sank down on her bed then decided to lay down to make sure she didn't fall over. What had she just done?

"Yes, you're still there or yes, you'll go with me?"

She pressed the phone to her ear and closed her eyes. Ben was asking her out. And it wasn't just any date. He wanted to take her to the premiere of his new movie. An actual red carpet movie premiere. Excitement bubbled up and Lily answered before she overthought it, before she let the voice of logic and reason talk her out of it. "Yes, I'll go with you."

She thought she heard him exhale on a whoosh. Did he actually think she was going to say no? The thought made her giggle and she slapped her hand over her mouth to cover the sound. Kate was going to freak out.

"Great. I'll call Noah and see if he can drive us."

He sounded so close, as if she could open her eyes and see him standing there. Whether she meant to do it or not, she had memorized his face. She knew the way his eyes crinkled when he laughed, the funny way he raked his hands through his hair when he got flustered. And now she was going to see him again. Nervous energy sizzled through her limbs. "Okay. It sounds like fun."

"I hope so. I'm looking forward to seeing you, Lily."

Ben was looking forward to seeing her. She barely heard the rest of the plan as he told her what time he would pick her up and where they were going for the after-party.

When they said goodbye and hung up, she stared at the blank screen on her phone. Had that really happened? Part of her wished she had let the call go to voicemail so she'd have evidence that she hadn't dreamt it.

Ben Prescott was taking her to a movie premiere. Grabbing her pillow, she hugged it to her chest and grinned like a fool. She didn't want to overthink it, she didn't want to dream too big, but at that moment she couldn't stop herself. She thought of Ben hugging Nate and building wooden block towers. She remembered him wearing the ugly Christmas sweater Noah had given him during dinner. Then she touched the necklace around her neck, the pendant he had given her, the one she knew he'd picked out himself. No matter what else happened in the future, for one night she would be the woman Ben wanted to be with.

"You're going out with Ben?" Noah stood in the door of her bedroom, his face as shocked as she felt.

"And apparently, you're driving us," she giggled.

Noah studied her carefully, weighing whatever it was he wanted to say next. The excitement she felt started to fade as she watched him. "Look, Sis, I like Ben a lot, too. He's a nice guy. But he lives in a different world. You don't know those people, Lily. I do. I've seen what goes on behind the scenes, when the cameras are gone and they think no one's watching. It's messed up."

Doubt burrowed its way into her heart. He was right. She didn't belong in Ben's world and he would figure that out soon enough. But for one night, she could pretend she had a chance. She could pretend there weren't a million different reasons why it wouldn't work out. "It's one night, Noah. He didn't even say it was a date. He's probably just being nice."

"I think one of you is on the way to a broken heart. But I don't know which one it is." Noah shook his head and she could see the worry on his face.

As long as she could remember, he had been her protector and her defender. He had given up a lot to come back here and work at the church. Looking at him, she wondered how much he kept inside, how many regrets he kept to himself. She wanted him to feel the same excitement and anticipation she'd felt when Ben called. God had a woman in mind for Noah, she knew it and she prayed that woman was on her way to him.

"Well," Noah's resigned tone broke into her thoughts. "I'll be in the driver's seat if you need me. Maybe this time I'll keep Ben and kick you out of the car."

Lily leapt off the bed and hugged her brother. "Thank you, Noah." She pulled back, panic seizing her. "Wait. What am I going to wear?"

He raised his eyebrows. "That's not your biggest problem. What are you going to tell Dad?"

Chapter Twenty-Two

LILY PACED THE LIVING ROOM in her bare feet. She wasn't putting on those fabulous, but painful three inch heels until it was absolutely necessary. Noah left two hours ago to pick up Ben and she'd been a nervous wreck ever since. It seemed silly for Noah to drive all the way to Ben's house, pick him up, and then come back for her, but Ben had insisted. He said he didn't want her stuck in the limo any longer than necessary. Lily chuckled, like being stuck in a limo would be a hardship.

And so she waited. In her simple, floor length black dress with an entire can of hairspray plastering her hair in place, she waited for Ben Prescott to pick her up and take her to a red carpet premiere. The reality of the situation hit her hard and she collapsed onto the sofa, deflated like a balloon that had been popped. What was she doing? She was nobody. She was a teacher and a worship leader from a tiny church in Hollywood. And now she was going to be sitting next to celebrities, walking past reporters and photographers. Panic began to dance in her chest. She was reaching for her cell phone to text Ben that she couldn't make it when her dad walked in.

He took one look at her and stopped cold, tears welling in his eyes. "You are so beautiful. You look just like your mom."

"Oh, Dad." Lily rose to hug him and in his strong arms, she found her peace. The worries and the fear began to disappear and she could breathe again. This was her life. This small house, their church, this was where she belonged. "What am I doing?"

Cupping his chin in his hand, he pretended to study her like she was a complicated math problem. "Looks to me like you're about to go on a date."

"It's not a date," she protested as she shook out her dress. For the hundredth time she wondered if she was dressed appropriately. She'd worn this dress to the last formal dance she and Kate attended in college. Kate had insisted she buy the dress, claiming the chiffon skirt floated like wisps of black smoke and the thin sleeves and drape neckline flattered her. But now she worried that she wasn't dressed up enough. Or maybe she was overdressed. Or maybe she should just admit she had no idea what she was doing.

Watching her as she toyed with the music note necklace Ben had given her, he asked, "Are you sure about that?"

She wasn't sure. She wasn't sure of anything where Ben was concerned. He hadn't used the word date. He hadn't said much of anything since he called and asked her to go to the premiere. The only thing she was sure about was that she wanted to spend more time with him. Even though she knew it was a silly, girlish fantasy. Ben Prescott could have the pick of any woman in the world. Why on earth would he pick her?

A car pulled up outside and she looked out the window. Noah was getting out of the driver's side in his fancy chauffeur's outfit. Reminding herself to make fun of him for it later, she bent down to put on her shoes, hoping her feet would survive the night.

A knock drifted down the hallway and she straightened. Why would Noah knock on his own door? She was about to call out to him to just come in when her dad waved at her to stay put as he opened the door.

She reached for her tiny purse. It was barely large enough for her phone and lipstick, but it would work for the night. She was making sure she had her photo id when she heard Ben's voice. Footsteps echoed on the hardwood floor as her dad walked him down the short hallway from the front door. Her heart hammered in her chest as she stood still and waited for them to step around the corner.

And then he was there, standing in front of her, every inch a movie star. He was dressed in a perfectly tailored black suit and tie and his hair was straight off a magazine cover. Up to that moment, she had seen him only in casual clothes, she had never been face-to-face with Ben the international celebrity, the man the whole world knew. Even that first night in the limo, he had been rumpled and travel-worn. Without thinking about it, she took a step back. This was a mistake.

Her head started to swim. Any minute he would realize what a mistake he'd made asking her to the premiere. He'd make up an excuse and walk away, taking a little bit of her heart with him. And she'd let him go. She'd take off the silly dress and go back to her life of ponytails and preschool and try to forget him.

Before she could run away, Ben was at her side. He took her hand in his and she was sure he could feel the staccato beat of her pulse. "You look beautiful, Lily."

In the flash of his eyes she saw the Ben she knew. Hidden under the celebrity veneer was the Ben who spent Christmas with her, the Ben who made her laugh, the Ben who washed the dishes in a silly elf sweater.

"Th-th-thank you." She heard the stammer in her voice and wanted to kick herself with her heels. So much for her plan to act calm and confident.

Her dad came close and extended his hand to Ben. "Take good care of my daughter."

Ben nodded once and shook his hand. "Yes, Sir."

Giving her a hug, his words were low and heavy, a comfort to Lily and a fatherly warning to Ben. "Have fun, Sweetheart. Call me if you need anything."

Ben offered his arm to her, walking her down the short flight of steps to the waiting limo. Noah winked at her as he opened the rear door. "Nice dress, Brat."

"Nice hat." She flicked the brim with her finger. Ben helped her in and then slid onto the seat beside her.

Butterflies swarmed through her veins as they drove into the neon night of Hollywood. The drive to the theatre took twice as long as usual thanks to the famous Los Angeles traffic, but Noah had planned for it and they made it to the queue of limos in plenty of time.

"6:12, right?" Noah asked and Ben nodded. It was 6:05. So Noah rolled down the window and waved for the cars behind him to go around.

"Nervous?" Ben asked when she unsnapped and re-snapped her purse for the fiftieth time.

"Very," she said and flipped the clasp again.

Ben put his hand over hers. "It's going to be fine. When we get there, I'm going to get out and do the interviews and photographs. Noah is going to let you out a little further down so you don't have to face the paparazzi. Is that okay?"

She exhaled the tight breath she'd been holding, relieved that she wouldn't have to face a sea of cameras and flashes. "That sounds great. Thank you. How will I find you?"

"My agent Zoe is going to meet you at the check in. She'll walk you in and I'll catch up with you just inside the theatre."

She nodded, her head whirling, as the limo rolled slowly forward. "One minute, Ben," Noah called as a din of voices and frenzied activity enveloped the car.

They had reached the red carpet. Ben re-buttoned his jacket as Noah pulled to a stop beside the crowd of paparazzi and fans. "You might want to sit on that side," he gestured to the row of seats beside the door. "So they don't get a picture of you."

Lily moved, gratefully turning her back on the chaos outside, happy to be hidden and protected from the cameras. Ben straightened his tie and positioned himself next to the door. She felt every beat of her heart as he leaned in and kissed her lightly on the cheek. "I'm really glad you're here, Lily."

Before she could reply, Noah opened the door and a flood of flash-bulbs filled the car. Ben squeezed her hand and stepped out. She had just enough time to glimpse the broad smile he plastered on his face, his hand raised in a wave to the crowd that shouted his name. Then Noah slammed the door, shutting out the noise and the light, but she barely noticed. She lifted her hand to her cheek. Even as her heart soared, her mind told her she was in trouble. The pastor's daughter had fallen for the movie star.

Chapter Twenty-Three

THE FRONT OF THE THEATRE was crowded with media, photographers, and fans hoping for a glimpse of the stars. Metal barricades and security guards turned the street into an obstacle course. Lily sat back, thankful Noah was driving. They inched past the chaos, and the noise faded as they left the red carpet production behind. The glare of the lights disappeared behind them and she wondered what it was like for Ben, facing the cameras, completely at ease and comfortable with the scrutiny and the attention, and absolutely certain that she would trip and fall flat on her face if she had to face that gauntlet of cameras and microphones.

Beyond the gated off areas, a side entrance was reserved for invited guests. No media or photographers were waiting as Noah opened the door and helped her out. It was a chilly night and somewhere in the midst of her nerves and worry, she had forgotten to bring a wrap so she hurried towards the check in sign.

A bored security guard sitting on a wobbly stool and holding a clipboard didn't even look up as she approached. "Name and ID."

"Lily Shaw." She hand him her driver's license. He looked at the name and photo and then up at Lily. Apparently satisfied that she was in fact on the list, he made a check mark on the clipboard and unhooked the red velvet rope. "Enjoy the movie."

Lily thanked him and walked into the theatre. It was crowded with people dressed in Hollywood finery. Sharp suits and designer dresses exploded in a riot of color. Everyone had someone to talk to. Clusters of people gathered in every inch of space, laughing, shaking hands, and hugging and immediately she wished that Kate were with her. Kate would have loved all of this. And with her bold personality and take-charge attitude, she would have known exactly what to do. She would have jumped right in and started making friends, heedless of whether she was welcome or not. Lily just wanted to find Ben and sit down so she could take off her gorgeous, but painful, shoes.

"You must be Lily." The voice belonged to a tall blonde in a chic blue evening dress. "I'm Zoe Waltham, Ben's agent. He asked me to make sure you got in okay." Her eyes raked Lily from the top of her head to the bottom of her shoes, and her lips pressed into a tense smile. "You wore black."

Lily glanced down, self-consciousness flooding her cheeks with heat. "Yes. Is that okay?"

The agent tipped her head to the side as if she didn't understand the question. "Well, Ben's wearing black." She paused as if that should have been enough of an explanation. When it was obvious Lily still didn't understand she continued. "So the two of you together, black and black, that's awfully somber. I mean this is a movie premiere, not a funeral."

Zoe paused and glanced around the room. When she turned back to Lily, her smile was bright. "Well, I'm sure you didn't know. Don't worry, it'll be fine. I mean it's not like he brought you on the red carpet with him."

The agent took her arm and Lily forced a smile onto her face. She was grateful she didn't have to find her way through the crowd alone, but Zoe's words dropped like stones in her stomach. Suddenly it felt like every eye was on her and her stupid, black dress. She had never felt more awkward in her life and that included the time she accidentally walked into the boy's restroom in first grade.

Zoe glided through the clusters of people with a grace Lily envied. She smiled and kissed cheeks as they passed. She would stop for a brief moment to talk to people Lily didn't recognize and then move on, never introducing her or giving people a chance to ask about her. Zoe knew everyone. She knew their children's names and Lily was pretty sure she heard the influential agent mention at least one dog during their long walk from the side entrance to the front of the theatre. She worked the room like a politician and by the time they found a quiet spot by the front entrance, Lily was drained.

"So obviously, this is your first premiere. Wasn't it sweet of Ben to bring you?" Zoe didn't look at her as she spoke, she was waving at someone across the lobby.

"Yes. It's very exciting." Anticipation filled the air. Loud, nervous laughter dotted the conversations. She may not understand the movie business, but she recognized stress and the room was filled with it. It throbbed and vibrated under the beautiful dresses and fancy suits, a monster ready to pounce.

But Zoe seemed unconcerned as they waited for Ben. "You know, this is an important night for him. If it goes well it could mean a lot of very big things for his future. I'd hate for anything to ruin that." An edge of criticism was buried under her friendly words. The nagging voice of doubt that had been following Lily reared its ugly head again. Zoe knew she didn't belong here. She knew Ben had made a mistake.

Lily searched for the right words, anxious to prove that she could hold her own, that she wouldn't embarrass Ben. "Well, it was so nice to spend Christmas with him and now this . . ." Lily looked around at the glittering lights and the posters of Ben covering the walls. The posters showed him in a dirty uniform, gun in hand and grim determination on his face as he looked towards the enemy's encampment. "I hardly know what to think."

Zoe stared at her for a long moment, her eyes going cold. "You two spent Christmas together?"

Lily paused, wondering if she said something wrong. "Just church and then dinner with my family." A hard smile froze on the agent's face as Lily caught sight of Ben walking towards them and she exhaled in relief.

"Thank you, Zoe." He took Lily's hand and tucked it under his arm. "I'll take it from here."

The warmth of his body next to hers banished the chill of Zoe's words. She stepped closer to him, seeking shelter in his strength and confidence, trusting that he wanted her here.

Zoe kissed his cheek, her voice a happy lilt again. "She's an absolute doll, Ben. You two have fun." Then she smiled and chatted her way back into the crowd, melting into the clusters of conversations until the blue of her gown vanished.

Ben looked down at her, his dark eyes diving into hers and his fingers closing around her hand. "Ready to sit down?"

Words failed her, stuck behind the tightness of her throat as she looked at her hand in his, so she nodded and let him guide her to the theatre. Every few feet, someone stopped him to offer congratulations on the new film. Ben was gracious but he moved steadily through the crowd, never letting go of her arm. She couldn't remember a time when she had felt so protected. More than once she had to remind herself that she was Cinderella and all of this magic was going to end at midnight.

Ben ushered her to their seats, then dropped heavily next to her. It was the first time that night she had seen a crack in his movie star persona.

"Are you okay?" She leaned close so she could keep her voice down. The crisp scent of his aftershave tickled her nose and she tried to memorize the smell, like spice and leather, knowing she would want to remember it when the night was over and he was gone.

He nodded. "It's a lot of talking and a lot of people all at once. I'm ready for a nap."

"You can't fall asleep in your own movie," she teased.

"Why not? I already know what happens." Sitting up straighter, he smoothed down his dress shirt, the black onyx of his cufflinks catching in the muted theatre lighting like ebony stars. She brushed a stray piece of fuzz off his jacket and he caught her hand, uncertainty flashing in his eyes. "The movie might be terrible. I'm a little worried you'll hate it . . . and then you'll see me for the charlatan that I really am."

Warmth spread through her fingers. She should pull her hand away, protect her heart, but she couldn't. "I'm sure it will be great. Besides, you've heard me sing. It's only fair I get to see you act."

Ben leaned in to her, his shoulder touching hers. His voice dropped to a whisper and her heart began to race at the closeness, the intimacy of the moment, as if they were sheltered, hidden on an island in the midst of a sea of people. "The difference is, you're actually good at what you do. I'm just a pretty face who can memorize lines."

"That's not true," she whispered back, aware of the people entering the row behind them, but unwilling to let the comment go. "God has a purpose for you here. You might not know what it is now, but someday it will make sense. All of this," she waved her hand and encompassed the theatre, the screen and the people, "this is what you do. It's not who you are. If all of this disappeared, if you never acted again, you'd still be you. You'd still be exactly who God created you to be and that's what matters."

People continued to pour into the theatre and the scent of extra butter on popcorn filled the air. Ben stood when the director Chris Johnston arrived. They hugged and laughed like old friends and Ben introduced her. Nicole Brant and her husband came in a few minutes later. As Ben greeted them and talked with Nicole about their hopes for the film, Chris leaned over. He had skipped the tie and the top button of his dress shirt was undone. He seemed much more at ease than anyone else and his calm presence drew Lily in.

"So Ben said you work at a church. Which one?"

He seemed genuinely interested and that surprised her. "The Hollywood Mission. My parents started it. I teach in the aftercare classes and lead worship."

Chris clapped his hands together. "Perfect. I just moved out here. I stalled as long as possible, but I couldn't avoid it any longer." He shrugged as if moving to Hollywood had been a last resort. "Maybe I can stop by your church one Sunday morning and check it out."

"I'd love that. Ben's helping us with our community outreach next month, he has the address and all the information."

Chris' eyes widened and he pulled back in shock. "Ben is helping at your church? Ben Prescott? At a church? I didn't think I'd hear that sentence today."

Lily leaned close and winked. "With God all things are possible."

Chris glanced over her shoulder, making sure Ben was still absorbed in conversation with his co-star and lowered his voice. "I've been praying for him for a long time."

She dropped her voice to an equal whisper. "Keep at it."

"You got it." He gave her a high-five and laughed loud enough to get Ben's attention.

He turned to them, a puzzled expression etched on his face. "What are you two talking about?"

Without missing a beat, the grinning director replied, "You."

Ben shot him a dirty look and Chris laughed it off. She decided right then that she liked Chris and she hoped he would come by the church. He and Noah would get along famously. And if Ben had another friend at the Hollywood Mission, maybe, just maybe, he'd show up again, too.

As the lights dimmed and the music started, Lily was swept away, not by the movie, but by the man beside her who quietly slipped his hand into hers.

Chapter Twenty-Four

BLOOD AND HONOR **WAS GOING** to be a hit. Lily loved it and judging by the raucous applause in the theatre when the credits started their slow crawl across the screen, everyone else did, too. Ben looked relieved and happy, the tension that had clung to him during the movie was gone and she was thrilled to be by his side as he accepted congratulations and positive comments from critics and celebrities alike. He kept a firm hold on her hand as they slowly made their way out of the theatre, and she made no move to pull away.

The studio had rented a nearby club for the after-party. As the crowd poured out of the theatre and into the chilly night, Zoe stopped them and insisted they sneak out the back exit to avoid the photographers. Ben's assistant led the way through the hallways and into the alley behind the theatre. Lily tried not to laugh at the cloak and dagger feel of it, like they were spies sneaking into enemy territory. Ben took it all in stride, as if he'd done this a million times before.

By the time they emerged from the alley and entered the club through the kitchen, Lily's pinched feet were ready to sit down again. Dance music was thumping from the DJ set up in the corner, the electric techno beat nearly shaking the walls. The lights were low and voices were loud. Ben said something to Derek that she couldn't hear, and the assistant disappeared into the crowd.

Excitement vibrated through the room. Producers who stood to make a lot of money off the movie, cast members who wanted to leverage their small roles into something bigger, and the young hopefuls who snuck into the party all merged together in a blur of suits and sequins that flashed by on the dance floor.

Derek reappeared and led them to a semi-secluded table. As they sat down, he vanished again. She slipped her shoes off under the table and sighed in relief as she wiggled her squished toes. Everything moved so fast she lost track of the people she met and the sea of faces. Beside her, Ben waved at someone across the room.

"Do you need to go mingle or schmooze or something?" she asked, raising her voice over the music.

Ben scooted closer so she wouldn't have to yell. "Schmooze?"

She leaned in, her arm brushing against his. "Isn't that what you're supposed to do at these things? Go shake hands and make deals."

He wrapped his arm around Lily's shoulder, drawing her near. It might have looked casual but it felt electric and she forgot what she had just said. The warmth of his touch was like a magnet pulling her closer to his heart and she would have happily spent the rest of the night right there.

"That's what my agent is for," he replied. He stared into her eyes and for a brief moment the music, the people, and the distractions faded away. There was only the two of them and if it had been up to her she would have kept it that way forever.

But, as if his words had summoned her, Zoe appeared at their table. "Well, don't you two look cozy."

"What did you think of the movie, Zoe?" If he noticed the pointed glance she sent their way he ignored it, keeping his arm right where it was.

"I think it's going to be a smash hit and will add another million to your next contract."

Lily's mouth dropped open and she was sure the deafening dance music had caused her to misunderstand. No one could mention that amount of money so flippantly. Back in college, she and Kate used to imagine what it would be like to suddenly have a million dollars. The things they would do, the changes they would make. Kate said she would travel the world and fight for oppressed people. Lily never thought beyond buying a small house and maybe starting a music school.

Now here she was, sitting in the flashing lights of a dance club listening to people toss around the amount like it was a lunch order. Maybe she should have been cool and reserved about it, but she couldn't stop the shocked question that leapt out. "Did you say a million dollars?"

Ben grimaced and shrugged, the self-conscious gesture shocking her even more than the staggering amount of money. "I'm highly overpaid."

Zoe frowned and glanced over her shoulder as if checking to see if they'd been overheard, then narrowed her eyes at him. "Don't let any of these producers hear you say that. Speaking of which, the reporters are set up by the entrance and they'd like a few photos of you with Chris and Nicole." She looked at Lily apologetically. "You don't mind do you? It'll just be a minute."

"No, it's fine," Lily said, knowing full well that the agent didn't want her anywhere near the cameras.

"Come with me." Sliding out of the booth, Ben reached for her hand.

Zoe blinked like an owl who had been woken up too early and started to stammer a protest, but he was already helping Lily out of the booth. They were halfway across the dance floor when she realized she left her shoes under the table. She could already imagine Kate's reaction when she told her she ended up barefoot at one of Hollywood's biggest parties. She'd probably be able to hear her laugh all the way from Boston.

Ben found an empty tall table near the media set up. Placing his hands on her waist, he lifted her up to the seat. "Be right back. Gotta go earn that ridiculous paycheck." He winked at her and she felt the tingling warmth of a blush creep up her cheeks. Suddenly, the dim lighting felt like a blessing.

Ben walked towards the reporters and the large *Blood and Honor* backdrop that was set up by the front door. Some of the other cast members were clustered nearby along with a bevy of assistants carrying clipboards and make-up bags. Chris greeted Ben with a hug then he caught her eye and waved. He clapped Ben on the back and walked towards her.

"Congratulations," she said when he arrived at the table. "The movie is great."

"Thank you." He rested his arms on the back of the chair opposite her. "Ben did a great job. So how do you like the party?"

Lily looked around the club. It was a frenzied mess of activity but there was an order to the chaos that she could perceive, even if she didn't understand it. The crowd on the dance floor undulated with a carefree abandon. But around the edges, people moved with deliberation and purpose, drifting in and out of conversations, their eyes always scanning the room.

"It's . . . " She paused, searching for a word that was honest, but wouldn't hurt his feelings. This was after all his world. She was the outsider trying to find a place to fit in. "Different," she finally said.

Chris nodded and she thought she saw a touch of sadness in the heaviness of the movement. Maybe he wasn't quite as comfortable in it as she thought. "Different sums it up nicely."

She would have asked him about it, but a flurry of white appeared out of the darkness as Giselle Ferris sashayed up to Chris and gave him a kiss on the cheek. "Chris! I'm so happy to see you."

Lily sat in stunned silence. This gorgeous vision in white was Ben's ex-girlfriend. Her platinum blonde hair was arranged in a twisting up-do with artful ringlets framing her perfectly made-up face. The white dress clung to her tiny frame in an intricate tangle of lace and crystals that caught the lights from the dance floor and reflected the colors back like tiny prisms. She draped her arm across Chris' shoulder and smiled with a confidence that Lily envied.

Shifting in her chair, she couldn't remember ever feeling so self-conscious. Compared to Giselle, she must look like a mousy wallflower. Lily shook her head, her hand fidgeting with her necklace. Who was she kidding? She didn't just look like a mousy wallflower, that's exactly what she was.

Chris slipped out from under Giselle's arm and motioned towards Lily. "Have you met Lily? She's here with Ben."

Giselle's icy blue eyes traveled from the top of Lily's head right down to her bare feet. The image of a spider stalking a fly popped into Lily's mind. She crossed her ankles and tried to hide her feet under the table, but judging by the smirk on the actress' face, it was too late.

Taking a sip of her drink, she turned away from Lily, dismissing her and focusing on Chris again. "The film is fabulous. Now, when will I get to be a part of that Chris Johnston magic?"

Stuttering, he glanced quickly over to the media set up. "Oh, it looks like they're calling me over for some photos. Excuse me, Giselle." He extended his hand to Lily and she took it. "Lily, it was a pleasure to meet you. I hope to see you a lot more often." Then he kissed her hand and gave her a wink before escaping to the cameras.

Giselle watched him walk away then turned back to Lily. "So you must be from that charity Ben has been working with. Derek mentioned he was doing some good deed publicity when we were working out the details for tonight."

Shame washed over her in a wave. Good deed publicity. Was that all she was? A chance for Ben to cash in on some Christmas goodwill and redeem his reputation? Holding her hand, wrapping his arm around her, had it all been an act? Phony staging by Hollywood's favorite leading man? Doubt assailed her as Noah's warning came rushing back. She didn't know these people. And maybe she didn't know Ben.

She was saved from trying to find an answer when Giselle waved cheerfully at a young woman. Giselle was all smiles, giving her a kiss on both cheeks, when she joined them. "Alyssa, this is Lily. She's here with Ben. Isn't that sweet?"

"Some party, huh?" Alyssa asked and Lily nodded.

"Would you two excuse me? I've got to say hi to a few more people." Without waiting for a reply, Giselle disappeared in a cloud of white.

"So you came here with Ben." Raucous laughter broke out across the club. Lily jumped but the woman across the table didn't seem to notice it. "Are you an actress, too?"

"Definitely not." Lily shook her head, distracted by the riot of emotions running through her mind. More than anything she wanted Ben to come back. She wanted to feel his hand in hers again, to look into his eyes and see something honest there, to know she wasn't a pawn in a celebrity game she didn't understand, to know that she meant more to him than a headline.

"Me neither." Alyssa smiled and twisted to look back at the photographers. Ben was standing to the side with Chris waiting for the photographers to finish setting up. "So if you're not an actress, how did you and Ben meet?"

Lily played with the clasp on her purse as she thought back to that first night. Her eyes settled on Ben as he stood in front of the bright lights, the photographers jostling to get the best shot. Who would have thought they'd end up here? "Well," she hesitated. "It's a little unusual."

"Those are the best kinds of stories." Alyssa propped her elbows onto the table and leaned in close.

Lily kept Ben in her sight, remembering how far they'd come, as she told her all about her first encounter with Ben Prescott.

Alyssa laughed out loud. "I can't believe you kicked him out of the limo and he had to walk home. You're probably the first girl to be immune to his legendary charms. You should get some kind of medal. Most of the girls in this room would jump at the chance to go home with Ben Prescott."

Lily ignored the little ball of dread that curled up in her stomach. She glanced over at the bright lights of the media reception. Ben was standing with Chris and Nicole smiling for the photographers. He didn't even flinch at the barrage of flashes and the glare of the lights. He looked right at home.

"So if you kicked him out of the car, how did you guys end up here?" The question dragged Lily's eyes away from Ben.

"We've been working on an outreach at my dad's church and we spent Christmas together. He invited me to come a few days after that."

"That sounds very romantic."

"Oh no, it's not like that. It's—" She struggled to find the words. How could she describe something that barely made sense?

"It's what?" Alyssa prompted and rested her chin in her hands.

From the corner of her eye she saw Ben standing alone in front of the backdrop. He looked every inch the movie star. But somewhere inside that celebrity mask, she could still see the man she had spent Christmas with, the man who had made her laugh. Reflexively, she touched the music note necklace around her neck. She may not know what was going on between her and Ben, but she was ready to find out.

She stood up and took a step towards him, towards the lights and the photographers and the world she didn't understand. Then she stopped. Giselle glided up to Ben in her nearly sheer white gown and the photographers went crazy. She leaned against him, her arm draped across his chest, as he looked down at her and smiled. She whispered something in his ear and he laughed, his arm wrapped around her waist. Giselle put her hand on his cheek and turned his face towards her. Flashes exploded everywhere and the reporters started shouting questions.

Alyssa turned around to see what caused the commotion. "Oh wow. Looks like everyone's favorite couple is getting back together."

Lily was frozen in place, mesmerized by the sight of Ben and Giselle. She didn't know which way to go. Alyssa stood beside her and put her hand on her shoulder. "I'm sorry. These actors have such short attention spans."

Ignoring the sympathy, she started walking towards Ben again. The voice in her head drowned out the music. *Did you really think you had a chance with him?*

The crush of photographers was an impenetrable wall. She worked her way along the edge of the reporters but was stopped by a stern security guard. She turned to try the other direction when Zoe appeared at her side.

"Let's take a walk." Zoe closed her fingers around her wrist and guided her away from the lights and into the shadows. "I'm glad you got to come to the premiere and have a little fun tonight, but I'm sure you can see that Ben has a lot of work to do here. This is a big night for him and he can't spend it all helping your little church, you know that right?"

Lily tried to clear her head, but she couldn't focus over the sound of her own stupidity. She had been wrong to come here. Wrong to think this was anything other than Ben taking pity on her.

Zoe sighed wistfully as the cameras captured Ben and Giselle together. "Just look at how great they are together. The perfect Hollywood couple. It's like . . . magic."

Involuntarily, her eyes slid back to Ben and Giselle, smiling and posing for the cameras. Giselle who knew better than to wear a black dress and who could navigate the movie industry without feeling like a panic attack might paralyze her. Giselle was the one he wanted by his side for the photographers. She hadn't been forced to sneak through back alleys and kitchens, hidden away because she didn't fit the image.

Tears threatened to fall, but she refused to let them. She needed to get away from the noise and the lights and everything she didn't understand. The music was too loud, the crowd too thick. She turned away from the lights and swayed.

"Are you okay?" Zoe opened the side door of the club and ushered Lily outside. "Maybe some fresh air will help."

She stepped outside, and breathed deeply of the night air, the rough concrete hard against her bare feet. Traffic raced down the street and Lily shivered, suddenly colder than she had ever been.

"Go home and get some rest. I'm sure you'll feel better in the morning." Zoe gave her a brief hug and a weak smile, then she disappeared back into the party, the door shutting firmly behind her.

Lily was left outside, staring at the closed door. Somewhere a clock was chiming midnight. The ball was over and no prince would come looking for her.

Chapter Twenty-Five

BEN CLENCHED HIS TEETH AND forced the smile to remain in place. Giselle's hand drifted up to his cheek, the cloying scent of her perfume rising with it. He captured her hand and brought it back down, ever mindful of the cameras and the reporters circling like sharks waiting for blood on the red carpet.

"What are you doing here?" he demanded, hissing the words through his locked jaw.

"I wanted to surprise you." Giselle cooed, leaning against him as the cameras clicked away. "The film is wonderful, by the way. It's going to be a huge hit."

"Thank you." He slipped his arm behind her waist to guide her away from the photographers. This was a conversation best had in private, even if Giselle did her best to linger on in the spotlight. "So where's Liam?"

She blew a flirtatious kiss to the cameras. "Oh, him. I told you, I made a terrible mistake. I was lonely and wrong. Can you ever forgive me?" She delivered the lines as skillfully as any actress on the screen, putting her hands on his chest, her face tilted up at him, the picture of sincerity. The cameras were clicking at lightning speed, and he could only imagine the picture they made. It was a pose meant for the front page.

He peeled her hands off his chest and steered her further away. Reporters called out questions as they left. "Are you back together?"

Ben waved and kept walking. Giselle tossed a sassy wink back at the reporter who shouted the question before linking her arm with Ben's.

When they stepped away from the harsh, white lights, Ben whirled on her. "What are you trying to pull?"

Giselle blinked in practiced innocence at him. "I told you. I made a mistake with Liam. I was wrong. I was wrong to do the interview and I'm sorry. I want to make it up to you."

He slapped his hand over his eyes and groaned in exasperation. "Make it up to me? Are you crazy? Giselle, you and me . . . it's over."

Tears glittered in her eyes and she stepped away. "How can you be so mean? I came here to apologize and you're treating me like garbage."

He raked his hands through his hair, frustration oozing from every tense muscle. "I'm not trying to make you feel bad. But I don't want this. I don't want to go back to the way things were. I want something different."

Giselle sniffed back the tears. "I can be different, Ben. We can be different. Just give me a chance."

There was only one person he wanted to be with, and it wasn't Giselle. He softened his voice. "I'm sorry if you're hurt, but we can't go back. Not this time. I need to go." He tried to turn away, but Zoe was right beside him, trapping him between the cameras and Giselle.

Looking past Zoe, he searched for Lily. The table he left her at was empty. Worry enveloped him as he scanned the club. "Where's Lily?"

"Oh, she wasn't feeling well," Zoe said. "She asked me to tell you that she went home with her brother and she'll call you later."

Disappointment settled on him. Lily was gone. "I guess I'll go see her tomorrow."

"Oh no," Zoe said in her clipped business voice. "You're on a plane first thing in the morning. You're going to New York for New Year's Eve, remember?"

Confusion crowded out the disappointment. He had no idea what Zoe was talking about. He hadn't agreed to a New Year's Eve event. "What?"

"You signed off on it two months ago. You fly out early tomorrow morning. You're hitting the daytime talk shows, plugging the movie, telling them how great it is and how much you love it. And since it's New Year's Eve . . ." Zoe paused, building up the suspense. "That night you'll be helping drop the ball in Times Square." Giselle squealed in excitement and Zoe preened. "Tell me I'm not the best agent ever."

Shaking his head, his brows drew together as he struggled to put the pieces together. There's no way he would have forgotten something like that.

With an exasperated sigh, Zoe pulled up her email on her cell phone. She scrolled down until she found the right email and showed it to him. "See? I sent this to you ages ago. Derek has all the details."

Ben looked at the email and wondered how he missed it. It wasn't like him to forget a trip, especially such a big one. But he had been finishing some reshoots so maybe the time change and the busy schedule had gotten the best of him. Times Square on New Year's Eve when his movie just hit the theatres was a major coup. He didn't want to guess how many favors Zoe had called in to make that happen. "I guess I need to pack."

"I'm sure Derek has already taken care of it and has your itinerary ready to go. At least *he* reads my emails." Zoe wagged a finger at him.

"You can ride home with me, Ben." Giselle looked up at him and gave him a seductive smile.

He stepped away, giving Zoe the pleading look he usually reserved for overzealous fans or pushy reporters.

Taking each of them by an arm, she skillfully placed herself between them. "Giselle, that is a lovely offer, but Ben has a lot to do tonight. I'll make sure he gets home safely."

They strolled into the chilly night air like a mother dragging her squabbling children away from a birthday party. Giselle's car was parked nearby so they went that way first.

"Now say goodnight like two actors who don't mind working together," Zoe chided and gave him a gentle shove towards Giselle. He pasted a smile on his face and opened the door for her. She took his hand and gave him an adoring look as she melted into the backseat. Then he closed the door without saying a word.

As the car drove off, he loosened his tie, ready for the night to be over. He wanted to drive to Lily's house, to make sure she was okay, but Zoe was already getting into her car and Ben didn't want to have this conversation with an audience.

Pulling out his cell phone he tapped on Lily's last text, but Zoe grabbed the phone away from him. "No one likes a needy date. I told you, she was overwhelmed by the whole thing and wasn't feeling well. You said yourself she wouldn't like all the cameras and attention."

Toying with the phone, she chatted about the itinerary for the following two days as the car left the premiere, the party, and Lily behind. He would be plugging the movie at every stop. The studio would be thrilled and Ben . . . Ben would be spending his time thinking about a blue-eyed girl with the voice of an angel.

Chapter Twenty-Six

LILY WOKE TO THE RINGING of her cell phone. Rubbing her eyes in the pre-dawn darkness, wondering who would call her so early, she fumbled for her phone and squinted at the called ID.

"Time difference, Kate. It's like five a.m. here."

"What happened last night?" Kate's words were tense and brisk.

"What?" She yawned and closed her eyes again. It was too early to remember how last night ended. Seeing Ben and Giselle, being escorted out of the club, then seeing Noah's pity filled eyes when he drove her home. Humiliation and stupidity teamed up to make her feel terrible. She'd been a fool to fall for Ben Prescott and look what happened.

"Last night, Lily." Kate's sharp voice ignited a fire of anxiety in her chest. "What happened? You're all over the celebrity news sites."

"What? That's impossible." She leapt out of bed and turned on her computer. As the screen glowed to life, she wrapped a blanket around her shoulders and sat at her desk.

"'Fraid so, Lils. Pick any site or blog you want. You're front page news."

Lily drummed her fingers against the wood, waiting for her computer to boot up. After a quick search for celebrity gossip, she clicked on the first search result and gasped.

Kate was right. There was a photo of her and Ben entering the back of the club for the after-party. So much for avoiding the paparazzi. In the photo, she was holding his arm and smiling up at him. The headline above the photo screamed "Mystery Woman Unmasked. Was Ben Cheating Too?"

"Did you talk to a reporter?" Kate asked.

"No. Of course not." She scanned the article, her stomach plummeting with every word.

Superstar Ben Prescott has been playing the victim in the wake of revelations that his then-girlfriend Giselle Ferris had been cheating on him with her hunky co-star Liam Donovan. But now it appears that Ben might have a few secrets of his own.

At last night's premiere of Ben's new movie, celebrity reporter Alyssa Harrison spoke with Hollywood resident Lily Shaw, the young woman Ben met up with on the night he arrived at LAX after Giselle's bombshell interview. Lily confirmed the alcohol fueled limo meeting and spilled that the two also spent Christmas together. One can only assume that Ben might not be as innocent as he claims.

Although judging by the cuddles and closeness Ben and Giselle shared last night, maybe the Hollywood hotties are ready to let bygones be bygones. Ben and Giselle were photographed looking very cozy as they left the party together. Limo Hookup Lily apparently left the party all alone.

The photos following the gossip blurb were all of Ben and Giselle together. The first was of them during the photo op, with Giselle's hand touching Ben's cheek. There was another of the two of them outside the club and getting into a car.

"Oh no," Lily moaned. She wanted the earth to open up and swallow her whole. She wanted to disappear into the floor and never show her face again. Limo Hookup Lily.

"I'm going to kill him." Kate sounded dead serious. "I'm a lawyer. I can kill him and get away with it."

Lily pulled her legs against her chest, squeezing into a tight ball under the blanket. She wanted to crawl back under the covers and pretend this was all a nightmare. Limo Hookup Lily. What was her father going to say? Embarrassment engulfed over her, and even locked in her room she felt the eyes of the world staring at her, exposing her for all to see. There was no place she could hide; her mistakes were on full display.

"It's not his fault, Kate. It's mine. I didn't know she was a reporter. I thought she was just another guest." Alyssa had been so friendly, so interested in hearing about her and Ben. Looking back, she could see the deception, but it was too late. The damage had been done and there was nothing she could do about it now.

"This is bad, Lily." The sympathy in Kate's vice was worse than the anger.

"What am I going to do? I have to go to church today. How am I going to face them?" She felt her whole world shift and flip. She was supposed to stand up in front of the church and lead worship. How could she sing about God's grace and His love when they all thought she had been a one-night stand for a Hollywood celebrity? Faces of parents at the church flashed across her mind. She was responsible for watching their children. Who would want a girl known as Limo Hookup Lily teaching their children?

"You're going to hold your head up high and ignore it. Do not talk to anyone you don't know and don't answer your phone." Kate had switched into lawyer mode. Lily was a client in need of rescue, and she hated it. "This will blow over eventually and then you can forget it. Okay?"

Lily sat in silence. She would never forget this.

"As for me," Kate continued. "I'm going to sue that reporter and kill that movie star."

Lily tried to laugh, but it didn't work. As Kate said goodbye and hung up, she clicked on another search result and found another version of the same story. Then another and another. They all sounded the same. She was a home wrecker. She was the other woman who tried to destroy Hollywood's favorite couple. Ben had cheated on Giselle but now they were back together and Lily was the scheming mistress who ended up discarded and dumped while the hero and the heroine lived happily ever after.

She told herself she didn't care if Ben and Giselle got back together. She had no claim on Ben. As far as she knew last night hadn't even been a real date, it obviously hadn't meant anything to him. She was a silly girl who read too much into it. And then she talked to a reporter and ruined everything.

Taking her phone she opened her text messages. There was nothing from Ben. She shouldn't have expected anything, but her heart had been wishing, hoping to see a message from him.

Zoe had been right, she had no place there. She didn't understand the rules of the game. She was foolish and naïve and now the whole world knew it. Ben knew it, too. Her throat constricted as she imagined what he would think when he saw the stories. How badly had she messed up? Would her words hurt the movie? His career? How could she have been so stupid?

Her fingers flew across the screen as she typed an apology. *I didn't know she was a reporter. I'm so sorry.*

She hit send before she changed her mind, then turned her phone off. Bringing the blanket with her, she curled into a ball on the bed with her Bible. Tears blurred the words, but she found comfort just knowing they were there. There was only one prayer she could offer in that moment, only one cry of her heart and she knew it would be enough.

"Jesus," she whispered, "please help me."

As much as she wished she could hide away in her room and never face the day, when sunlight filtered through the curtains she forced herself to get dressed. Thoughts about pretending to be sick so she could stay home tempted her, but that wouldn't be right. Bad news doesn't get better with age, as her mother used to say. There was nothing to do but face the consequences. Quietly, she slipped out of her room, dreading the look on her father's face when she told him what happened. What would he think of her?

She tiptoed towards to the kitchen. The smell of coffee wafted down the hallway and she knew he was awake. Her feet moved forward and she whispered the prayer that had been her companion ever since Kate's call. "Jesus, please help me."

Uncertainty pulled at her like a lead weight. Her dad was leaning against the kitchen counter, his head bowed over his phone, his brows knit together as he read something on the screen. She stood in the doorway in silence. He knew.

The urge to run away and hide, the instinct to cower in her shame was almost overpowering. She didn't want to see the look on his face, to see the pride she usually saw there replaced with the anger and condemnation she deserved.

Looking up, her dad met her eyes. Without saying a word, he dropped his phone on the counter and swept her into his arms. Pressing his head against hers, he held her against his chest, his arms wrapped tightly around her, holding her like he'd never let her go.

The tears that she'd kept locked away spilled over. She buried her face in her father's shirt and wept, crying in his arms until there were no more tears to shed.

"I'm so sorry, Dad." The words were muffled, whispered into the soft flannel fabric.

Holding Lily's face in his hands, he spoke with conviction and strength. "You are my daughter, and I love you. Nothing will ever change that."

A tide of emotion rose in her throat and she swallowed hard. "I didn't know she was a reporter. I can't believe I was so stupid. I'm so sorry."

Her dad hugged her again. "This is not your fault. What the enemy intends for evil, God will use for good. You will get through this and your brother and I will stand by you no matter what." He used his thumbs to dry her tears. "Now get some water, you have to sing today."

Lily stared at him, dumbfounded by his simple declaration. She had been prepared to see disappointment in his eyes. She had been prepared for him to ask her to stay off the platform, maybe even to stop teaching. She deserved it. But he didn't want her to stay home and he hide. After everything she had done, he still wanted her to lead worship. "But what will people think? The church—"

"The church will be fine. God is at work, even in this. Trust in Him and let Him fight your battles."

Noah had a much harder time letting the gossip go. He agreed with Kate's plan to sue one person and murder another. They made quite a trio walking to the church that morning. Lily's eyes were dry, but red and puffy, and Noah's face was set in a hard line, his fists clenched at his sides. Only their dad walked with the familiar peace that followed him wherever he went. Lily stayed close to her father, drawing strength from his calm and unshakable faith that God was at work.

They weren't expecting the crowd of photographers that were waiting at the locked gate to the church. Ignoring their questions and the cameras that flashed in his face, her dad unlocked the gate and pushed it open.

"Church starts at ten a.m., folks," he said. "You're welcome to join us for service. But leave your cameras at the door."

Chapter Twenty-Seven

BEN HADN'T SLEPT. BY THE time they got back to his house, Derek was waiting to go over the itinerary for the trip and Zoe wanted to give him talking points to hit during the interviews. When the car service arrived at four a.m. to take him to LAX, he thought about arranging a detour to stop by Lily's house. He hated that he had to leave without talking to her. Last night had not gone the way he'd planned, and he wanted to talk to her, to make sure she was all right, to tell her how much it meant to him that she was there.

But as he checked his phone and saw there were no messages from her, he realized she was probably sound asleep, like any normal person would be at four a.m. Better to let her sleep. He hoped Zoe was right about giving her time. He tried to remember his first premiere and how overwhelming it had been, the stress of it all. Deciding to call her from New York instead, he slipped his phone into his bag and settled into the car for the ride to the airport.

Traffic was light and he was ensconced in his first-class seat by six a.m. He had barely buckled his seat belt when he fell asleep. He didn't even notice the delay as they sat on the ground waiting for clearance to take off.

It was the bump of the wheels hitting the tarmac in New York that startled him awake. He yawned and stretched. It was going to be a busy day. Maybe the busyness would help keep his mind off Lily. Looking out the window at the snowy New York day, he thought that she would have enjoyed being here. Maybe if he'd remembered the trip sooner he could have brought her. New Year's Eve in New York City was quite an adventure. He imagined what Lily would look like bundled up in a heavy coat and scarf with snow clinging to her long lashes. They could go to the top of the Empire State Building and see the whole city spread out before them, maybe take a horse drawn carriage ride through Central Park. Ben was swept up in the idea. Even if it wasn't New Year's Eve, he could bring her back here someday when the snow was on the ground and the grey winter sky stretched out to the sea.

The flight attendant's voice cut through the quiet of the plane. "Ladies and gentleman we'd like to welcome you to New York. We apologize for the delay. If you need any help making your connecting flight or rescheduling a missed flight, please let our customer service representatives know. They will be glad to assist you in any way. The current time in New York is 3:38 p.m."

Ben didn't hear the rest of her comments. 3:38. He was going to be late to the first taping.

He yanked his cell phone out of the bag. There were no messages or missed calls littering the screen so hopefully the studio wasn't panicking about him yet. He stuffed his phone into his back pocket and raced through the airport. Calling Lily would have to wait.

A car was waiting outside the terminal to drive him to the first studio. Inside the dark vehicle, he opened his garment bag and changed into his first television outfit. The minutes ticked away as he struggled to change in the cramped space. He hated being late.

The car pulled up to the studio an hour later than planned. He was rushed through hair and makeup. There wasn't time to prep him on the questions so Ben would be doing the interview cold. Less than thirty minutes after he arrived, he was sitting on a hard fabric couch under the glare of studio lights.

Martina Mendoza, host of *Mornings with Martina*, was getting her makeup touched up by fluttering assistants who buzzed around like bees. One of the makeup girls decided Ben had too much glow and needed a bit more powder. He tried to relax as the dust flew around his face, and the studio audience fidgeted in their seats, anxious for the next segment to start.

The lights, the noise, and the stress of the morning had given him a headache that throbbed relentlessly behind his eyes. He sipped tepid water from a plastic bottle and hid it back behind the couch, wishing he could disappear just as easily.

The director called everyone back and the assistants vanished in a cloud of foundation and lip gloss. Martina adjusted her skirt and sat up straighter in the chair opposite from him. She gave him a quick smile, then squinted her eyes and checked the teleprompter that was hidden just off camera.

Theme music swelled and a stagehand ran in front of the audience encouraging them to clap. When it wasn't loud enough he raised his hands to get them to make more noise. The director cued the camera to his left and it moved in slowly, zooming in on Martina's face. She smiled broadly and the show began.

After a clip of *Blood and Honor* and a few standard questions about filming and preparing for the role of the soldier who gets lost behind enemy lines and has to fight his way home, Martina put her hand on her chin and grew serious.

"Okay, Ben, let's get to the real story here." A knowing smirk crossed her face and that made him nervous. He had no idea what was coming next. He snuck a glance at the teleprompter, but it was angled away from him. "Everyone here is dying to know, are you and Giselle back together?" The audience erupted into applause. Keeping his eyes fixed on the host, he couldn't tell if it was genuine applause, or if it had been cued by the guy in charge of getting the audience to sound enthusiastic about whatever was happening on stage.

He waited for the applause to die down before replying. "You know, Martina, sometimes things don't work out. The truth is Giselle and I are just friends."

The audience moaned in disappointment and Martina picked up on it. "You looked awfully cozy at last night's premiere to be just friends."

"Now, Martina," he said with as much lightness in his voice as he could muster. "You know better than to believe everything on the gossip blogs."

"Fair enough." Martina uncrossed her legs and leaned in like she was about to share a secret. "But I wonder if the new woman in your life has anything to do with that." He stared into her narrowed eyes and caught the glint sparkling there. She had a scoop. What did she know? "So Ben, what about this other girl you've been spotted with? This Lily Shaw. Is she the reason you and Giselle aren't together?"

A hush fell over the audience. The moment stretched on as he tried to formulate an answer. He was shocked, unprepared to answer questions about Lily. How had Martina found out about her? The silence turned awkward and the astute host swiveled to face the screen behind her. "Audience, what do you think?"

With a dramatic flick of her wrist, a collage of photographs flashed on the large screen behind the couches. There was the photo from the night they met in the limo, another of them entering the club last night, and one of Lily standing outside alone. Across the top the words "Ben's Latest Fling" screamed in bright gold letters.

Anger raced through him as the audience rumbled behind him. It was the sound of gossip and speculation taking off like wildfire across dry land. He prayed to a God he didn't believe in that Lily hadn't seen this, but in his heart he knew it was too late.

"Well, Ben?" Martina looked like a cat who had stumbled across a wounded bird, stalking him from her armchair perch under the hot, electric lights. "Who is she?"

He took a deep breath while he scrambled to find the best answer. How could he protect Lily? What could he say that wouldn't force her into a media circus? The story must be everywhere.

Drawing on every ounce of the charismatic movie star image he had honed over the years, he draped his arm on the back of the sofa, looking completely relaxed and at ease. "Lily is a wonderful woman. She works with disadvantaged children at a church in Hollywood. I've been privileged to help her over the past few weeks with a large event they are putting together for the community."

Martina glanced at the teleprompter, looking for guidance. This obviously wasn't what she had expected so he pressed his advantage. "The real story here is that there are people like Miss Shaw who are willing to give so much of their time to help people who really need it. You know, just a week ago I was with Miss Shaw and her family when they prepared and served meals for hundreds of homeless families. It was right before Christmas and isn't that what the season is all about? Giving to others." He turned to the studio audience, inviting their opinions and when they murmured their approval, Ben saw his chance. He turned back to the flabbergasted host. "Isn't that what's truly important right now, Martina? People coming together to help each other?"

The audience burst into applause and he gave them a quick wave. He casually crossed his leg over his knee and looked at Martina, daring her to disagree.

The television host who had been expecting an exclusive on a new love triangle looked disappointed and Ben didn't feel bad about it at all. After fumbling through a quick story about her own charity work, she finished with a question about Ben's upcoming projects and the interview was over.

Red, hot anger coursed through his veins as Martina thanked him and the music started. His jaw clenched so tightly he thought his teeth might break, he shook her hand and walked off the set with a parting wave to the audience.

Once he was safely back in the green room, he dug his phone out of his bag. The screen was still blank. No messages, no missed calls. That couldn't be right. He checked the settings as he slammed the door shut, rattling the signs hanging on the walls that asked for quiet during taping. Airplane mode. His phone was in airplane mode. When had he done that?

The thick carpet muffled his footsteps as he paced the length of the room while his phone loaded everything he had missed.

It was worse than he imagined.

Limo Hookup Lily.

He collapsed into the nearest chair. What had he done to her? There was only one message from Lily. It glowed on the screen and he could hear her voice as he read the words. *I didn't know she was a reporter. I'm so sorry.*

He punched her number into the phone and waited, his heart dropping with every ring. An automated message answered saying that her voicemail was full. He hung up and sent her a text instead.

I had to fly to New York this morning. I just saw the news. None of this is your fault. Please call me.

He sat in the abandoned green room reading all the horrible things people were saying about Lily. No one seemed to remember or care that Giselle had been cheating on him, that she had left him for an up and coming hotshot looking for his big break. Lily was painted as a Hollywood schemer trying to steal Ben away from a woman he didn't even want to be with. Guilt gnawed at him. This whole mess was his fault. Lily might not know how to play the game, but he did.

So he fought back in the only way Hollywood would understand. He made a few calls of his own.

"Hi, Kiki, it's Ben Prescott."

"Well, well, aren't you the popular kid in class this morning."

Ben met Kiki back when he was a stuntman and she was struggling to find work as an actress. Eventually they went their separate ways and they each found success, Ben as a leading man and Kiki as a popular gossip blogger. They had kept in touch off and on through the years and if anyone would be willing to help him, it was Kiki. At least that was what he hoped. "And I'd rather not be. I need your help."

Calculation echoed in the silence. Kiki may not have been much of an actress but she was savvy businesswoman. "Give me an exclusive behind the scenes interview on your next movie with spoilers."

He exhaled in relief. Kiki was on board. Now it was just a matter of negotiating the favor. "On set interview, no spoilers."

"Deal. What's your plan?"

Ben gave her the same answer he gave Martina. He pushed the charity work the church did and Lily's good heart.

"So she's Hollywood's very own Mother Teresa." Exasperation colored the blogger's words. "If you really want to deflect this story, you've got to give me something more."

"There isn't anything more. She's sweet and kind and she doesn't deserve this." Ben dropped his head into his hand. Helplessness threatened to swallow him whole.

"Wow." The cynical voice on the other end of the phone, the author of snarky words that had launched viral scandals, lowered to a reverent whisper. "You've really fallen for this girl."

The words hit him like a cold ocean wave. He'd fallen for her. Lily with her gentle spirit and her innocent laugh. The girl who thought he was worth saving had burrowed her way into his heart. He couldn't admit it to anyone, not even to Kiki, but the truth of it hovered in the air, unspoken and real.

She sighed. "Fine. I'll do what I can. Give me an hour and I'll have an article up on the blog. I'll pass it on to a few other writers and see if we can get your version some traction. But forget that interview, I want an invite to the wedding."

His nervous laugh echoed in the empty room. Lily wouldn't want anything to do with him after this and he didn't blame her. "You're assuming she'll ever speak to me again."

"You're Ben Prescott. I'm sure you'll figure it out."

Trusting that Kiki was on his side, he hung up and checked the time. He had only a few minutes before he had to leave for the next interview. This time he knew what was coming and he'd be prepared.

His phone lay quiet in his hand. Lily hadn't responded. His texts were unread and her voicemail was still full. There was nothing more he could do from here. Ben stared at his reflection in the mirror across the room and made up his mind. He had one more call to make.

Chapter Twenty-Eight

"BEN PRESCOTT, DON'T YOU DARE."

He held the phone away from his ear. Zoe was in a rage. He couldn't remember ever hearing her so angry. But at that moment he didn't care. He had made up his mind and none of her cursing or threats could stop him.

"Do you have any idea how many favors I had to call in to get you on the ball drop? Do you know what this would mean for you? For your career? Do you know how much publicity you're throwing away? And for what?" she screeched.

Standing in the fourth green room of the day and cradling the phone with his shoulder, he stumbled as he changed clothes. "Look, Zoe, I'm sorry. But I'm doing this."

He had no idea how much Lily had heard or what she was going through. It was his fault she had been exposed to the nasty side of his business and he had to make it right. So between the second and third interviews of the day, he'd booked a flight back to LA. It hadn't been easy to find an empty seat on New Year's Eve, but he'd be back on the West Coast by eleven p.m.

Zoe was not taking his plans well.

"If you bail on this, I will never forgive you. Do you hear me, Ben? You will never get a chance like this again."

He stared at the plain beige walls. Lily told him at the premiere that if he never acted again, he'd still be the same man. But she was wrong. If he wasn't famous, if he didn't have a star by his name, he'd be just some lost kid from Indiana trying to escape his demons. Bitterness clung to his heart as he considered what it might cost him. No one had ever sacrificed anything for him. His own parents hadn't even been willing to pass up a beer for his sake.

As he wrestled with resentment, Zoe fed his doubts. "Ben, no one will even remember her name in a week. You have to look out for yourself. Don't throw away everything you've worked for because some girl you just met blabbed to a reporter and got her feelings hurt. Are you sure she didn't do it on purpose?"

The thought was like a punch in his gut. Trust was a rare commodity in this business. Relationships changed, loyalties shifted. It was an industry built on survival. The thought that Lily could be part of it, that her family could have an agenda was too much. It sucked the energy out of him until he didn't know which way to turn.

"Think about it," Zoe said. "This is her big chance. Maybe this was her plan all along. You said yourself the church was small and struggling. What better way to build a church in Hollywood than to get a celebrity involved?"

But they hadn't involved him. Not really. They hadn't used his name at all. Lily had been devoured by the press. Mocked, humiliated, and blamed for his mistakes. The fiery anger that had been building since his interview with Martina turned to ice hardened resolve. He was done letting other people run his life. His words were sharp and unyielding. "I am going back to Los Angeles, Zoe. You can get on board with it or I can find a new agent."

Tense silence stretched between them, but he didn't care. The only thing that mattered was getting back to Lily.

"Well," she spat the word into the phone. "It sounds like you've made up your mind. Maybe you don't need me after all."

"Zoe—" But she had already hung up. Staring at the blank screen, he blew out a long breath. "Happy New Year to you, too." He grabbed his bag and headed outside to find a cab back to the airport.

*****

Lily was wearing her comfy pajamas, sipping hot chocolate, and watching the New Year's Eve festivities with Noah and her dad. She couldn't muster any excitement about the New Year, but she had never been so glad to see a day end. Exhaustion pulled at her and she wanted to go to bed early. Maybe when she woke up this whole mess would be over and forgotten.

The host in Times Square was bundled up against the snowy night. "It's a shame Ben Prescott couldn't be here tonight." Lily sat up straighter. As much as she hated it, he was a flame and she was the moth about to get burned.

"Yes," the female co-host agreed. "Unfortunately Ben had to get back to LA. He's in the midst of promoting his new movie and we can't wait to see it. But we're excited to have another Hollywood superstar join us tonight. Giselle Ferris is here with us."

Noah wrapped his arm around her and squeezed. "We're going to need more ice cream," he said and disappeared into the kitchen.

Giselle looked stunning in a long coat with a fur collar turned up against the wind. "Thank you for having me. I'm sad I'll miss my

New Year's kiss from Ben, but maybe I can find someone else to ring in the New Year with." Cheers went up from the crowd and Giselle blew kisses to the spectators in the streets below.

Lily watched the shifting scene with a hollow ache in her chest. Of course Giselle was there. She wondered if they had flown out together. While she had been crying her way through the morning, had Ben and Giselle been sipping champagne and jetting across the country? Had they slipped into the car outside the club and gone straight to the airport?

She didn't want to think about it. Noah and Kate had tried to warn her but she didn't listen. She thought . . . she thought what? That she could change him? That she could help him? And all that got her was a front-page photo and a nasty nickname.

Closing her eyes, she tried to shut out the memory of the day. Standing in front of the church had been one of the hardest moments of her life. She hadn't imagined the whispers or the hard stares that greeted her when she stood up to sing that morning. Families that had hugged her and wished her a Merry Christmas only a few days ago avoided her. Nate had been there to give her a big hug and his mom hadn't seemed disturbed by the news at all. But others looked at her differently. She could feel the questions burning to be asked, but remaining unsaid. Not that she blamed them, it wasn't every day your worship leader was accused of being a rebound girl for a movie star.

With God's grace and her family's support she made it through the service. They stayed in the church until the photographers left. The reporters had given up and left after only an hour. Apparently Lily wasn't as interesting as they had hoped. She walked home surrounded by the two people who loved her most. And more than anything Lily wished for her mom. She needed a hug. She needed advice. She needed to be reminded that she wasn't alone. Her mom had always had a way of putting things in perspective. Even when she was fighting cancer, suffering the side effects of chemotherapy and facing the dire predictions of doctors who had given up hope, her mom was the one reminding her that God was still in control. Nothing surprised Him. Nothing could shake Him. God was still God, even in the face of cancer, even in the face of death. And God was still God, even when she felt like her world was falling apart.

So she sipped her cocoa, watching the last minutes of the year pass away, trusting that God would be there for whatever the New Year brought.

The loud knock on the door startled them all. Her dad motioned for her to stay put. If it was another reporter looking for a story, he would deal with them the way he had dealt with all of the others. By telling them about Jesus and inviting them to church. Her dad's impromptu sermons usually got them off the porch pretty fast.

Lily heard a rumble of male voices. Guilt rose up, sharp and brutal. She hated what her family had been through today, all because she had made a foolish mistake. In truth it had been two foolish mistakes. One was talking to the reporter. But the bigger mistake was falling for Ben Prescott. She should have listened to the warnings instead of her heart. Resting her head against a throw pillow, she waited for the reporter to go away.

"Lily." Her dad came back to the living room. She opened her eyes, concerned by the weight in his voice. "Ben's here."

"You don't have to talk to him." Noah's defenses were up. Earlier that day he confessed that he blackmailed Ben into helping with the outreach and now he blamed himself for everything. If he had just let Ben walk away he would have walked right out of their lives and none of this would have happened. Lily gave her big brother a weak smile. Apparently there was plenty of blame to go around.

She walked to the front door, patting her dad's arm as she passed. It was time to face the music. Ben had been on the entertainment shows that evening, cleaning up her mess. It didn't even bother her that he made it sound like she was nothing more than charity work, because really, had she ever been anything more than that to him?

The midnight air was cold and cruel as she stepped outside. Sitting on the top step of the porch, his head in his hands, exhaustion radiated off Ben's body. With the rumpled clothes and the bag at his feet, he looked the same as he did the first night they met, travel weary and worn out. And after everything that had happened, the rebellious butterflies in her stomach still leapt to life at the sight of him.

The wood porch creaked under her weight and in one swift movement he rose and crossed the planks that separated them. Warmth seeped through the thick fabric of her pajamas as he put his hands on her shoulders.

Fatigue lined his face as he looked at her and his voice was rough. "Lily, I am so sorry. I came back as soon as I could."

She blinked back tears. There was no reason to cry. Not now. The worst was over. "It's not your fault," she said. "It's mine. I didn't know Alyssa was a reporter. When Giselle brought her over I thought she was just another guest."

Echoes of a New Year's Eve party somewhere on the street danced by and he frowned. "Giselle introduced you to her?"

"I was talking to Chris while I waited for you. Giselle joined us and after Chris left she introduced me to her friend." She stumbled on the word. That reporter was hardly a friend. "You were busy with the photographers . . . and then Giselle." She hated the sadness she heard in her voice. She had no claim on Ben. She had no right to feel hurt or jealous. He was free to be with whomever he wanted.

"That wasn't my idea. She just showed up. But it was in front of all the photographers and I couldn't get away without causing a scene." He studied her face, searching for answers. "I tried to find you afterwards, but Zoe said you left. If you'd told me you wanted to leave I would have gone with you."

She stepped away, her shoulders slipping from his grasp. She put her hands on the painted white railing and stared towards the lights of Hollywood, lights that were so close but felt a world away. "It doesn't matter. I didn't belong there."

"Don't say that." He crossed to the railing and leaned against it so he could look at her, but she refused to meet his gaze. "I was so happy you were with me. I still am."

Hurt ignited, fresh and raw, and she faced him. "So you could show off your good deeds?" Her words were harsh and she knew it, but she didn't stop. "I saw the interviews today. I'm an amazing woman who works with disadvantaged kids and gives food to the homeless, right? You sounded very proud of your work at the church. Even if you never actually said it was a church."

He paced away, dragging his hands through his hair. "I was trying to protect you. I didn't want them to think that we . . . that you . . . "

"That I'm Limo Hookup Lily?"

The words cracked like a whip in the night. His hand closed gently around her arm and he waited until she lifted her eyes to his. "I never wanted that for you. It's not right. It's not fair, but it's the way this business works. People think they have a right to your soul. They think they can say whatever they want and that it won't hurt. You can't let it get to you. It doesn't mean anything. They're just words."

She shook her head and pulled her arm back, the pain of the day catching up with her. "Words I have to explain to my family. To the people who love me. To the children I teach."

"It won't always be like this." When she retreated further, he followed her, closing the distance that separated them. "Give me a chance, Lily. Give me a chance to show you it can be different."

Her heart leapt at the words. Ben was standing in front of her asking for a chance. A chance for the two of them to be together, a chance for a future. Her hands trembled and she balled them into fists. She looked into his eyes, but in her mind all she saw was Giselle and all she heard were the words of the gossip sites playing on a loop in her head.

"I can't." His hands fell to his sides and her heart fell with them. "I can't be a part of that world. The fake smiles and the nasty comments. It hurts too much. I wouldn't know who to trust. I'd always be afraid of saying the wrong thing or doing the wrong thing and messing up your career."

"But I would be with you, every step of the way."

"You were with me last night and look what happened." She wrapped her arms around her waist, insulating herself from him, from the words she was going to say. "I don't want to be a part of that world. You should be with someone who understands it. Someone like Giselle."

He grabbed her hands, holding them so she couldn't pull away again. "I don't want to be with anyone else. How can I make you understand? No one makes me laugh like you do. When I'm with you, I can just be me. You give me a freedom I've never had before. Lily, please, don't push me away over what one reporter said."

Warmth ignited where their hands touched, but she ignored it. Her heart hammered in her chest but she ignored that, too. "It's not the reporter, Ben. It's you and me. We're too different. My life revolves around God, my family, and the church. That's what's important to me. Your world is fame and fortune and publicity. There's no middle ground for us. I want to be with a man who loves God more than he loves me."

As sirens wailed in the distance, Ben dropped her hands and sat on the step again, defeat dragging at his weary limbs. "So it's not the business, or the gossip. It's me. The one thing you want is the one thing I don't have."

Lily sat beside him. Their legs brushed and she felt the moment ending. She wanted to lean against him, to believe that it was possible, that they had a chance, but she didn't. He was sitting only inches away from her, but he was already gone.

"I don't have your faith, Lily. I probably never will." He stared at the cracked concrete sidewalk at the bottom of the steps, his shoulders sagging as the year slipped away. "I can live without God. I don't want to live without you."

She knew what she had to say, but the words lodged in her throat. As soon as they were spoken it would be over. Every dream she cherished, every secret hope she clasped to her heart, would be gone, shattered by the weight of a few simple words. Her heart ached, but some things weren't meant to be, no matter how badly she wanted it. The tears she had held at bay began to fall. "I'm sorry, Ben. I can't."

Finality descended on them like a curtain closing on the last act of a play. He walked to the bottom of the steps and picked up his bag. Slowly, he turned back, and Lily knew she would never forget the pain in his face as he looked up at her.

"Happy New Year, Lily." Then he walked away, a shadow fading into the darkness, a dream crushed by reality.

Tears slid down her cheeks as she poured out her heart under stars she couldn't see, telling God she didn't understand. Why bring Ben into her life just so she could watch him walk away. She cried and she prayed, and when she heard fireworks in the distance and voices raised in celebration along the street, she knew the old year was gone, disappearing into memory, and Ben had disappeared with it. She closed her eyes, shutting out the hope of a new year. She'd been wrong. The worst wasn't over.

Chapter Twenty-Nine

LILY SPENT NEW YEAR'S DAY at home, while her dad and Noah went to the church to start work on preparations for the block party. There was a ton of work to do, but neither of them argued when she said she wasn't up for it. They closed the door behind them, and Lily sat in the lonely silence replaying her last conversation with Ben. She remembered how tired he looked, the slump of his shoulders as he walked away. She didn't have to remember how it felt to say goodbye. The pain was still there, just as fresh and just as suffocating as it had been last night.

Aimlessly, she wandered through the empty house. She turned on the television and flipped through the channels, but it took only one commercial for *Blood and Honor* for her to shut it off again. How could she forget about him when his face was on billboards and posters and even showed up on the television in her living room?

She spent the day feeling sorry for herself. She didn't even want to call Kate. Kate would find a long list of terrible qualities about Ben. She'd do her best to make her hate him because that's what best friends do. But she didn't want to hate him. She didn't blame him, not really. Some people just aren't meant to be together and no amount of wishful thinking or sappy, romantic movies could change that. Ben belonged in the Hollywood fast lane and she belonged here. Recognizing that reality didn't stop the hurt, but it steeled her resolve to forget the handsome movie star. She might have been Cinderella for a night, but it was time to forget the fairy tale and focus on real life instead.

The next day, she was ready to face the world again. The church's after care classes were back on schedule after the holiday break and the kids needed her. She'd used up her allotted time for self-pity and pouting. Stuffing her heartbreak way down deep inside, she headed to the church. At least there she knew what to expect. Predictable and safe was better than exciting and unknown. Or that's what she told herself as she walked down the sidewalk in the crisp, late morning.

Noah had taken down the Christmas decorations in the church the day before. The hallway that had been filled with Christmas joy now looked empty, and she felt a pang of guilt for leaving him to do all the work while she moped in the house. But there was nothing she could do about it, and she was certain Noah would extract some sort of payback later. The best thing she could do was focus on her job and her family and try to forget that for a few brief days she had thought something else was possible.

She was setting up activities in her classroom and inventorying craft supplies when the high-pitched whir of a power saw tore through the silence. Worry flared and she hoped the old building wasn't falling apart. They often talked about being able to update the church and even expand it, but there was never enough money in the church's tight budget. She peeked out the window but she couldn't see anything.

Dropping the crayons she was holding back in their color-coded mason jars, she went to investigate. Leaving by the back door, she crossed the parking lot. Her dad and Noah were standing beside a pile of two by fours and talking to a man bent over a table saw. The blade spun and whined and sliced through a fresh piece of wood. Noah grabbed the long end and carried it to another pile. The man at the saw tuned off the blade and wiped his brow.

Halfway across the asphalt, she froze. Her lungs forgot how to draw in oxygen and her heart skipped and stuttered.

Ben.

She knew she should turn around. She should run back to her classroom before he spotted her, but her feet wouldn't cooperate. Every inch of her body was stuck, rooted to the spot in panicked paralysis.

He pulled a tape measure off his belt and knelt by the pile of boards waiting to be cut. Lily's scarf fluttered in the breeze, a dash of color that leapt around her face, and he looked up. Their eyes met, and the loss and sorrow that had kept her awake at night was mirrored in his gaze. The knowledge that he was hurting too almost drove her to her knees. It wasn't fair. How could she move on if he was standing right in front of her?

Her dad waved at her. "Look at this. Ben came by to help build a stage for your kids' performance at the outreach. Isn't that great?"

She should cross the parking lot. She should at least say hello. She should say thank you. But the distance was too great and she was afraid of what would be waiting on the other side. She didn't have the strength to say goodbye to him again.

So she ran.

She fled to the church and hid in her classroom. She was a coward, and she knew it. She just didn't care.

Ben followed her. He stood in the open door of the classroom, not crossing the threshold, held back by some invisible line he couldn't cross. "Lily, I'm sorry."

"Why are you here?" She asked, her voice raw with emotion, her hands clasping the edge of the desk behind her.

Dropping his head, his dark hair fell over his forehead as he shoved his hands into the front pockets of his jeans. He stared at his shoes as if the answer was there. Then he lifted his face, sleepless lines crinkling at the edges of his eyes. "I made a commitment to help you guys. That's what I'm doing."

Regret filled her until she couldn't feel anything else. Looking at him, the undisguised hurt in his expression, the flakes of sawdust that coated his shirt, she wanted nothing more than to go to him, to lay her head on his chest and throw caution to the wind.

But nothing had changed. There was still no way forward for them, no way for her to love a man who didn't love God. The best thing they could do was go their separate ways.

"Look Ben, the story is out. You don't have to do this. There's nothing left to cover up."

"Lily, I—" But whatever he was going to say was drowned out by the rush of footsteps and childish squeals.

"Mr. Ben!" Nate raced down the hallway and launched himself at Ben.

His smile was tired, but genuine as he looked down at the boy wrapped around his legs and Lily's heart ached at the sight of it. "Hey, buddy. How's it going?"

"Going good. Are you gonna build blocks with me today?"

Ben hesitated and looked at her, waiting for her to say something, letting her make the decision. Excitement radiated off Nate as he bounced up and down, wrapping his hand around Ben's finger, but she couldn't do it. She couldn't be in the same room as him, breathe

the same air, hear the timbre of his voice and know that it was hopeless. It was better not to draw it out, to close the door and walk away.

"Nate, Mr. Ben has work to do so he can't stay today." Ignoring the disappointment on his face, she ushered Nate into the classroom. She looked up at Ben but there was nothing left to say. More kids started arriving, so Ben stepped further back, the gulf between them widening with every passing second.

She let the kids walk past into the classroom then she closed the door, leaving Ben on the other side.

*****

Evan and Noah were waiting for him by the now-silent table saw. Without saying a word, he knelt beside the next plank to be cut, measuring the length and marking it with a pencil. He tried to focus on the number in front of him, but the image of Lily closing the door in his face was seared into his brain. He'd been a fool to come here.

It hadn't been the reporter, or the gossip, or even Giselle that had driven her away. It was him. He was missing the one thing she wanted. He looked up, but the cloudy, grey sky didn't offer any answers. If there was a God up there He certainly didn't care about him. He hadn't shown up when his dad was using him as a punching bag, and He hadn't been there when he was sleeping in his car and wondering where his next meal would come from. So why would He show up now? It was simply too late for him. God had given up on him just as surely as he'd given up on God.

He hadn't known how much he cared for her until the confession slipped from his lips on New Year's Eve. He was a man who didn't know he was drowning until someone reached for his hand. But standing in the doorway to her classroom, so close he could smell the vanilla of her perfume, he was afraid it was all slipping from his grasp and he was going to be lost to the waves again. Because in his heart he knew she was wrong. He wasn't worth saving.

Evan put his hand on his shoulder. "Give her some time. Sunday was a pretty bad day."

He double-checked the measurement before lifting the plank and carrying it to the saw. "I don't think time's the problem." He flipped a switch and the saw spun, cutting through the board without resistance, severing the unwanted piece and letting it fall to the ground. "She wants something I can't give her."

As the hum of the blade slowed, his phone rang. Slipping off his gloves, he saw Derek's name and answered the call. His assistant had been acting as a mediator between he and Zoe since their argument on New Year's Eve.

"Hey, Ben, what are you doing at the church? I thought that was over and done with?"

Tension gathered in the back of his neck. He was going to have to do something about Derek tracking his phone. He needed an assistant, not a spy and definitely not a nanny. "What do you need, Derek?"

"Look, I know things have been tense between you and Zoe. I'm just trying to keep everyone happy. Can't you step back from that church thing for a while? Just until things calm down."

Fatigue and irritation made him impatient. He stepped away from Evan and Noah and walked to the corner of the concrete dock. Leaning his back against the cool stone he closed his eyes and tried to find his way out of the mess he had made. Everything he touched recently turned to ash in his hands. First Giselle and the disaster in Rome, then the limo photos, and now the story about Lily. It was like he was being attacked from all sides, but he didn't know who the enemy was. It was a war he didn't know how to fight. The one place he was comfortable, the one place he could let his guard down and be himself was this church.

He'd simply have to make Derek understand what he was doing here. Maybe then he could explain it to Zoe, make her see that this wasn't a career killer, it wasn't a scandal in the making, it was one good thing he could do in the midst of everything he had done wrong.

"Listen," he began, trying to keep the frustration out of his voice. It wasn't Derek's fault, Zoe was the one pulling the strings. "This is something I have to finish. The story's been contained so we don't need to worry about it getting out of control. A few more weeks and it'll be done."

Derek was quiet and he wondered what the aspiring actor would do if their roles were reversed. Would he blindly follow the machinations of his handlers, or would he put his foot down and risk the consequences?

"Zoe isn't going to like it. And Ben, you need to remember who she is."

And just like that, he had his answer.

Chapter Thirty

LILY DAWDLED BEHIND HER DAD and Noah the next morning. Ben was going to meet them at the church to continue work on the stage they were building for the block party. She should have been happy for the help. She'd been working on a fun musical number with the children for the past three weeks. It would mean the world to them to have a big stage to perform on. She tried to imagine how excited the kids would be, how much their parents would enjoy seeing them perform, but the only thing she could focus on was Ben. How was she supposed to move on when he kept showing up?

As she walked, she prayed for strength. Strength to get through this day. Then the next day and the next. She would get through each day until she finally forgot him. But it was a lie. She would never forget Ben Prescott.

Stumbling to a halt, she nearly crashed into her dad's back as he stopped abruptly. Silence and shock paralyzed her as she stared across the small, front parking lot. Even from this distance she could see the damage. The sliding metal gate had been forced open, the sides twisted and broken from the tracks. Shards of glass glistened on the asphalt where the windows of the church had been shattered, and trash littered the parking lot. The trees and potted plants on the loading dock had been tossed over the railing and lay in heaps of broken pots and tangled roots on the ground. Graffiti marred every wall and the front door. She stared at it, unable to blink as the words "Limo Hookup Lily" stared back at her in red spray paint.

Her stomach dropped. Dizziness swept over her and she reached for her father's hand. Anger clenched his jaw, tension rippling through his body as he gripped her hand. She and Noah looked to him as he stared at the destruction laid out before them. Stunned silence enveloped them, wordlessly they held on to each other.

Taking a deep breath, her dad looked beyond the church. Lifting his eyes to the sky he said, "Let's pray."

*****

Police cars blocked the entrance to the church. Panic seized Ben as he slammed the car to a stop alongside the curb. He leapt from the car and ran to the gate, a thousand terrible scenarios playing through his mind and at the center of all of them was Lily.

Yellow crime scene tape stretched across the parking lot entrance and a uniformed police officer stood guard, keeping anyone except police from getting in. A handful of reporters were clustered to one side snapping pictures of the front of the church.

Seeing the chaos and destruction made him move faster. "Can I get in?" he asked the officer.

"Sorry, church employees only," he said, barely looking at Ben, his focus scanning the crowd that was growing on the sidewalk.

"I do work here," he said, figuring that was technically an honest answer and hoping Evan would back him up.

The conversation caught the attention of the reporters. One of them recognized him and started snapping pictures. The others followed his lead and the group started to circle him. Planting himself in front of Ben, the police officer tried to force the cameras back.

Ben used the distraction to slip under the caution tape. If the cop saw him, he didn't try to stop him. He walked quickly past the police officers making notes and marking evidence searching for Lily. When he made his way around to the back of the church, he found the Shaw family sitting together on the steps of the dock. Sorrow had settled on them like a coat.

"What happened?" he asked, and all three of them looked up.

The tears in Lily's eyes propelled him forward. It didn't matter what they had been through, or that she didn't want to be with him. He saw the heartbreak on her face and he couldn't stop himself from taking her in his arms. She didn't resist and he soaked up the feeling of her head against his chest. If this was all he could offer her, he would do it.

"Vandals," Evan said. "Probably kids out looking for trouble."

Noah said nothing, but the hard set of his jaw told Ben that he didn't agree with his dad's opinion.

"Was anyone hurt?" he asked.

"No, it was like this when we got here this morning." Lily stepped out of the circle of his arms and wiped her eyes. Missing the warmth of her body against his, he reached out to her, but she backed away and he let his hands drop.

"What can I do?" His heart ached. After the hours they invested in this church, in this neighborhood, the love they had shown, who would do this to them? Who would cause such damage to a family that wanted only to help?

"Just pray," Evan said.

Ben crossed his arm and didn't reply. That was the one thing he couldn't do.

A detective in a brown suit approached and leaned against the side of the building. "This just sucks, Evan."

"Can't say I disagree." Evan stood. "Ben, this is Joe Sullivan. He's a good friend and one of LA's finest detectives."

Ben shook the older man's hand, surprised by the iron grip. "And you must be the movie star. My daughter Kate and Lily go way back." The grip on his hand tightened by another fraction and Ben could only imagine what the man had heard about him.

Lily blushed and looked away. Clearly she was thinking the same thing.

Detective Sullivan dropped his hand and turned back to Evan. "We don't have a lot to go on, but I'll keep my eye on the investigation and let you know what we find."

"Thanks, Joe." Evan and the detective walked off, Lily following close behind, their voices trailing away as they headed into the church.

Ben started in that direction, but Noah stopped him. "There's something you should see." They walked in the other direction heading for the carport where Noah kept his limo. The headlights and taillights had been smashed and shards of splintered plastic littered the ground. Bright red paint dripped and glowed along the black walls of the car. *For a good time call Lily.*

Cold, hard rage coiled in Ben's gut. This hadn't been vandals or kids. This was personal.

*****

"Ben, you can't be a part of this anymore." Zoe said the words flatly, without emotion, as if she were reciting a line from a contract, a simple fact that couldn't be disputed or denied. "This is ridiculous."

He was too tired for this argument. His back ached and his head pounded from trying to figure out who had attacked the church. Detective Sullivan wasn't hopeful about finding the culprits. In spite of the personal messages left on the door and the limo, he said it looked like a random attack. Maybe a gang initiation or vandalism that went too far.

After the police finished their investigation, he stayed to help the Shaws with the clean-up. Evan went into the church office to call the insurance company and start a claim for damages and a tow truck dragged the limo away for repairs. While Lily swept away broken glass from the shattered windows and Noah cleaned up the parking lot, Ben found a bucket of paint in the garage and painted the front door. He didn't want Lily to see that slur on the door ever again.

His muscles ached and fatigue pulled at him. It had been a long, frustrating day and Zoe was turning it into a long, frustrating night. She was trying to look out for him, to protect him and his career, but he was running out of patience. There had to be a line somewhere. There had to be some part of his life that was his and his alone.

He paced the floor, unable to sit still, anger and adrenaline keeping his body moving. As soon as he sat down he'd fall asleep and he wasn't ready to let the day go. Not yet. "I'm not going to abandon them now."

"You've got other things to focus on. I want you in New Mexico for the film festival next week."

Ben stared beyond his reflection in the windows to the dark Los Angeles sky hovering above the bright lights of the city. "I'm not going. Lily needs me here."

"No, she doesn't. She needs a check from the insurance company and a good handyman." When he didn't reply, she rose from the chair and stood beside him at the windows, their muted reflections staring back like faded stills from a forgotten movie. "Look, Ben, I know you like this girl, but this isn't the right time to get involved in this kind of story. There are pictures of you standing in front of that church door. Ben Prescott and the word 'hookup' should never be in the same sentence."

Turning from the view that suddenly seemed empty and hollow, he went to the kitchen and grabbed a bottle of water from the fridge. But there was nowhere he could go where he didn't see the memory of her face, the dried tears staining her cheeks, and the haunted look in her eyes as she stood in the midst of the wreckage of the church. "This isn't her fault."

Zoe followed him, as she always did. "Of course it isn't. I know that. But if you really want to help her, step back. If this is some crazed fan of yours taking aim at Lily and her family, the best thing you can do is get away from her."

Her words struck home. Was this his fault? Had he brought all of this on Lily and her family? "What are you talking about?"

"Derek, show him."

His assistant hesitated for a second before disappearing into his office. When he came back, he had a stack of letters in his hand that he held out to Ben.

Scanning through the collection of printed emails and crinkled hand-written pages, a sour taste filled his mouth.

I love you, Ben. We're meant to be together.

How can you be with someone else when I know you love me?

If you don't stop seeing that girl, I will make sure she pays.

His stomach churned as he read the twisted declarations of love, the misguided fan letters, and the threats. Each letter was worse than the one before, fan letters that escalated from admiration to adoration to instability. Every word he read widened the yawning pit of fear growing in his gut.

"How long has this been happening?" he demanded.

Derek glanced at Zoe before answering, but the agent didn't say anything. "The most threatening ones are new. They started arriving after the premiere. After the story about Lily broke."

Derek tried to take the letters back, but Ben pulled them away. He couldn't stop reading them. The vile words and dark promises on the pages swam through his mind. Even when he tried to do something good, when he tried to protect her, he had only made things worse.

His hands trembled with the urge to tear the letters to shreds, to destroy them as if that would erase the horrible words, as if he could paint over it as simply as he had painted over the church door, hiding the evil that was underneath.

But he didn't. He stared at the words in his hands, confronted by the irrefutable evidence of the devastation he'd caused, knowing that once again, Lily was paying for his mistakes.

Helplessness curled in his gut, a weight threatening to crush him. "I don't know what to do."

Zoe gently pulled the letters from his grip, her hand patting his as she whisked the words away. "That's why you have me. Let me take care of it."

Ben let the wave of condemnation swallow him whole. He had done this to Lily as surely as if he'd been the one who attacked the church. Maybe Zoe was right. Maybe the best thing he could do was walk away.

Chapter Thirty-One

BEN SAT IN THE SUNLIGHT beside the pool. Even in Los Angeles, January was too cold for a swim, but the fresh air and the sound of the water were as close to relaxing as he could get. Images of the destruction at the church were stuck in his mind, an endless loop playing over and over set to the soundtrack of the threatening letters Derek had showed him. The words of a disturbed and violent fan had been meant for him, but Lily was the one who suffered.

Zoe had wanted to keep the letters quiet, to keep them from the papers, but he insisted on giving the letters to Detective Sullivan. The investigator's hard stare told Ben exactly what he thought of the movie star who had brought so much trouble to the Shaw family. No doubt he blamed him for everything. And he was right.

A cold wind blew across the pool, rippling the still water. He tried not to think about Lily and her family still cleaning up the mess he left behind, but he couldn't escape it. Zoe called him that morning and let him know that she sent a large check to the church in his name to help with the repairs. She assured him it would be more than enough to fix the building and Noah's limo. In the end, maybe that was all he was good for; a name, some cash, and staying far away from everyone he cared about.

"So this is where you've been hiding."

Ben didn't turn around. He wasn't in the mood for company. Regret was something he preferred to indulge in alone. He'd already sent Derek home for the day, and he was looking forward to a lonely afternoon of self-pity.

But instead of taking the hint, Chris walked out the sliding glass door with a pizza box in his hands and a smirk plastered across his face.

"I'm not hiding. I'm thinking."

"If you say so. But from my trained director's eye, thinking looks an awful lot like hiding." Dropping the pizza box onto a glass table between the lounge chairs, Chris sat and made himself comfortable, apparently planning for a long visit.

"How did you get in here?" Ben asked.

"Maria likes me." Opening the box, Chris grabbed a slice of pizza and bit into it with a groan of satisfaction. "You know," he said between bites. "You made the news last night. And not just the entertainment segment. You were on the legitimate, journalism stuff."

Ben raised his eyebrows, afraid to ask, but knowing Chris was going to tell him anyway.

"They ran a story about the vandalism at the Mission. Apparently it's a big deal since there's some famous movie star who hangs out there."

He wanted to laugh, but he couldn't. The sound was stuck in his throat, strangled by the guilt that had taken up residence there. He closed his eyes and rubbed his temples. "Everything is so messed up."

Chris clapped him on the shoulder, seemingly unconcerned about the damage Ben had caused. "Don't worry, God knows what He's doing. He's still in control." Then he kicked his feet up on the lounge and laid his head back, pulling his sunglasses over his eyes as he stared at the cool sky above.

God.

Ben frowned. He didn't see much evidence of God in this. If God really knew what was going on, if He truly saw and cared, wouldn't He have stopped it? Who deserved His protection more than Lily and her family? And if God couldn't be bothered to help them, what hope was there for the rest of the world?

"If you say so. But if you ask me, it doesn't look like there's much of a plan here."

Chris waved away the theological debate and took another slice of pizza. Then he slid the box towards Ben. "So how's Lily?"

"Better off without me." Untangling a piece of pizza from the gooey strings of cheese, he tried to ignore the truth in those words and the pain it caused. Her life had been turned upside down from the moment he got into the limo outside LAX. What had he done except drag her into the spotlight, ruin her reputation, and make her the focus of a confused and violent stalker? Anyone could see she was better off without him.

"Is she mad about the premiere? Limo Hookup Lily was a pretty harsh headline, even by Hollywood standards."

His appetite gone, Ben dropped the crust he was holding back into the cardboard box. "She's not mad. She's hurt. And I don't blame her. I'm sure Giselle set her up with that reporter at the club. I can't prove it, but I also can't fix it."

"There's nothing to fix, it's not your fault. She knows that."

"And the church? I suppose that's not my fault either?" Anger spilled into his words, fueled by a potent mix of frustration and helplessness.

"No, it's not. Did you smash the windows? Did you do the graffiti?"

"Of course not. But—"

"But nothing." Chris dropped his feet to the ground and faced Ben. "People make their own choices. And sometimes they make stupid ones. You're responsible only for your own stupid choices. And giving up on Lily, that would be a stupid choice."

Ben stared across the hills, an endless horizon that led further and further away before disappearing entirely. "She doesn't want any part of this. Movies, the business, my life . . . " He waved his hand to encompass his house, the pool, everything he had worked for, everything he had fought so hard to gain. And in the end none of it mattered, not to Lily. "She doesn't want any of it."

"I don't blame her. It's a rough gig being a movie star's girlfriend."

"You're not helping."

Chris grinned and helped himself to more pizza. "So when are you going to see her again?"

"I'm not."

"Well that sounds like a dumb plan."

"I told you, she's better off without me. I destroyed her life. She ended up all over the tabloids, she was called horrible names, and her church was vandalized. All because of me." Ben sat up and faced Chris. "And to top it off, she said quite clearly that she doesn't want to be with me."

The director considered that, his head nodding slowly. "Those are all very valid reasons for staying away. But you're forgetting one tiny detail."

"What's that?"

Chris brushed the garlicky crumbs off his hands then pulled his sunglasses down to look at his best friend. "You love her."

The words echoed in his head. They were so loud he was sure Lily could hear them from here. He loved her. The realization wrapped around him like a blanket. It surrounded and enveloped him. He loved Lily Shaw. There were a million reasons why he shouldn't, why it wouldn't work, but in spite of it all, he loved her.

So what was he going to do about it?

He looked up and saw Chris watching him. The director clapped his hands and rubbed them together the way he did when he planned a shooting schedule for a new movie. "That's the look of a man who needs a plan. Let's get to work."

Chapter Thirty-Two

THE SETTLEMENT FROM THE INSURANCE company was going to take a few days. Lily didn't want to admit it, but it was Ben's check that was getting them through. When his agent showed up the day before with that check and her sincere apologies on Ben's behalf, Lily walked away knowing that he had given up. The story in the press, the vandalism, it was too much for him. She knew that. She knew his career was more important, and Zoe had made it very clear that he wouldn't be coming back.

She should have been relieved that she wouldn't have to hide in her classroom to avoid seeing him. But she wasn't. She felt his absence in the silence of every passing second. So she did the only thing she could. She kept going.

That afternoon, she took the kids outside on the loading dock to rehearse their song for the block party. Her dad was adamant that the outreach would go on as planned. They painted over the graffiti and boarded up the broken windows. Her dad hoped to have new glass installed before the event, but even if they didn't, they would move forward. She hated seeing all the trees and flowers gone from the dock, some of those flowers her mother had planted. They'd bloomed and survived for years. And now they were gone.

Noah had been able to salvage most of the tables and chairs, and he was thrilled that by some miracle, the grill hadn't been damaged.

"As long as we have hot dogs, people will show up," her brother declared as he tested the grill.

Lily kept the kids outside while workmen repaired the damage inside the church. They were all lined up, ready to go through their song while her dad and Noah worked to finish the stage Ben had started.

"Okay, kids, let's do this again. You're going to be so great at the block party!" Nate raised his hand and started bouncing up and down. "What is it, Nate?"

"Look, Miss Lily." He pointed excitedly behind her. "Mr. Ben's back. And he brought a friend."

Anticipation rose like a fire before she could trample it back down. She turned slowly, knowing what she would see, but still unprepared for the impact she felt when she saw him. Ben was walking across the parking lot with Chris Johnston beside him and they were headed right towards her. Her heart hammered in her chest and she didn't know if it was joy or fear that she felt.

They stopped at the bottom of the dock, and Ben looked up at her through the railing. "Hey guys. How's rehearsal going?"

The kids all ran towards him and he passed out high fives and fist bumps while Chris looked on. Lily hadn't moved, she was trapped, caught by the shock of his sudden appearance.

Then Ben turned to her and she scrambled to remember all the reasons why she was supposed to be happy he was gone. "Hi, Lily."

She swallowed hard. "Hi. Zoe said you weren't coming back."

Holding her gaze, intensity burned in his eyes and her legs wobbled beneath her. "Some things are worth fighting for."

She wanted to say something but she couldn't find the words. Ben was here. In spite of everything she said, everything that happened, he'd come back. She didn't know what it meant, she didn't know how it would end, but at that moment, she chose to believe God was working in Ben Prescott's life. Maybe there was still hope that he would find his way back to God.

"I hope it's okay, but I brought some extra help." He raised his hand towards Chris. "Do you remember Chris Johnston?"

"Of course." Lily nodded at the young director, ignoring the amused expression on his face as he glanced from Ben to her and back to Ben. "Thanks for coming."

"Oh, I wouldn't have missed this for the world," he said, his words heavy with implication.

She was saved from replying when her dad appeared. Ben introduced him to Chris as she shifted on her feet and tried to figure out what to do next.

"Chris is one of the best directors in the business," Ben said.

Shaking his hand, her dad grinned. "I'm happy you're here. How do you feel about manual labor?"

Chris laughed and stuffed his hands in the pockets of his leather jacket. "As long as you keep me away from the power tools, we should be okay."

"I think we can work something out. We'll all be grateful for the extra help. We've got only a week to get ready for this shindig and there's plenty of work left to do. And you're welcome to join us at the block party."

"We'll both be here for church Sunday morning and then we'll stay to help out, right Ben?"

All eyes turned to Ben and she watched the play of emotions that crossed his face. He'd been cornered and he knew it. Shooting Chris a look that promised retribution, he nodded.

Lily felt like dancing. Ben was going back to church. It was a start.

*****

"So what do you think?" Lily asked, dreading the answer. Kate was silent for a longtime and she could imagine her sitting in her tiny Boston apartment trying to organize her thoughts.

"I think it's great he came back to help. But," she paused again and Lily knew bad news was coming. "It doesn't change all the other stuff. He's still a celebrity, he's still followed around by the same gossips that spread those nasty rumors about you, and he's still not a believer. Do you really want to be a part of that?"

Sighing, Lily hugged her pillow to her chest, wishing for the thousandth time that Kate had never gone to Boston. She needed her friend right here. If she could meet Ben in person maybe then she'd understand.

"Look, Lils, I'm not saying it wouldn't work out, I'm just saying it would take a miracle."

In the semi-darkness of her room, she smiled. Fortunately, she believed in a God who still worked miracles.

Chapter Thirty-Three

BEN AND CHRIS SAT ON the loading dock for lunch after a long morning. Over the past few days, they had fallen into a comfortable routine. Show up at the church right around the time Lily arrived to set up her classroom, help Evan and Noah for a few hours with building projects and preparations for the outreach event, stop for lunch when Lily moved to the church to catch up on office tasks, work a little more, and leave when Lily and her family locked up.

Ben was grateful to have Chris with him, but the director hadn't exaggerated when he said he should stay away from power tools. Twice, Ben had to stop him from nearly shooting himself in the foot with the nail gun before he finally took the tool away and passed him a measuring tape instead. So with Chris holding the pieces and Ben using the tools, they finished the frame for the stage. All that was left was to lay the planks for the stage itself and sand it down.

That morning, Lily said hello to them when they arrived, then she disappeared inside the church, and she hadn't emerged since. Every once in a while Ben would look towards the door, wondering what she was doing, but it never opened.

After his fifth poorly disguised glance at the side door of the church, Chris laughed. "You know the door opens both ways, right?"

"What?" He'd been so focused on what Lily might be doing that he hadn't heard the question.

Chris shook his head and tore open a bag of chips. "You know, you could just go in and see her instead of waiting out here like a lovesick puppy."

"I'm not lovesick." He fiddled with the cap on his water bottle and resisted the urge to check the door again. Surely he'd hear it open when she finally emerged.

"If you say so," Chris said, clearly enjoying his friend's torment.

"And I'm not a puppy."

The director shrugged. "Puppies are cute. You should embrace your cute puppy-ness . . . it can only help you at this point."

Ben glanced at the door again, still firmly closed, and tossed his napkin at his friend when he laughed at him. Lily had seemed happy to see him. There were still photographers that stopped by the church to take photos but they were few and far between. Apparently, the story of Ben's work at the church and his possible interest in the pastor's daughter had run its course. The bloggers and reporters had moved on to the next big thing.

Ben chuckled to himself. According to that morning's tabloids the next big thing turned out to be Liam dumping Giselle for a much younger, and much blonder, pop star. That would explain the slew of messages from Giselle currently clogging up his voicemail. Messages he had no intention of listening to.

"Did you tell Zoe you wouldn't be going to New Mexico?" Chris asked as he took a bite of his sandwich.

Ben shuddered. "Not yet. I'm not ready for that amount of yelling and guilt." The New Mexico Film Festival was starting that weekend, the same time as the church's block party, and he had no intention of skipping out on Lily and her family. Zoe would just have to understand. And if she didn't, maybe it was time for him to find a new agent.

Surprisingly, he didn't find the idea frightening. In fact, for the first time since he arrived in Los Angeles, he wasn't worried about his career. He wasn't worried about losing a part or sabotaging his celebrity. An odd sense of peace had snuck up and settled around him. Looking back at the door again, he had a very strong sense that the peace he felt had nothing to do with him and everything to do with the blue-eyed girl on the other side.

He stood up and brushed off his pants. "I'll be right back."

"It's about time," Chris said with a dramatic sigh.

Ben ignored him and went to find Lily.

She wasn't in her classroom. So he poked around until he heard her voice coming from the music room behind the sanctuary. He stood outside and listened to the song. It reminded him of the first time he had come here. The wonder and awe in her voice captivated his heart now just as it had done then.

He waited until the song was over before opening the door. She was focused on the sheet music propped up on the music stand in front of her. When the door shut behind him, she looked up and he knew he didn't imagine the blush that crept up her cheeks.

Standing beside the door, looking at her across the small room, he remembered the first day he had come here. He had bungled it so badly. The same nervous anticipation was churning in his stomach, but this time there was so much more at stake. All the carefully chosen words he had practiced, all the things he wanted to say flew out of his mind as the echo of her voice faded away and he was left to stare at the woman he had been dreaming of all his life. "That was beautiful."

"You were listening?" Her cheeks turned even redder, her hair falling across her shoulders as she rearranged the papers on the music stand.

"I was waiting outside. I didn't want to open the door."

"Why?"

"I wanted to hear the end of the song."

The air in the room seemed to vanish when her eyes finally met his. Every instinct in his body screamed to go to her, to take her in his arms and never let go, but he waited. He caught sight of the necklace he had given her for Christmas peeking out from under her scarf.

She stacked the sheet music on a side table and tucked her long hair behind her ears. When she turned back to him, a polite smile fixed on her face, he knew he'd waited too long. "It means a lot to all of us that you and Chris are here. We couldn't have done all of this without you."

"It's our pleasure, really. It's a great cause." He wanted to kick himself. That wasn't what he wanted to say at all. He was an actor who had forgotten his lines, and his moment was passing him by.

"Lily, I know things haven't gone well between us. I messed it up, and I'm so sorry." He crossed the small room until he was right in front of her, his hands yearning to reach for hers. "Can we start over? Will you let me try to do it right this time?"

The silence of her reply was as painful as the words she'd said on New Year's Eve. Stepping closer, he risked taking her hand. "I know I'm not the man you want me to be. I can't pretend to have your faith, but I'm here. And I'm staying, for as long as you'll let me."

Her fingers twined with his and she studied them for a long time, her small hand joined with his. "I'd like that," she whispered.

Relief flooded through him. She was giving him another chance. They had another shot to make it work. Taking her in his arms, he held her close, and felt something he hadn't felt in a long time.

He felt home.

Chapter Thirty-Four

BY SATURDAY MORNING, THE HOLLYWOOD Mission was a frenzy of activity and preparation. The whole parking lot had been transformed. Noah's limo was still in the shop being repaired, so they used the shaded area under the carport to set up raffle tables. Bouncy houses were being delivered early Sunday morning and they were expecting two face painters, a juggler, and a balloon animal artist to arrive right after the church service ended.

Ben and Chris finished the stage and set it up on the side of the parking lot near the playground. The plan was to add plastic folding chairs in front of the stage on Sunday morning. It was going to be an outdoor church service, with worship starting at ten a.m. Her dad would give a very short message and then they'd kick off the fun.

In the flurry of last minute errands, planning, and cleaning, Chris disappeared for an hour and re-appeared with a car full of hot dogs and buns and every condiment he could think of. Lily's dad was thrilled when he realized how many people they would be able to feed on Sunday afternoon. It was going to be the church's biggest event and everyone felt the anticipation building in the air.

Lily was exhausted, but excited. And she knew it wasn't just because of the outreach.

Ben had been at the church every day. They worked side by side, preparing for the event. Then each night after her dad locked up, Ben would walk her home. By unspoken agreement, they slowed their steps, lagging behind her family, drawing out the sunset conversations as long as possible. In the evening shadows, things seemed easier. The obstacles they faced in the light all disappeared in the gloaming of the day.

Saturday evening, he stopped at her classroom, ready for their walk home, and Lily looked up from a maelstrom of cotton, glue, and giggling children.

"So this is where the party is," he said and her heart skipped. His dark hair was disheveled, a look that made him appear roguish and wild, and sawdust coated his jeans, but to her, he looked perfect.

"Mr. Ben!" The kids charged him and he ended up on the floor with his arms full of fluffy sheep.

Lily clapped her hands and the kids went back to sitting in a circle on the rug, their tiny bodies barely containing the nervous excitement thundering through them.

"So, I'm guessing you're not ready to go home," Ben said once he was free of the kids and their costumes.

She shook her head. "No. We've got a few more run throughs to do before their parents pick them up. Tomorrow is the big day." The kids screamed and cheered, and she squeezed her eyes shut against the noise. It was going to be a long night.

"I can wait with you," he said as he picked up a pile of cotton fluff.

She put her hand on his arm and electricity danced between them. "You don't have to do that. Why don't you go home with my dad and get something to eat. I'll meet you there when we're finished."

"I don't mind staying."

Lily felt the tug, the invisible string that kept drawing her ever closer to him. Yes, she wanted him to stay. She wanted him to stay forever. But she held back. "It's okay. Let me finish with them and then I'll head home."

Lowering his voice, he whispered beneath the rumble of the kids. "I don't want you walking home alone. I'll meet you back here. What time?"

Flutters of anticipation raced through her. "Eight o'clock. Is that okay?"

"I'll be here." He reached up and tucked a stray strand of hair behind her ear, his fingers brushing against her cheek. The kids noticed and broke into a loud chorus of oohs and aahs. He laughed and bowed to the class. "Break a leg little sheep."

Nate furrowed his brow and frowned at him. "That's not very nice, Mr. Ben."

"Sorry, Nate. In acting, saying good luck is bad luck. So people say break a leg instead."

Nate didn't look convinced. "Actors are weird."

Lily giggled. "You are absolutely right, Nate. But we love him anyway." Too late she realized what she said. Her mouth dropped open and embarrassment threatened to drown her.

A slow smile spread across Ben's face, there was no chance he hadn't heard what she just said. He took her hand and brought it to his lips, his warm breath brushing across her knuckles before he kissed the back of her hand, sending the kids into a wild round of kissing noises. "I'll see you at eight."

Lily gulped and nodded her head so hard her ponytail bounced. She didn't trust herself to say anything else. In fact, she might never speak in front of Ben again.

He gave her a wink and disappeared down the hallway, whistling as he went.

Turning back to her room full of sheep, Lily silently counted the hours until she could see him again.

*****

Ben ignored the text alerts on his phone. Zoe had not taken the news of his decision to skip New Mexico so he could stay here to help the church well. Her messages had gone from "call me" to "your career is over" in a remarkably short amount of time. He sent Derek to talk to her and try to smooth things over, but his assistant hadn't come back. He assumed Zoe had either fired the poor kid or was still yelling at him. He assumed Zoe had either fired the poor kid or was still yelling at him.

But he didn't care. He'd been so happy working with Lily that he wouldn't have traded those days with her for the biggest blockbuster in the world.

He sat at the kitchen table with Evan and Noah and drummed his fingers on the coffee mug, anxious to go back to the church and see Lily. He was certain they'd come back here and spend the night talking, just as they had every night that week.

The Shaws were a family like he had never seen or experienced. They talked, they laughed, their house was welcoming and relaxing. Ben sat back, sipping a cup of coffee as Noah shared a story about a man he had prayed for that day. A homeless man had come to the church looking for food. Noah had given him lunch and then sat at the table with him while he ate.

"It was so sad, Dad," he said. "He was a vet. His wife left him while he was in combat and he was medically discharged due to injuries he got in Iraq. He ended up addicted to pain killers, not working, and eventually he lost everything. He doesn't even know where his kids are."

The story picked at Ben's conscience. How many times had he walked by people who were suffering? How many times had he looked the other way, unwilling to see and unwilling to help because he was too busy, too distracted, or too wrapped up in his own problems?

"I don't know how you guys do it," he said and both Evan and Noah looked at him. "How do you look at all that pain, that suffering, and still believe that God loves everyone." The question had been bothering him since the day he helped in the soup kitchen. If God was all-powerful why didn't He just step in and fix things? How is it loving to let people suffer?

Evan took his time before answering. "If I didn't believe that God exists and that He loves us, all of us, then I couldn't face another day. It's knowing that I'm loved for who I am, no matter what, that makes each day possible."

Ben considered Evan's words, looking at the pastor, a man who had watched his wife die of a terrible disease, but had never lost his faith. He was so sure of the fact that God loved him, not even death could shake him.

It didn't make much sense to him. But maybe that was the point of faith, a person had to leap before he could believe. His grandmother had believed, her faith had radiated out from her like sunlight on a cloudy day. She told him time and time again, "Benny, all you have to do is trust God and He'll be there." The older he got the harder it seemed to give up control, to trust his life to someone he couldn't see and didn't know.

But there was a gentle, yet persistent pull on his heart. He hadn't told Lily or Evan, but he felt it more and more, a knock on a door that was waiting to be opened. It sounded so simple, just believe. But he couldn't do it. It was too simple. Nothing could be that easy. After everything he had done, why would God want him? He didn't have anything to give to God, there was nothing he had to offer. And if Hollywood had taught him anything it was that nothing good was free.

Still his grandmother's words clawed through the years of his memories. "Jesus loves you, Benny. He will always be with you, you just have to ask."

Sirens wailed in the distance, screeching through the night somewhere close by. He glanced at the clock. If he was going to walk to the church to meet Lily, he should get going.

"None of this makes sense to me," he said as he pushed away from the table. "But I can't deny that your family has something special. Something I've never seen before."

"You can have it, too," Evan said, but Ben didn't reply. There was nothing he could say. Not yet.

As he opened the front door, the smell of smoke filled the house. Scanning the horizon, fear closed his throat. A sinister red glow lit up the sky from the direction of the Hollywood Mission.

"Evan! Noah!" he yelled, and heard the rough scrap of chairs against wood.

He didn't wait for a response. He didn't wait for them to see the flames. He leapt off the porch and started running, only one thought racing through his mind. He had to get to Lily.

His feet pounded against the asphalt as he ran down the street. The smoke grew thicker and more acrid as he got closer to the church. Sweat beaded on his forehead and trickled down his back. He didn't know if it was from running or if the air itself was getting hotter. Skidding to a stop in front of the gate, he shielded his face with his arm.

Fire. Angry red and orange flames were devouring the back of the church. The smoke was thick and hot, ash raining down like fiery snow. He looked at the scene spread before him and knew no movie would ever show how bad it really was. This wasn't a staged and controlled burn. There were no stuntmen or safety precautions. This was an inferno destroying everything in its path.

Panicked crying came from the side of the parking lot. Children huddled together in a tight knot, tucked away in a corner of the fence, clinging to each other.

Lily.

He ran to them and dropped to his knees. "Mr. Ben!" Nate threw himself at him and clutched his chest, fresh tears streaming down his face. "I'm scared. I want to go home."

Ben hugged him as his eyes darted over the group. Lily wasn't there. "It's going to be okay, Nate. Pastor Evan and Noah are on their way. Where's Miss Lily?"

Nate rubbed his eyes, soot and tears smearing his cheeks. "In there." He pointed to the burning building and Ben's heart dropped. Lily was still inside.

"Nate, I want you all to stay here. Do you know how to call 911?" The young boy nodded and Ben gave him his phone. "Call them now."

He tried to take a step away, but Nate grabbed him again, his fingers digging into his with a force born of terror.

"Don't leave!"

Ben held Nate's shoulders, the sobs of the other kids cutting through him. "I'm going to get Miss Lily. I'll be right back. You keep all the kids together. That's your job, got it?"

Nate clutched Ben's phone and wiped his tears. "And we'll pray."

Ben smiled weakly and patted his head. Then he ran into the fire.

Chapter Thirty-Five

EVAN AND NOAH WEREN'T FAR behind. They arrived to a scene of fire and chaos. The kids were still huddled together and in the midst of the cluster of terrified children Nate was talking on a cell phone.

"We need lots of fire trucks. And water. You have to hurry."

Evan grabbed the phone. "Nate, let me talk to them." He heard the sound of a dispatcher and relief washed over him. The little boy had called 911. Evan gave the dispatcher their address and described he scene as best as he could.

Noah knelt in front of the kids and they mobbed him. "Is everyone okay?"

"We're okay." Nate nodded. "Mr. Ben told us to wait here for you and Pastor Evan."

Noah checked the kids, looking for injuries, but other than the tears and the frightened faces, they all looked fine. "Where did Mr. Ben go?"

Nate pointed at the church. "He went to get Miss Lily."

At the sound of Lily's name, Evan stopped talking, the phone frozen by his ear. He and Noah turned to the fiery building, the flames spreading like a hungry monster, swallowing it whole.

"Oh God, help them." His whispered words lost in the rumble of the smoke and shattering glass.

*****

The foyer was dark and filled with smoke. "Lily!" Ben forced his voice to carry above the noise of the flames, calling into the darkness as he ran to the sanctuary, but the room was empty.

He flew out the glass side door out to the loading dock. The heat was brutal. From there he could see behind the church. The stage he and Chris had built was completely engulfed in flames. The fire leapt from the stage to the back wall of the church, eating through the roof and crawling along the walls. The whole church would be enveloped soon.

Darting to the children's church door, he headed for her classroom. Paint was bubbling and melting off the walls while the roof cracked and popped above him.

"Lily!" he called again. There was no answer.

He threw open the door to her classroom and skidded to a stop. Part of the ceiling had collapsed and lay scattered in pieces on the floor. Flames on the roof danced overhead, bright and threatening against the night sky.

Crying broke through the roar of the flames, panicked wails full of fear coming from the far side of the classroom. Two little girls crouched in the corner, coughing and wheezing in the smoke. He knelt beside them, and then he saw her.

Lily was pinned under the remains of the roof. A gash crossed her forehead and her waist and legs were buried under debris and stone.

Terror gripped him and he shook her arm as firmly as he dared. "Lily, can you hear me?"

Her eyes struggled open and he brushed the dirt and dust from her face. "I'm going to get you out of here," he said, tossing pieces of roof and wood away.

"Ben, get them out." A trembling hand pointed toward the two girls.

"I'm getting all of you out of here." He dug through the debris that trapped her, ignoring the cuts on his hands, as he grabbed jagged pieces of the shattered ceiling and tossed them away.

A sickening crack ripped through the sound of the fire. Another piece of the roof broke free and fell. He covered her body with his as the charred wood exploded on the ground beside them.

The girls screamed and clung to each other, shrinking in the corner as if the shadows could save them.

The roof was being eaten away by flames, inch by sickening inch, burning fragments raining down on them. They were running out of time. Attacking the rubble as he coughed, he scooped away the smaller pieces, desperate to get her free.

Putting her hand on his, Lily stopped his frantic movements. "Ben, please." Her voice barely carried over the tumult that surrounded them, a whisper that pierced his heart. "You have to take them. Now."

His hand gripped hers, willing her to understand. "I'm not leaving you."

"You have to." Tears glistened in her eyes, but she was unwavering. "Please Ben. Get them out of here."

He looked at the frightened little girls. Dirt and ash clung to their hair and covered their faces. He couldn't remember their names, but he had seen them in this very room, singing and playing with Lily. He had seen them in their sheep costumes on the dock getting ready for the performance they would never give. Terror twisted their faces and broke his heart.

The weight of the decision pressed down on him. He kissed her forehead, feeling the unnatural chill of her skin beneath his lips, and conviction filled his words. "I'm coming back for you."

Tears rolled down her cheeks, cutting through the ash like a river through a dry land. Squeezing his hand, she nodded.

He touched her face, and though it ripped his heart out, he left her. Scooping the sobbing girls into his arms, he ran through the fire. Their cries echoed in his ears, but he didn't listen. He focused on each step, running through the smoke, looking for a way out. He shoved the back door open and a wall of fire blazed in front of him, the heat licking at his skin.

His shoulders burned and his lungs ached for air as he turned and ran along the loading dock, sticking close to the undamaged side of the building. Smoke stung his eyes, but he didn't stop.

At the front of the church, Evan and Noah and a group of people had gathered with the other kids, the firelight bathing their faces in red and orange. Ben swayed as he passed the kids to Evan. A mother wailed as she grabbed one of the girls and wrapped her in her arms.

"Mama!" the girl cried and clutched her mom.

Noah grabbed his arm. "Where's Lily?"

Ben ignored the pain in his body and the dizziness that crowded the edges of his mind. "I'm going to get her."

Before Noah could stop him, he ran back into hell.

Sirens chased him, as he raced back across the parking lot, but they wouldn't make it in time to save her. He grabbed the door to the children's church wing. Pain ignited in his hand as the burning metal seared his palm. The smoke was thicker as the flames closed in, it settled above his head like an impenetrable cloud of ash and acid.

His lungs gasped for air, tears and smoke blurred his vision, and he couldn't see more than a few feet in front of him as he shuffled down the dark hallway, feeling for the open door to her classroom.

The gaping hole in the ceiling had grown, debris and embers covered the floor. The sky above was red, ignited into an inferno that blazed like a dying sun.

He slid to his knees beside Lily and touched her face. "Lily? Can you hear me?"

She didn't move. Blood trickled down her forehead, tracing a path down the side of her face.

He shook her harder. "Lily? Lily, wake up."

A chunk of drywall dropped to the floor by the window. Flames licked their way into the classroom and the wall behind him burst into flame, the heat burning his back as the fire crawled closer. They had to get out.

He pushed and shoved the pile of debris that buried her body, but a broken section of the ceiling joist was lying across her chest, the thick, wood beam pinning her down. He braced his legs against the ground and tucked his hands under the splintered wood. The muscles in his arms, shoulders, and back burned as he strained against the weight, but it was too heavy.

He collapsed on his knees, struggling to breathe, his eyes burning. His hands were ripped and bloodied, so he pushed his shoulder against the beam, crying out with effort, but it refused to move. The wall behind them was brilliant with flames. Death was stalking them, laughing with every snap of the fire, intent on dragging them into its fiery depths.

Ignoring the pain in his palms, knowing it was futile but refusing to give up, he forced his hands under the wood again. He wouldn't leave her here. The heaviness of the weight he bore, the impossibility of it, the emptiness of his effort descended on him. He couldn't do it. He couldn't save her. He couldn't save himself.

He screamed in frustration, but he had nothing left to give. His strength was gone. Lifting his eyes to the flame-framed sky, he saw an endless blackness stretching before him.

"Jesus, help me!" he cried. "Help me."

From the depths of his childhood, an image filled his mind. His grandmother reading him a story of three men thrown into a furnace, consigned to a brutal, fiery death. But in the midst of the flames, a fourth man walked with them.

God hadn't spared them from the fire, but He'd endured it with them. He stood by their side and led them through it because they trusted in Him. He never left them, never abandoned them, and never stopped loving them.

A cool breeze washed over him and suddenly he knew. He wasn't alone. He knew it as certainly as he felt the heat of the flames. He'd never been alone.

He turned his back on the fire and strength surged through him as he gripped the beam and tensed his muscles. It shifted an inch, then another. Gritting his teeth against the pain, he forced the broken wood to the side.

The window on the far wall exploded in a shower of glass, and fire filled the empty space. He lifted Lily into his arms, her head rolling back as he staggered through the burning haze. The hallway was clogged with smoke, but he knew the way, he had walked this hallway with her too many times to forget it. Holding her tight against his chest, he forced the door open, stumbling from the fire and into the night.

Water showered over them, washing away the dust and the grime as he carried her towards the flashing lights of a fire truck.

A firefighter spotted them and ran over. "I've got her," he said and gently took Lily from his arms. With her weight gone, he slipped, his legs giving out and he started to fall, but Noah wrapped his arms round him.

"It's okay, Ben."

He leaned against Noah, swaying unsteadily. Behind him, fire fighters worked to save the church while a crowd of people watched helplessly.

He didn't notice the cameras. He didn't see the crowds. All he saw was Lily's limp body being loaded into the ambulance.

Chapter Thirty-Six

BEN SAT IN THE ASHES of the ruined church. The back of the building was a blackened husk. The children's church wing was gone, reduced to ash and rubble. Dust choked water flowed across the parking lot carrying away the ruined remnants of the Hollywood Mission. Police and firefighters whispered that it looked like someone had set the stage on fire and the flames spread to the church, carried by the dry Los Angeles wind.

Noah had gone to the hospital with Lily. Ben wanted to go. He wanted to see her, but he couldn't move. He sat in the water and dirt, watching the firefighters roll up the long hoses that snaked across the asphalt and tried to understand.

Exhaustion lined Evan's face when he sank to the ground beside him. He had stayed to make sure all of the kids were reunited with their parents. Not one child had been injured. Even the two girls Ben had rescued were unhurt.

The police arrested a young drug addict who had been in the crowd watching the fire. Evan identified him as the same man who had threatened Lily and the church before Christmas. Detective Sullivan came by and took charge of the investigation and promised to keep them informed, but that was small comfort at the moment. The church was gone.

The exhausted pastor rubbed his hands across his soot-covered face as a police car disappeared around the corner, the bedraggled drug addict in the backseat. "I won't ever be able to thank you enough for what you did, Ben. You saved my daughter's life. There aren't enough words to tell you how grateful I am."

Ben raked his hand through his wet hair, hissing at the sting in his burned and broken palms. "It wasn't me."

Evan looked at him. "What do you mean, it wasn't you?"

A tear rolled down Ben's cheek. He brushed it away but another took its place. "Lily told me to leave. She told me to get those two girls out. When I went back for her, the fire was getting closer. I—" He stopped and looked up at the sky. "I cried out to God. I begged Him to help me. I wanted Him to save her."

He was quiet for a long moment. The words were heavy on his tongue. He knew saying them would change everything and some last part of his heart wanted to hold them back. He wanted to forget what had happened. Already his mind was trying to explain it away, to make excuses, to steal the truth from him before he set it free. But you can't explain away a miracle.

"I was so wrong," he said. "About everything." Tears broke free and he dropped his head, sobbing into his blistered and bloody hands. "All these years I thought God hated me. My grandmother tried to tell me the truth, but I didn't listen. I didn't want any part of a God who would stand by and watch me suffer. But in there . . . " He stared at the burned out church, the building that could have been his tomb. "I finally got it. He was there all the time. In spite of everything I said, everything I did, He was always there. As soon as I said His name, I knew. God was there."

Evan wrapped his arm around Ben's shoulders, drawing him close, heedless of the dirt and the ash, the firefighters and the police, pulling him into his arms like a son coming home. "Thank You, Father," he prayed. "Thank You for saving him from the fire. Thank You for bringing him home."

The simple prayer resonated in Ben's heart. It filled him, banishing the shadows and the emptiness he had carried with him for so long in the light of God's perfect love. He wept in the ashes of everything that had been destroyed. Evan prayed for him and he let the words seep into his heart. The sun broke through the darkness of night and as the first rays of a new day crested the horizon, Ben turned to the God he had rejected and offered him the rest of his life.

*****

Lily opened her eyes and blinked against the brightness. Sunlight stung her eyes and she turned her head away from the light. Confusion filled her mind. Starched white sheets. A hospital curtain. The steady beep of a heart rate monitor.

"Hey, you're awake." Noah's voice startled her and she turned her head. Dark circles ringed his eyes and the faint scent of smoke clung to his clothes.

She moved her arm and winced as an IV embedded in her hand pulled against her skin. The beeps of the monitors raced as fear skittered through her heart. Taking a deep breath, she tried to calm down, to make sense of everything. She had a vague memory of waking up last night and seeing a doctor hovering above her bed. She had disjointed images of her dad and Noah and . . .

Ben. Ben had been here. She tried to grab on to the image of him, his face dirty and his hair wild and messy, but it disappeared before she could hold on to it.

She tried to sit up, but her body wouldn't cooperate. Noah reached for the bed control and pressed a button that slowly raised the back.

"What happened?" The last time she had been in a hospital room was the day her mother died. This room had the same white walls, the invasion of machines and wires, the same hushed whispers in the hallway. Panic started to build in her chest. She didn't want to be there. She wanted to go home.

"You've been unconscious since the fire." As he spoke, he pressed the button for the nurse. "Smoke inhalation, a few broken ribs, and a concussion."

Fire. The word opened a floodgate of memories. Closing her eyes, she could see the flames again, feel the searing heat. She heard the screams of the kids, remembered holding the door open as they ran past her, then the ear splitting crack and the rush of air as the ceiling collapsed.

"The kids—" she began.

"They're all fine. Every one of them."

"But Jennifer and Beth—" The girls had been hiding in the corner, too afraid to move. She'd been trying to get them to leave with her when the roof collapsed.

"It was, Ben, wasn't it?" His voice had pulled her out of the darkness. In the midst of the fire, somehow he had found her. "Ben saved them."

Noah nodded. "He told us you made him take the girls and leave. He got them out. And then . . . then he went back for you."

She pressed her fingers against her eyes and she was back in the classroom, trapped under the rubble, the weight crushing her chest, helpless to save the little girls who trusted her, depended on her. Their frightened cries were the last thing she heard as she slipped into blackness.

Then suddenly Ben was there, his gentle eyes looking into hers. The smell of the smoke and the heat of the flames edged at the corners of her mind. But she watched him leave. He picked up the girls and disappeared into the smoke. Looking through the hole in the roof into the sky, feeling the lick of the fire as it crept closer, she knew she was going to die. She prayed. She prayed for her family, she prayed for the kids to be safe. The last thing she remembered was praying for Ben.

"He was a real life hero, Sis. He ran back into the building right before the fire trucks arrived." Tears gathered in his eyes as he held her hand. "The fire was so bad, I didn't think we'd see either of you ever again. And then wouldn't you know it, here comes Ben, covered in soot, carrying you in his arms."

She tried to picture it, but she couldn't. Ben had come back for her. He went back into the fire . . . for her.

"Knock, knock." Ben stood in the doorway holding a big bouquet of flowers, the pinks and yellows bright against the stark white of the hospital room walls. "Can I come in?"

Noah stood and clapped him on the back. "Absolutely."

Crossing the small room, he sat in the chair Noah vacated and set the flowers on the rolling table beside the bed, their spring scent drowning out the lingering smell of smoke and ash. Neither of them noticed when Noah quietly slipped out and closed the door.

"How are you feeling?"

"I'm okay. Thanks to you."

He reached for her hand and she gasped when she saw the bandages that crisscrossed his palms. "From the fire?" She turned his hands over. Thick, white gauze was wrapped from his wrists to his knuckles. The parts of his fingers that extended beyond the bandages were cut and scraped.

"No stuntman this time."

She traced a pattern on the bandage on his hand. "When I told you to take the girls. I . . . I didn't think you'd come back. I didn't want you to come back. I wanted you to be safe."

Ben gripped her hand. "I'm never leaving you again."

She shifted in the bed and uncertainty washed over her. "Ben—" She tried again, uncertainty turning to fear and fear turning to horror.

"Lily, what's wrong?"

The panic that had taken root in her chest bloomed and spread until she thought she would pass out. She tried to move, but she couldn't. She told herself to move, to get out of the bed, to run away from the cords, the machines, and the smell of antiseptic and death. But her body betrayed her. She was trapped in the bed.

She looked at Ben, too afraid to even cry. "I can't feel my legs."

Chapter Thirty-Seven

LILY STARED AT THE BLANK, white walls. Her room was awash with flowers. From her dad and Noah, from Kate, even Chris Johnston had sent a big bouquet of daisies. But most of the flowers were from Ben. He brought her flowers every time he came to visit. And he came every day. He was there when she realized her legs weren't moving and he was there when the endless parade of doctors came through to poke and prod her.

She had tried to listen as Dr. Fernando talked about damage to the nerves in her spinal column, but the only word she heard was paralysis. The word echoed in her mind, replaying over and over until she thought her head would explode. *Paralyzed.* She was paralyzed. Dr. Fernando said it could be temporary. With enough time and physical therapy, the nerves might be able to heal and restore the connection to her leg muscles.

"But," the sympathy in his voice made her skin crawl. He could use all the nice words he wanted, but his tone told her enough. She would never walk again. "I also want you to understand that we can't be certain of the extent of the damage just yet. It could be temporary inflammation pressing on the nerves and interfering with neural communication that will eventually subside. Or it could be permanent damage to the nerves. There is just no way of knowing right now. Only time will tell if the nerves can be healed."

The doctor was gentle and compassionate as he examined her legs. Her heavy, useless legs. He talked about physical therapy and surgery, but all she heard was that she might never walk again.

Ben had been beside her the whole time, listening to the diagnosis, asking questions, telling her that everything would be fine. But he didn't know that. He was saying words that didn't mean anything.

When he tried to take her hand, she pulled away. She wanted to ignore the hurt on his face so she turned to the wall. And for the past three days that was what she had done. She stared at the wall and waited to fall asleep so she could forget for a few hours that her life was over.

*****

Ben sat in a stained chair beside a stack of expired magazines in the hospital waiting room. Helplessness engulfed him. Lily was lying in her hospital bed, withdrawing more and more every day, retreating into a space he couldn't reach. He didn't know how to talk to the God he had just met, but he tried. So far all he could manage was a desperate plea for Lily to be okay.

Picking at the bandages on his hands, he wished there was something more he could do.

"Mr. Prescott?"

His head flew up, expecting a doctor with more bad news, but instead he saw a short, balding man dressed in jeans and a flannel shirt, twisting a worn ball cap in his hands.

"Yes?" Ben was tired, he was worried, and he didn't know if he had it in him to sign an autograph.

"I'm sorry to bug you. My name's Pete. I'm a photographer."

Ben stiffened. The last thing he needed right now was a reporter looking for a story. "Listen Pete, this isn't a good time."

"I'm not looking for a photo." Pete shifted his weight and he looked over his shoulder. "I just . . . I was at the church that night. I was sitting there waiting for you to come by." The ball cap twisted more, crumpling beneath his sweaty palms. "It's nothing personal, really, it's just a job."

Ben didn't say anything and the photographer shuffled on his feet like a jittery child who'd been caught stealing cookies. "While I was waiting I took some practice shots. Checking my settings and stuff for when you got there. Anyway, I was there when the fire started. I got a bunch of photos, even got some of you carrying the girl out. I hope you don't mind, but I already sold those ones."

Ben didn't reply. There was nothing he could do about it anyway. His phone had been destroyed in the fire and he hadn't gotten a new one. He had no idea what the press was saying and he didn't care. Let them print whatever they wanted. The only thing he cared about was Lily.

"I went home to email the photos to the magazine and see what else I had. And that's when I noticed something on these pictures." Stuffing the wrinkled hat back on his head, he pulled a manila envelope out of his bag and handed it to Ben.

A series of photos spilled into his bandaged hands. In the first photo, the stage still standing behind the church. And there, next to the stage was the image of a person. The second photo was an enlargement. As he looked at the picture, cold, hard rage exploded behind his eyes. He stared at the grainy image, the unmistakable blonde hair, unwilling to believe what he saw.

Noah came to the waiting room with two cups of coffee, his eyes settling on the photographer. "What's going on?"

Stuffing the photos back in the envelope, Ben stood quickly. "I've got to go. Tell Lily I'll be back soon."

"Where are you going?"

He turned a hard stare towards Noah. "I'm going to talk to an old friend."

Chapter Thirty-Eight

BEN WALKED INTO THE BISTRO like he was walking onto a battlefield. A week's worth of stubble darkened his face and the hard set of his eyes chased away both friends and autograph seekers.

The maître d' retreated behind his fancy podium when Ben yanked the front door open.

"Mr. . . . Mr. Prescott." He stuttered, clearly unnerved by his famous patron's entrance. "We weren't expecting you."

Without a word, Ben walked past the maître d' to the dining room. He didn't have time for fake charm or celebrity swagger. Heads turned his direction but he was focused on only one table and nothing was going to stop him.

Dropping the manila envelope on top of a stack of papers on the table, he pulled out a chair and sat down between her and Derek. The stunned silence that reigned when he walked in graduated to hushed whispers that swirled around his back.

A young waitress approached the table, but he raised his hand and stopped her before she could give him a menu.

"I'm not staying." His words were cold and clipped. Pivoting on her heel, the waitress disappeared just as quickly as she had appeared leaving the three of them in tense silence.

"That was unnecessary." Zoe cleared her throat and set down her delicate silver fork, a patronizing smile fixed on her face.

Derek started to rise, quick to make an escape, but Ben stopped him. "Sit."

Ben's hands fisted under the table and he welcomed the pain as his fingers dug into the raw skin under the gauze bandages. Images of Lily trapped in the fire, the sound of two little girls crying in fear, the resignation on the doctor's face as he tried to explain the damage to Lily's legs, it all came rushing back in one swift wave of rage and he threw caution to the wind.

Grabbing the manila envelope, he pulled out the photos and spread them out on the table. Then he looked at his assistant. The fear he saw in his eyes was all the confirmation he needed. He wanted to leap across the table, to punch him until the anger passed, to make him pay for what he'd done. Instead, he stared at him, daring him to deny it.

Derek turned pale. His hands shook as he tried to pick up his water glass. The icy liquid spilled onto the tablecloth and splashed his sleeves. Tiny beads of sweat glistened on his forehead and he licked his lips.

"I . . . it was an accident." The words burst forth like a dam breaking free. "You weren't supposed to be there. I checked your phone. You were gone and Lily . . . she always went home with you. No one was supposed to be there."

Hysteria tinged his words, but Ben was beyond feeling sorry for the man he had trusted, the man he had promised to help. "You're going to pay for this."

"I didn't have a choice," Derek whimpered and shoved a stack of papers into his hands. The first was a contract naming Zoe as Derek's agent and manager. The second was an offer from a major film studio. "I just wanted my shot. This was my chance."

The room tilted and Ben sat back, feeling drugged by the horror of it. Zoe. It had always been Zoe. The emails he thought he forgot, Giselle's sudden appearances. Zoe had been playing him all along, toying with his life, using Derek to manipulate him into doing what she wanted, nearly killing Lily, and for what?

He looked at her with fresh eyes and it was as if a mask had been ripped away. Everything he had ignored, denied, or excused was laid before him in all its stark and vile reality.

"Why?" The words were a strangled whisper, forced past the guilt that snaked around his throat.

"Why what?" She swirled her wine, watching the red liquid make circles in the glass. "Why do I put up with a client who ignores my advice and seems intent on ruining not only his career, but mine as well? I took a chance on you, Ben. I made you what you are. So yes, I protected you. Your career was about to tank. That church would have been the end of everything we'd worked for. You couldn't see it, but I did, and I made sure we'd stay on top."

"People could have died. Lily is in the hospital. She might never walk again, and you don't care about anything except yourself. How many lives have you ruined to stay on top?"

"Don't play the hero with me. I know who you really are." Venom dripped from her lips. "You didn't care how it happened, as long as you got rich and famous. You can pretend to be the nice guy, but your hands are just as dirty as mine." She tossed her napkin on to her plate. "I make stars. That's what I do. If you don't like the way the game is played then you should go back to that tiny town in Indiana and make way for someone who has the guts to do what it takes."

He reached for the photos, but Zoe snatched them from his grasp, tucking them into her bag, one more scandal she'd make disappear. "You won't get away with this."

"You can't touch me, Ben. Everyone in this town owes me." Triumph glittered in her eyes as she stared at him.

Leaning back in his chair, he loosened the top three buttons of his shirt, pulling apart the collar to reveal a thin black wire taped to his chest. "Not everyone."

The front door of the restaurant slammed open as four uniformed police officers rushed in, Detective Sullivan following in their wake.

As the officers surrounded the table, her mouth moved, but no words came out. For the first time since he'd known her, Zoe Waltham didn't have an answer. The woman who spun stories and turned the tides of bad publicity was staring into the face of her own demise.

Voices erupted in the restaurant, cell phones flew out and started recording.

"Thank you, Mr. Prescott." Detective Sullivan shook his hand. "We can take it from here."

Zoe and Derek were handcuffed and led through the restaurant. Ben followed, heedless of the cameras and unconcerned by the chaos he left behind.

A large crowd was already gathered outside the restaurant, drawn by the flashing lights, eager for a front row seat. Zoe tripped as the officer holding her arm led her to a waiting police car. "Don't do this, Ben. You need me. We can still fix this."

Even as she tried to negotiate, the officer pushed her into the back of the police car.

"Wait." Ben put his hands on the hood, leaned down and peered into the darkness of the car. "One more thing, Zoe." Hope blossomed in her face. Hope that flared for an instant then vanished. "You're fired."

Disgraced Agent Arrested for Arson

By Alyssa Harrison

Zoe Waltham, once known as Hollywood's Star Maker has become Hollywood's Inmate Maker. She and an assistant were arrested yesterday at LA hot spot, The Bistro, on suspicion of arson. Witnesses say that her star client, Ben Prescott, walked into the restaurant and confronted Ms. Waltham about a fire that had taken place at the church where he and his mystery woman, Lily Shaw, had been preparing for a community event.

Ms. Waltham has denied any involvement in the fire that left Ms. Shaw hospitalized, but the Los Angeles Police Department disagrees. Ms. Waltham and Prescott's former assistant, and aspiring actor, Derek Phillips, were arrested in front of a dining room full of Hollywood power brokers and celebrities. Inside sources have confirmed that Phillips has agreed to a plea bargain in exchange for his testimony against Ms. Waltham.

Actors and actresses represented by Ms. Waltham have fled the disgraced agent like rats jumping from a sinking ship. The Alleged Arsonist Agent's assets have been frozen pending an investigation and she is currently in custody unable to post bail.

Ben Prescott has not returned requests for a comment and the hospital where Ms. Shaw was admitted has not released any details about her condition.

The owner of The Bistro's reaction to the unfolding drama was, "I'm going to be very nervous whenever Ben Prescott steps foot in my restaurant."

Chapter Thirty-Nine

BEN CAME INTO THE HOSPITAL room carrying another bouquet of flowers. She didn't say anything. She just watched as he searched for an empty space, finally pushing a few other vases together to make room for the newest addition. Then he sat in the chair beside her bed.

"The doctor said you could go outside today. Are you up for some sunlight?" When she didn't respond, he forced a smile onto his face and tried again. "It's a little chilly, but I've got a blanket for you. What do you say?"

She shook her head, her gaze fixed on the ceiling. She knew every chip, every scratch, every ripple in the cold, white walls that surrounded her. As much as she hated the hospital room, the idea of going outside and facing the world in a wheelchair was too much. She couldn't do it. So she'd stay in her whitewashed prison and let life go on without her.

Ben toyed with the edge of the sheet dangling off the bed, his bandaged hands still clumsy and awkward and she resisted the urge to reach out and touch him, to feel the warmth of his hand under hers. Emptiness yawned like a chasm inside her and she wanted to scream, but even that seemed too hard.

"Lily." His voice was soft and low, the same gentle tone everyone had started using around her. Like she was a child that had to be coddled.

"I know this is hard. But you can do it. I'll be with you the whole time, but you have to fight. You can't give up. Not now."

Years of patience, of being strong, of being the good girl, snapped like a twig crushed under a careless foot.

"You know?" She whipped her head around to stare at him, every emotion she had kept locked inside, exploding in a torrent. "You know what this is like? When was the last time you were paralyzed? When was the last time you couldn't walk?" She dragged herself up to a sitting position and tossed her hair out of her eyes. She hated that she couldn't move. She couldn't walk out of the room, she couldn't even stand up and face him. She was confined to a bed, trapped in a body she couldn't use. "Don't tell me you know what this is like. Because you don't."

He reached for her hand, but she pulled away. Hurt broke across his face, but he didn't back down. "You're right. I don't know what you're going through. So tell me. Tell me how I can help you."

The kindness on his face was more than she could bear. She was suffocating under the sympathy in his expression, crushed by the shattered pieces of the dreams she had dared to believe in. Dreams that died in the fire.

"You can't help me. You should just go."

Across the room, the second hand ticked on the clock. It shuddered and jumped every time it moved, like every second it forgot how to move forward so it lurched awkwardly ahead, trying to keep up with time speeding by. She focused on the jerky movement, waiting for him to get up and walk away.

But he didn't move. "I told you before, I'm not leaving you."

He laid his hand on the bed, not touching her, but close enough that she could reach him if she wanted to. Instead she pulled further away, building wall after wall until even the few inches that separated them were a canyon too wide to cross.

"Why not? I don't have anything to offer you. Are you planning to wheel me down the red carpet at your next premiere? Won't that be a touching scene for the gossip sites? Famous movie star throws his life away on paraplegic girlfriend."

Shock drove him back and he recoiled from her words. "Stop it, Lily."

"No." Anger took over and the words flew off her tongue. She didn't care about the consequences. She didn't care who she hurt. She just wanted to be left alone. "You can't write a check and make this okay. I don't want your pity, Ben. I don't want your guilt. And I don't want your stupid flowers. Just go away. Go away and leave me alone."

She choked on a sob and turned back to the wall. Squeezing her eyes closed, she forced herself to hold back the tears. She listened for his footsteps, waiting to hear the door to close, waiting for him walk out of her life. Then she would cry. Then she would sob and scream and mourn for the life she lost.

But there was only silence. He hadn't moved, she was sure of it. She didn't want to turn around. She didn't want to face him. So she kept her eyes closed and waited for the end.

He stayed by her bed as the minutes crept silently past. She refused to face him, but she felt his presence as surely as if she was staring at him. Noah's words echoed in her mind, *Ben went back into the fire. Ben carried you out.*

He didn't deserve to be treated this way.

If it had been anyone else sitting there so quietly, she might have thought he was praying. But she knew better. A sinister whisper burrowed into her heart, maybe he had been right all along. Maybe she had been the fool, putting her hope in a childish fantasy. After all, look what happened. She had served God her whole life. She prayed, read her Bible, she did everything she was supposed to do and still she ended up here, broken and empty. Maybe she *had* been wrong all along.

The sun was setting when her dad walked in the room with a take out bag of non-hospital food. He looked from her to Ben. "Well, this looks fun."

Ben stood, his body radiating weariness. "I'm going to head home. Good night, Lily."

A lifetime of politeness forced her to speak and she mumbled "Good night." As he left the room, she caught sight of a book in his hand. It was the Bible she had given him for Christmas. Her breath stuck in her throat. Had he been reading it the whole time?

Her dad dropped the bag on the table and sat in the chair Ben just vacated. "Sweetheart, what are you doing?"

She rubbed the tears from her eyes. "I don't know."

He climbed onto the bed and held her as she cried, wrapping her in his arms the way he had done when she was a little girl. She heard him praying over her, soothing words full of faith. She tried to speak, but she couldn't. The words that had once come so easily vanished before they formed. She wanted to cry out to God. She tried to find the words, but they were gone, burned up in the fire that had taken her legs and her freedom. She had lost her legs, she had lost Ben, and now she was losing her faith.

Chapter Forty

BEN LOOKED UP FROM THE Bible he was reading. Cold, forgotten coffee sat on the table beside him. He'd been sitting in this same corner of the couch in the hospital waiting room for nearly a month. Lily might not want him in her room, but he said he wouldn't leave her, and if that meant long days under the fluorescent lights of the chilly room so be it.

Every day anxious and worried parents, friends, and loved ones silently dropped into the scattered chairs and sofas, waiting for news. Tears of relief and loss littered the floor and he had seen them all. Evan and Noah took turns sitting with him and he was struck by the thought that they were nursing him back to health as much as they were caring for Lily.

On most days, Chris came by for a few hours to keep him company. On one of those days a terrified mother had come into the room, weeping into her hands. As her sobs grew, Ben couldn't stand to watch her suffer any more. He sat beside her and asked if he could help.

That one question opened a floodgate and she poured out her heart to him. Her seven-year-old son was fighting cancer. Things had taken a turn for the worse and he had to be admitted. The agony of watching him endure so much pain and the draining side effects of chemotherapy had overwhelmed her and she just needed to get away for a few minutes. So when the nurses came to check on him and update his vitals, she escaped to a place where she could cry without her son seeing it.

No one had been more surprised than Ben when he asked if he could pray for her and her son. She gripped his hand like a lifeline as he prayed, the words coming from deep within. He didn't think about it, he didn't script it, he just let the words flow and he knew God was listening. Somewhere in the quiet of the waiting room, in the days spent reading the Bible Lily had given him, he started to trust the words he read. They seeped into his heart and took root like seeds settling into fertile soil.

"So you're the movie star." The woman standing in the doorway in black pants and a pinstripe blazer, her intense stare focused on him, was not a grieving mother. Arms crossed over her chest, she regarded him with speculation and appraisal in her eyes. Beside him, Chris drew in a sharp breath as they both looked at her.

"I'm sorry?" The first few days he'd been here, he'd attracted some attention from the hospital staff. A few had ventured in to ask for autographs, but after a week they'd gotten used to him and left him alone. He'd become less of a novelty and more of a fixture.

She crossed the room in quick, determined steps and stopped right in front of him, looming over him in a black-clad tower of authority. "I'm the best friend."

While Chris was paralyzed in mute shock, Ben put the pieces together and smiled. "You must be Kate." He extended his hand, and she shook it firmly. "I'm Ben. This is my friend Chris."

The unusually quiet director mumbled something that sounded like hello, but Kate's attention was fixed on Ben.

"How's Lily?" Pulling over a chair, she sat across from him. Her dark, red hair hung in waves past her shoulders and intelligence sparked in her green eyes. She sat straight in the chair, like a lawyer preparing for cross-examination.

Her expression didn't give anything away and Ben knew he was probably on shaky ground with her. But he also knew how much her presence would mean to Lily. "Physically, she's improving. They started her on physical therapy and she's learning how to use a . . . " He paused, struggling to get the word out. "A wheelchair."

He lifted the coffee cup, remembered that it had gone cold and set it down again as Kate waited for him to continue. "But emotionally . . . " He rubbed his hand over his eyes, feeling the familiar pull of helplessness that had become his constant companion. Over and over he reminded himself that God was in control. Under her searching gaze, he chose that trust again. "She's struggling. It will mean so much to her that you're here."

Kate nodded and the tension that had kept her back stiff and rigid relented and she relaxed a little. "I wish I could have come sooner. When my dad called and told me what happened, I tried to book a flight, but the firm is pretty strict with time off." She glanced around the waiting room, her eyes lingering briefly on Chris, before skipping past.

Ben heard his friend suck in a breath.

"So what are you doing out here? Have you been banished?" she asked with a knowing smile.

"She doesn't want to see me." Saying the words didn't make them hurt any less. Lily didn't want to see him. She didn't want him near her.

"That sounds like Lily. And she thinks I'm stubborn." Kate rolled her eyes and he found himself liking the straight talking lawyer. "So you sit out here? Every day?"

Hearing someone else say it made Ben question his sanity. Spending his days on this uncomfortable couch, and for what purpose? She didn't even know he was here, and if she did find out, she'd probably tell him to go. But he had no plans to leave. If that meant living in this waiting room, he'd do it.

"I'm not leaving her."

Kate crossed her legs as she watched him, her free foot bouncing in time with whatever thoughts she was working out in her mind. If there were more questions coming, he was ready for them. He wouldn't let anyone chase him away, not even Lily's best friend.

"Well." Standing abruptly, she straightened her jacket, and slung her purse over her shoulder. "It was nice to meet you." Without waiting for a reply, she turned and left the room, her flaming hair dancing behind her.

Ben watched her go, a pang of jealousy that she was going to see Lily churning in his heart.

"What was that?" Chris was still staring at the empty doorway, as if he expected her to suddenly appear again and drag them to court.

The dumbfounded look on his friend's face was priceless and for the first time in almost a month, Ben laughed.

*****

Lily sat in a wheelchair, staring out the window. Sunlight was trying to peek through the bleak February sky, but thunderous grey clouds continued to roll in. Pulling the hem of the lap blanket up, she looked at her toes, willing them to move. Her heart raced with the exertion as she tried to force them to cooperate, to obey the command in her brain, but nothing happened. It was like they were disconnected from her body. Like her legs had been severed.

But they were still there. Lifeless and numb.

Like her.

The door opened with a soft whoosh and she closed her eyes. She didn't want to see any more nurses or doctors. They all plastered happy smiles on their faces, their voices positive and upbeat. It made her want to scream. The therapist who worked with her legs kept up a steady stream of motivational quotes as he worked, but she knew the therapy was useless. She went only to keep the doctors happy so they'd let her go home. Once she was home she could hide away and finally be left alone.

Gripping the cold metal of the wheels, she forced the chair away from the window in a jerky semi-circle. When she faced the door, she gasped and tears pricked her eyes.

Before she could speak, Kate crossed the small room and wrapped her in a hug. The tears that had gathered burst forth and ran down her cheeks and onto her friend's blazer. She'd been holding so much back, but just by her presence, Kate drew it all out. The fear, the anger, the hurt rushed out of her soul and into the arms of the one person who already knew her secrets. Her best friend took it all, absorbing it as she cried.

When the tears ran dry, Kate sat beside her and handed her a wad of tissues. "I go away for a few years and look what happens."

"How did you know?" Lily was ashamed that she hadn't called Kate, that she hadn't told her about the fire or the paralysis. It was as if keeping the news from Kate meant that in at least one person's mind she was still whole and healthy.

"My dad called me the night it happened. I would have been here sooner, but my boss was being a stickler about the case files on my desk. I've been kind of a wreck, but Noah was texting me updates." She took a tissue from Lily's crumpled pile and dabbed at her smudged mascara.

Self-consciously, Lily tucked a stray hair behind her ear. Kate was perfectly made up, stylish as always and she was sitting in a hospital gown. She couldn't even remember the last time she looked in a mirror.

"Thank you for coming."

Kate went to the rolling bedside table and poured water into a plastic cup. She handed it to Lily before sitting back down. "So I met your handsome movie star."

The cup froze at Lily's lips. Sadness crashed over her as his face flashed across her mind. She'd spent a month trying to forget him, to convince herself that she had never really cared for him, that she was right to chase him away. "You met Ben? How?"

Kate waited until she had taken a sip of water. "I saw him in the waiting room. He's in there with a cute friend . . . a director or something."

Disbelief and confusion warred for her attention. How could Ben be here? She hadn't seen him in weeks, not since she told him to leave her alone. He'd walked away and disappeared. Kate had to be wrong.

Unless . . .

A flicker of hope dared to breathe within her. What if he really was there?

But just as quickly as it flared to life, that hope was crushed again. She looked down at the wheelchair, the prison she had been consigned to and let the bitterness win. She'd heard the doctors and the therapists comparing notes, and she knew the chances of her ever walking again were becoming slimmer every day.

"He probably just feels guilty." Tiny pieces of cotton floated in the air as she shredded the tissues in her hands, picking them apart bit by bit until Kate reached over and covered her hand.

"I don't think that's it."

Lily wheeled the bulky chair to the corner and dumped the pile of torn pieces into the trash can. Dusting off her hands, she watched the tiny white particles dance in the thin shaft of light that broke through the clouds.

"He obviously cares about you . . . a lot. Are you sure you don't want to see him?"

Fresh pain ripped through Lily's heart. The more she tried to move on, the more Ben refused to disappear. "Of course I want to see him, but look at me." She waved her hands at the metal wheels. "Does this look like the cover of an entertainment magazine to you?"

Kate shook her head, her forehead wrinkling as she looked at the chair. "What does that matter?"

"It's his career. I don't want him giving it up to play nursemaid to me. I don't want to see him looking at me with pity every day. And I definitely don't want him staying with me because he feels guilty and blames himself." How she wished she could get out of the chair and pace. She was vibrating with anger and energy, but she was stuck, trapped in her own body, unable to get it out so it festered inside, like a parasite eating her away.

"And what if he's staying because he loves you?"

The words dove straight for her heart, squeezing until she thought it would burst. She looked away, studying the walls, the dying flowers on the window sill, the scratched medical notes on the whiteboard, anywhere but at her friend. "Why would he love me? Even God has forgotten about me."

"Oh, Lily." Kate pulled the chair over so she could face her. Gripping her hands, like she could will her to believe, she looked at her with every ounce of Irish stubbornness she possessed. "God loves you. He hasn't forgotten you."

Holding her best friend's hands she finally asked the question that had been plaguing her, haunting her dreams, and eroding her faith. She couldn't bring herself to ask her dad, not when she was supposed to be the good girl, the one with all the answers. But she didn't have an answer this time. "Then why can't I walk?"

Kate dropped her head and her shoulders slumped, and Lily knew it was wrong to put this on Kate. She had suffered so much, run from her family and from God when she sought the same answer Lily desperately wanted now.

"Do you remember when Megan died? I was so angry. I kept telling you that God could have saved her, but He didn't. My little sister died on that street because some drunk got behind the wheel of his car and God was watching, letting it happen." Kate's voice was raw with emotion, scraping the words as they slipped out. "Do you remember what you said to me?"

Lily shook her head, the memories of those days, the funeral and the fractures in Kate's family. The anger and the grief had exploded, tearing them all apart.

"You told me that God is still God even when everything falls apart. One man made a terrible choice and it cost me my sister, my family, and my faith. And when I wanted to give up on everyone and everything, you reminded me, God is still God."

"Then why won't He heal me?"

"I don't know. But I do know that He hasn't forgotten you. Lily, I saw the building . . . or what's left of it. It's a miracle you survived. God was right there with you. And He's with you now." Kate tugged on her hands so the chair rolled closer. Putting her hand under Lily's chin, she lifted Lily's face. "Don't let that twisted agent and her boy band reject henchman steal anything else from you."

In spite of herself, she laughed. "Boy band reject?"

"Did you see his hair?" Kate stood and pushed the wheelchair over to the window, then she brought her chair over to join it. "Look, I know I'm not a great example of holding on to your faith in the middle of the storm, but I'm trying. I do know that you're going to get through this and there's a supremely handsome movie star in the waiting room who wants to help you."

Lily watched the clouds shifting across the sky. Everything was changing and there was no going back. "I'm scared."

"That's okay." Kate wrapped her arm around her shoulder, and they sat side by side, two friends who had seen the best and worst of each other, staring into the horizon, waiting to see what it would bring. "You have to be scared before you can be brave."

Chapter Forty-One

LILY WAS DISCHARGED ON A Sunday morning. She looked at the calendar with a sharp pang of bitterness. She should have been at the church getting ready for service, her dad flipping through his sermon notes one more time and Noah working with the media team to set up. Instead she was sitting on a hospital bed waiting for someone to help her into a wheelchair so she could face the world again. And she wasn't sure she was ready to do that.

The doctors said there was nothing more they could do in the hospital. She needed time, therapy, and rest, so they were sending her home. She had a stack of discharge papers, a white, paper bag of medications, and a list of physical therapy appointments that seemed to go on forever.

While she waited for her dad, she tried to find God's hand in this mess. Thanks to Kate's visit and her gentle reminders, she didn't doubt that God loved her, and she didn't doubt that He was real. But she couldn't see the plan behind this pain. She was a teacher, she was a worship leader, but how could she continue to serve Him like this? Over and over she told herself, "God works all things for good," but the words felt hollow. How could this be good? How could any good come out of this? Who would take care of the kids after school? Who would sing on Sunday mornings and serve lunch to the hungry? If she couldn't do those things anymore, what purpose did she have?

The door opened and she tried to shake off her melancholy thoughts. She stuck a smile on her face, ready to pretend that she was okay. But when Ben walked in pushing a wheelchair, she was definitely not okay.

"What are you doing here?" The words flew from her mouth before she could stop them.

In spite of everything Kate said, she thought he had finally come to his senses and realized he was better off without her. To see him standing there, his hair a little longer, but still adorably disheveled, a warm smile on his face, it was like walking into a memory. As if none of this had happened and they could walk home in the sunset like they had so many times before.

Then she looked at the wheelchair he was pushing and it all came crashing back.

"I'm your ride," he said, setting the chair beside the bed and locking the brake. "Are you ready to go?"

Lily stared at him, trying to separate her feelings, but there were too many of them hitting her at once. "Where's my dad?"

"It's Sunday morning. He's at the church of course."

"Noah?"

"Church."

"Kate?" she squeaked.

He smirked as he looked at her. "I'm your guy, Lily. Everyone else is at church. I'm in charge of getting you out of here." Gently, he lifted her into his arms.

She fought the urge to melt into his embrace. Warmth radiated from his chest and for the first time since she had woken up in a hospital bed with no feeling in her legs, she felt safe.

All too soon, the warmth was gone, as he settled her in the chair. Grabbing a blanket from the basket underneath, he tucked it around her legs.

"Let's roll," he said.

They went through the front door of the hospital and she squinted against the sunlight. She'd been outside only a few times in the past month, quick trips for a bit of fresh air, but the promise of that small hospital room had always been hanging over her. Now that she was finally going home, the world seemed so much bigger. Too big for a girl who couldn't walk.

Scooping her out of the chair, he put her into the passenger seat of his car. As he collapsed the wheelchair and stored it in the trunk, she rolled the window down and breathed in the morning air. After all those weeks in the hospital, the unfiltered Los Angeles air was heavenly . . . smoggy, but heavenly, nonetheless.

He drove cautiously through the empty streets. It was a quiet Sunday morning, and she stared out the open window watching as the streets became more familiar. She was going home.

Then he drove past her house. Lily looked over her shoulder, watching her home fade into the distance. He couldn't have forgotten where she lived. "Where are you going?" she asked, but part of her already knew the answer and she was terrified.

"To the church."

Anxiety rippled through her. She imagined the stares she would get. She could already hear the murmurs that would follow her as she was wheeled into the sanctuary, and she felt sick. "I can't go there. Not yet."

He looked at her, his eyes darting between her and the road. The peace she saw there quieted some of the doubt that filled her mind.

He reached over and touched her hand, just a light caress, a whisper of his skin against hers. "Trust me, Lily. Please."

Worry wound its way around her heart. She wasn't ready for this.

They arrived at the church and Lily couldn't stop the gasp as she got her first glimpse of the devastation. The debris and soot had been washed away, but what remained still bore the scars of the fire. All the years they had spent here, all the memories they'd made rushed at her like an avalanche. Looking at the blackened walls, the empty space where the roof should have been, she remembered how many hours her mom had spent walking those halls. How long had they spent picking out a paint color? Lily and her mom had put up so many color samples the walls had looked like a patchwork quilt of browns and beiges. To see it all destroyed broke her heart.

"Ready?" Ben asked.

She wasn't. She wasn't ready at all. She sat in the car and stared at the building in front of her. She'd always assumed she'd spend her life there. And now it was gone. Burned up in a blaze of hatred and jealousy.

"Lily," his gentle voice wrapped around her. "It's going to be okay."

She took a deep breath and nodded. All too quickly, he set up the wheelchair and brought it around. He lifted her out of the car and set her in the chair. The warm blanket was back and wrapped around her legs before she even noticed the cold.

As he wheeled her up the sloping ramp of the loading dock, she thought she could smell the faint memory of smoke hovering over the church. After all the conversations between her parents about getting rid of the ancient concrete ramp, Lily was struck by the irony that she was the one who needed it.

The roof over the dock had been destroyed, but the wide, concrete platform itself had survived. There was a small podium at one end of the dock and Noah was setting up neat rows of plastic folding chairs. It looked like they were going to have an outdoor service.

A flash of yellow caught her eye and she looked to the back of the church where a giant bounce house was slowly inflating. Nearby a face painter was laying out her supplies and a colorful clown was blowing up a huge pile of balloons. It was the block party. They were finally having it. Joy welled up within her and for a second, she forgot about the chair she was sitting in.

Her dad was standing by the podium and he came over to give her a hug. "I'm so glad you're here, honey."

"Thanks, Dad."

"So," he said, his hand resting on her shoulder, "Are you up for a few songs?"

"Me? But, I . . . I'm . . . " She fumbled for the words, her hands gesturing limply to her legs.

Kneeling in front of her, he cupped her face in his hands, his eyes filled with love. "You are blessed by God. You are precious and honored in His sight. You have a gift to worship Him. Satan tried to silence you, but God rescued you. God hasn't given up on you and neither have I."

Swallowing the emotion that rose up in her throat, she looked at their makeshift church beside the ruins of the empty building. It was no mistake she was discharged that morning. It was no mistake that she was here. It might not make sense to her, but God was at work. No one could not stop what God had planned. The only question was whether she was willing to be a part of it.

"Okay, Dad. I'll do it."

"Well, hallelujah," he said and kissed her cheek. "I'm not going to preach today. After worship, we're going to have a special testimony. Once everyone arrives, I'll say a few words and then you can start."

She smiled through the worry while butterflies filled her stomach. "Do you think people will come?"

Her dad squeezed her shoulder. "Even if it's just us, that's enough. But I think God has something else in mind."

As her dad went back to his notes, Ben pushed her to the front of the dock and the music stand that was waiting there. "Now if you'll excuse me, I have to do something real quick." He winked at her and disappeared behind the church.

He was gone only for a few minutes when she heard a wild cheer followed by a flood of child-sized sheep racing around the corner. The kids surrounded her, everyone talking at the same time and fighting for a chance to hug her.

"We're so happy you're back, Miss Lily."

"Me too, Nate," Lily said as she looked at all of them in their costumes. "Have you been practicing?"

"Mr. Ben was in charge of us," Nate said proudly and pointed.

She looked over the crowd of cotton balls and saw Ben standing against the wall watching the happy reunion. Ben Prescott, movie star and international celebrity, had spent the past month helping a group of children rehearse their song.

"He even showed us some special acting tricks so we'll be extra good." Nate scooted closer to Lily and whispered in her ear. "Did you know he's in movies?"

She laughed. "Yes, I'd heard that."

Ben clapped his hands and the kids turned. "All right, little sheep, time to go backstage so no one sees you and ruins the surprise." The kids hugged her again then followed him back behind the church.

"Where do you want this?"

Lily looked over the railing. Chris was pushing a brand new grill through the parking lot.

"Chris?"

"Hey, Lily, I heard you were breaking out today. You look great."

Noah ran down the steps to check out the new grill. "Dude! This thing is awesome. Let's set it up over there." Together they walked to the far side of the parking lot where Kate was setting up a table with buns and condiments. She waved at Lily and blew her kisses.

"Well, look at that," her dad said, nodding towards the street.

Lily followed the direction of his gaze. People were streaming in to the parking lot. Families she recognized from the neighborhood mingled with celebrities she knew only from their pictures. The trickle became a river as more and more people arrived.

Ben returned and stood next to her.

"Did you do this?" she asked.

He shook his head. "Word about Zoe's arrest and what she did spread pretty fast. They all want to help."

She couldn't believe the turnout. She thought their work in Hollywood was over, burned up in smoke and fire. But here they were, with nothing but a slab of concrete and plastic chairs, and people were coming. She looked at the burned out building, the charred remains of the playground and classrooms. The building had been destroyed, but the presence of God remained.

As everyone settled in, nerves fluttered in her stomach. There was only an acoustic guitar to accompany her and she hadn't thought to ask who would be playing it. Looking at the sheet music in front of her, she exhaled in relief. They were all songs she knew by heart. Her dad had chosen them well.

There was laughter and tears as people saw the damage that had been done. Some of these families had been coming every day to clean up. Others brought food and water. Even more had stepped up to help keep the ministries going. The enemy thought he had defeated them, but they rose up stronger than before. Lily was overwhelmed by the outpouring of love she saw all around.

People filled the rows, and when they ran out of chairs, they stood against the railing. A gentle breeze began to blow, and she turned her face to the sun. Ben touched her shoulder then sat beside her and picked up the guitar.

She didn't have time to question him as her dad started to speak. "Good morning. Before we begin, I want to thank you all for your hard work and most especially for your prayers. God is good. We are blessed to be here. What Satan intended for evil, God is using for good. Right this minute He is using it for good." The congregation applauded and cheered. "And most importantly, He has brought my daughter back."

Tears gathered in her eyes as they applauded again. She looked out on the sea of faces before her. Noah, Kate, and Chris stood in a line by the railing, each of them smiling at her. Friends who were more like family, visitors who came just because they wanted to help, and somewhere in the crowd were people who would meet Jesus here today and leave forever changed.

Her dad nodded to her and she adjusted the microphone. She glanced at Ben who gave her an encouraging smile as he started to play.

Closing her eyes, she let the music fill her. She didn't think about the wheelchair or the burned walls. She didn't even think about the people in front of her. Opening her heart, she sang for God. She worshipped the God who saved her from the fire, the God who wasn't done with her yet.

As she sang, she gave Him her legs. If she never walked on this earth again she knew she would run to God in Heaven. She gave Him her future, her hopes, and her dreams, knowing He could be trusted with all of them. She sang because whatever He had planned was so much better than she could imagine.

The words flowed from her mouth and rose to the heavens. She sang of a love that surpasses everything else. And as she sang, she gave God her heart. She looked at Ben playing beside her, perfectly in synch with her, and she surrendered him to God. She would trust God with her life and her heart and she would not fear.

Worship rose from the ashes of the Hollywood Mission as her voice drew even more people. They heard the music and drifted in. They heard her voice and came without even knowing why. She didn't need her legs to serve God, she just needed to hear His voice and follow.

When she finished, she felt the change in the atmosphere. The Hollywood Mission was no longer a place of destruction and loss. It was holy ground.

Her dad walked to the front. "Instead of listening to me preach today, I have a special treat for you. Please welcome our guest speaker, Mr. Ben Prescott."

The congregation clapped and Lily stared as Ben set the guitar in its stand and took the microphone from her dad.

"As most of you know, I was here when the fire hit. You may also know that it was my agent, well, my former agent, who was responsible for starting the fire. Hatred, greed, and fear drove her to do it. What you may not know is that for a long time, I felt the same way." A hushed attention flowed through the crowd as they listened.

"I didn't know God. I knew only a lie about Him. I thought God hated me. I thought God wanted to control my life and then punish me when I messed up. Jesus was just another curse word to me. I didn't understand sacrifice, I didn't understand grace, and I certainly didn't understand love." He glanced at Lily and she was too stunned to even blush. She was as captivated by his words as the congregation.

"Then I came here. I'd like to tell you I came here because I wanted to change, but the truth is I came here because I was trying very hard not to change. I was trying to stop a scandal and I ended up being blackmailed into helping with this event. If you don't believe me, you should ask Noah." Noah's eyes popped open and a deep red stain spread across his cheeks. Kate smacked him on the arm, and he blushed even more. Lily didn't mind seeing her brother so uncomfortable and judging by the grin on Ben's face, he didn't ether.

"Then I met Pastor Evan. And Lily." She felt his eyes on her and she looked up. "This family showed me what it means to love. They showed me what it means to trust. They told me about a God I never knew. I didn't believe. Not for a long time. I was afraid of what believing would mean, what it would cost me. Some of you may know that I have a pretty fun job. And it pays a lot." The congregation laughed. "I didn't want to lose that. But then I found something that I loved even more." Ben turned towards her. "And I almost lost her."

His voice broke and he paused. "But God saved her. God was with us in the fire. You may think it was me carrying her out of the fire that night, but the truth is, God was carrying me. I didn't save anyone that night." He looked at her, his next words meant for her alone. "I was the one saved."

The words were like music, a balm to her soul, an answered prayer. Joy filled her heart and she wanted to jump and shout with thanksgiving.

"God pulled me out of the fire and brought me home. I stand here today to tell you, I believe."

Applause erupted and filled the air, and Lily was sure she could hear the angels rejoicing. Ben had come home.

Chapter Forty-Two

BEN SAT ON A BENCH beside Lily. Her cheeks were pink in the chilly afternoon and she couldn't stop smiling. All around her children ran and played, families sat and talked. Chris and Noah took turns grilling the hot dogs while Kate dished up the chips and drinks. The church was filled with laughter. She watched her dad pray with people she had never met. The kids finally got to perform their adorable sheep song. Everyone clapped and cheered for them and she couldn't remember ever seeing them so proud and full of life. It was a beautiful day.

"How are you doing?" Ben asked. She heard the concern in his question, but she felt great.

"I'm good." She marveled at her own words. "For the first time, I think I'm going to be okay."

"I never doubted it." He draped his arm over her shoulder and pulled her close.

Excitement spread through her and she embraced it. She didn't try to crush it, she let it flow, enjoying the freedom to dream again. Linking her fingers with his, she looked up at him. "Why didn't you tell me?"

"I was going to. That last day I visited you in the hospital. But you weren't really in the mood for talking."

"I didn't think you were going to come back."

"I was busy shepherding a bunch of overactive sheep."

Looking at the ground she searched for the right words. "I'm sorry. For the things I said."

"You have nothing to apologize for. You needed time. I get that. But seeing you here, seeing you smile again, hearing you sing . . . it's an answer to prayer."

Smirking, she elbowed him in the stomach. "Listen to you getting all Christian."

He laughed self-consciously. "I have no idea what I'm doing, but your dad is helping."

Nate ran past, his battered sheep costume shedding cotton balls. They watched him sprint by and Lily admonished him to be safe. Ben turned on the bench so he faced her fully and took both of her hands in his. The serious set of his jaw worried her.

"I thought we weren't going to make it. The fire was so close and I couldn't move you. I thought we were going to die in that classroom and my biggest regret was that I never told you . . . " He looked down at their joined hands then lifted his eyes to hers. "I love you, Lily Shaw."

She couldn't breathe. Her heart raced and her head began to swim. Ben loved her.

"Ben—" she started, but he stopped her.

"Before you say anything, there's something else I want to tell you." He smiled and she gasped at the change on his face. Joy radiated from him. His eyes were filled with a peace she had never seen there before. "You showed me that I could be different. You showed me that it wasn't too late. If I hadn't jumped in that limo at LAX, I don't know where I'd be now. Still angry, still hating a God I never really knew. I know I'm not perfect. I know I have a long way to go. But I want to go with you."

Lily clapped her hands over her mouth. She didn't care about the tears that fell, she didn't care about people who were watching or the grin on her brother's face as he pointed at them and slapped Chris on the back. God had answered her prayers.

Ben leaned forward and wrapped her in his arms. As he ran his hand down her hair, she rested her head against his shoulder and let all the dreams that she had kept locked inside spring to life. If it were up to her, they would stay just like this forever.

"What were you going to say?" he asked.

Lily smiled into his shirt before she pulled back to look at him. "I love you, too."

He put his arms under her legs and lifted her into his lap. Whatever else came, wherever God led, them, they were going to face it together.

She nestled into the security of his arms, her legs dangling off his lap as they watched the activity going on all around the church. Lily laughed as the kids squealed in the bounce house. As she leaned forward to get a better view, a tingle zipped down her right leg. It wasn't pain, just a tingle.

Gasping, she looked down at her foot.

"What is it?" Ben asked, his arms tightening around her.

"Look," she whispered.

Ben followed her gaze. It was so small, so subtle no one else noticed. No one else saw the spark of hope that leapt between them. Her foot moved.

And there, in that church parking lot on a bright Sunday afternoon, Lily knew they were surrounded by miracles.

Epilogue

AS THE LIMO ROLLED FORWARD, the muffled din of the crowd outside grew louder. Even through the darkened windows, Lily could see the pop of flashes dancing like electric fireflies.

She opened and closed her purse, flipping the tiny clasp back and forth as they inched closer to the paparazzi gauntlet. Doubts assailed her and she wondered again why she had agreed to this. Panic crawled closer and she nearly broke the metal snap off the purse.

Warmth stole across her hand as Ben laid his hand on hers. "It's going to be okay."

The certainty in his smile stilled her nervous fingers. "You know this is going to change everything." She was giving him a way out, the chance to change his mind. And part of her wanted him to take it. Taking her on the red carpet was going to start something entirely new for them. It wasn't too late for him to back out, to decide to keep their relationship hidden from the press for a little bit longer.

She loved him more every day and her favorite place to be was by his side. But memories of the last Hollywood event she attended and the scandal that followed it, kept her on edge.

Lifting her hand to his lips, he kissed her knuckles. "That's my plan."

Squinting her eyes, she gave him a sideways glance, but Noah's voice stopped her from asking any questions.

"We're up." He turned in the driver's seat and looked at Ben. "I can give you about three minutes before the driver behind us starts getting irritated."

"Perfect," Ben replied and Noah leapt out of the car.

The trunk opened and she knew he was getting the wheelchair. But judging by the ruckus he was making, he was having some trouble with it. Why on earth was he stalling?

She was about to ask Ben to go help him, when he took her hands. His jaw was set in a firm line and the intensity in his eyes chased every other thought from her mind.

"I've thought about this a hundred times. Being with you here, in the place where it all started, shows me how far we've come. I don't know how you put up with me back then or why you let me be a part of your life . . . part of your family. There's no other explanation except that God was trying to get a hold of me and you were compassionate enough to help. You've changed my life forever, and I want you to keep changing it, everyday."

Her stomach flipped and her throat tightened as he slid from the seat and dropped to one knee in front of her.

"I love you, Lily, and if you give me the chance I will spend the rest of my life showing you how much." He reached into his pocket and pulled out a small velvet box. "Will you marry me?"

Tears stung her eyes, but it was joy that drew them up from the depths of her soul, joy like she had never known before.

The trunk slammed shut, startling her. Ben was still on his knee, looking up at her, and she realized she hadn't answered him. "Yes. Yes, I'll marry you."

Slipping the ring onto her finger, he exhaled heavily. "I'm so glad you said that." Laughing, he gathered her into his arms and kissed the top of her head.

He held her close and she breathed in the promise of the moment, the days that spread out before them, the future that was suddenly so clear.

Noah knocked on the door and she remembered the night hadn't even started yet.

Caressing her cheek, he smiled only for her, letting the rest of the world wait. His finger brushed against the diamond on her hand. "Ready to cause a scene?"

For the first time, she wasn't nervous. Nothing could shake her happiness, nothing could steal what God had planned. In the midst of a broken world, they had found each other. Whatever the night held, whatever the next day brought, they would face it together, walking side by side in the light of God's love and grace.

Acknowledgments

This book could not have happened without the love and support of so many people. First, my husband, Paul, and my children, Emily and Brett. Thank you for giving me time to write, for encouraging me when I struggled, and for loving me through it all. The three of you are my greatest treasures.

Special thanks to my critique partners; Christa, Kellie, and Emily. Thank you for sharing your time, your talent, and your wisdom with me. Each of you made this book better and I am profoundly grateful to you.

Thank you to Ambassador International for believing in *Mission Hollywood* and to my editor, Daphne, for her hard work and encouragement.

Thanks and hugs and high fives to my writing community. This book began as a project for National Novel Writing Month and I want to thank the organizers and the NaNoWriMo community for their support, as well as the awesome fellowship of writers who have shared the ups and downs of this journey with me. Never underestimate the power and blessing of community.

Most importantly, my thanks and praise to God for His boundless love and endless grace. I'm here only because of Him.

Finally, a huge thank you to all of you, the readers who have shared Ben and Lily's story. From my heart to yours . . . thank you. I hope you'll be back when Noah gets his turn in the spotlight.

Soli Deo Gloria

For more information about
Michelle Keener
&
Mission Hollywood
please visit:

www.michellekeener.com
www.facebook.com/mkeenerwrites
@MKeenerWrites
www.instagram.com/mkeenerwrites

For more information about
AMBASSADOR INTERNATIONAL
please visit:

www.ambassador-international.com
@AmbassadorIntl
www.facebook.com/AmbassadorIntl

*If you enjoyed this book, please consider leaving us a review on
Amazon, Goodreads, or our website.*

Made in the USA
Las Vegas, NV
17 May 2021

23188828R00164